Had Adam always

Of course he had. He l...
with shorter hair, more ...
was somehow more attractive than his brother's
charming grins had been.

Why was he here?

"This way," he said before Madison could ask, and
jerked his chin toward the end of the building from
which he'd come. He reached for her bag, and in her
confusion over his appearance, she didn't release it
fast enough.

The heat of his hand covered hers on the handle and
the contact zapped her. She snatched the tingling
extremity away, and her pulse skittered out of control.

Static electricity. That's all it is.

Who was she trying to fool? Warmth pooled low in
her belly. She squashed that reaction.

His gaze snapped to hers, his eyes narrowing
suspiciously.

She carefully blanked her expression until he
pivoted and headed for a pair of glass doors on
the opposite side of the building from where she'd
parked. A slow breath leaked from her lungs. For
pity's sake. You'd think she'd never been touched
by a man before. She hadn't in a long time. Years,
actually. But still, celibacy was no excuse for her
neglected hormones to start tap-dancing now, and
for Andrew's brother no less.

Dear Reader,

There are those who say you only get one chance at true love, and if you choose unwisely romance is over for you forever.

I'm not one of those people.

I believe in second chances. I believe that growing older makes us wiser and teaches us what's really important in life and in a partner. Sometimes we find the one we were meant to be with only after we've earned a few bumps and bruises on our heart. I finally found my soul mate, and in this story Madison finds hers, but to do so she must face her painful past, overcome her fears and risk her wounded heart to see past the superficial and into the heart of the man who was meant for her.

Come back to Quincey, North Carolina, with me. It's a fictional town in the countryside through which I love to drive.

Happy reading!

Emilie Rose

EMILIE ROSE

—

The Secrets of Her Past

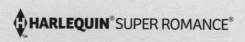
HARLEQUIN® SUPER ROMANCE®

Recycling programs
for this product may
not exist in your area.

ISBN-13: 978-0-373-60833-1

THE SECRETS OF HER PAST

Printed in U.S.A.

ABOUT THE AUTHOR

Bestselling Harlequin author and RITA® Award finalist Emilie Rose lives in her native North Carolina with her own romance book hero and two adopted mutts. Her four sons have flown the coop. Writing is her third (and hopefully her last) career. She's managed a medical office and run a home day care, neither of which offers half as much satisfaction as plotting happy endings. Her hobbies include gardening, fishing and cooking (especially cheesecake). She's a country music fan because she can find an entire book in almost any song. She is currently working her way through her own "bucket list." Visit her website, www.emilierose.com, or email her at EmilieRoseC@aol.com. Letters can be mailed to P.O. Box 20145, Raleigh, NC 27619.

Books by Emilie Rose

HARLEQUIN SUPERROMANCE

HARLEQUIN DESIRE

SILHOUETTE DESIRE

*Monte Carlo Affairs
**The Payback Affairs
***The Hightower Affairs

Other titles by this author available in ebook format.

To my own romance book hero.
We have traveled some very bumpy roads to find
exactly where we were meant to be—with each other.

CHAPTER ONE

"BRING MADISON HOME."

Tension and loathing snatched a knot in Adam's gut at the sound of his former sister-in-law's name. He stared at his father across the motor home's small galley table. "I know your diagnosis was a shock, but bringing her back into our lives would be a mistake."

"I disagree. At times like this we need family support."

"She's not family, Dad. Not anymore. By her choice."

"Madison wasn't responsible for your brother's death. The ice storm was."

"Even if that was true—" and it wasn't "—she betrayed you. After all you and Mom did for her, Madison took the life insurance money and disappeared immediately after Andrew's funeral, and she hasn't bothered to call and check on you since. *Family* wouldn't do that."

"Madison was grieving, too, son, in her own way. She lost her husband and her son that night."

"A baby she didn't want." His father's stubborn

refusal to accept reality made Adam want to punch something.

"You can't know that, son."

"I know what Andrew told me. He said she resented the pregnancy."

"You only heard one side of the story. The pregnancy might have been unplanned and the timing less than ideal, but Madison would have been a good momma once the little one arrived."

"Damn it, Dad, her carelessness killed—" An abrupt slicing motion of his father's hand made Adam bite back his words. Danny Drake had never been willing to hear anything negative against the woman he'd loved like a daughter.

Adam tried again—this time with cold, hard facts. "She was ticketed for 'driving too fast for conditions.' Your son and grandson died in that wreck, and she walked away with barely a scratch. How can you not hold her responsible?"

"Not all wounds are visible. She was injured enough to miscarry her baby. Placing blame doesn't change what's happened. Andrew is gone. Holding on to your anger won't bring him back.

"You asked what you could do for me, Adam. I'm telling you. If I'm going to devote all my energy to beating this cancer, then I need to know my practice is in good hands. Madison is the only veterinarian I trust to do things my way while I'm out of commission."

"But you know nothing about what she's been doing since she left."

"Wrong. I've been keeping tabs on our girl. Bring her home, son, or I'll skip the surgery and take my chances with the chemotherapy radiation treatments. At least then I won't have to miss as much work."

"The odds of a nonsurgical approach—"

"I know the damned odds," his father snapped, then took a deep breath and slowly exhaled. "Ripping my rib out to get to my lung is going to sideline me for months. I need backup. Reliable backup. This is *my* cancer. *My* fight. And I'll do it *my* way. Bring. Madison. Home."

His father snatched up his newspaper and stormed from the galley down the short hall and into the bedroom, his footsteps shaking the motor home in which Adam's parents had been living since beginning the renovations on their house. The door slammed shut.

Frustrated by his father's refusal to listen to reason, Adam balled his fists. What choice did he have except to comply if he wanted his father to take the most successful course of treatment?

Adam had to go after the one woman he never wanted to see again. If he succeeded, would he finally win his father's approval?

A GHOST ROSE from the rocking chair on Madison's front porch, freezing her fatigued muscles with icy horror and chilling the sweat on her skin.

No. Not a ghost—ghosts weren't tall and tanned. They didn't plant fists on lean hips and scowl with hatred-filled blue-green eyes and flattened lips.

The man on her front porch wasn't her dead husband. It was his identical twin. Adam Drake. Adam so strongly resembled the man she'd once loved with every fiber of her being that looking at him made her chest ache.

Resignation settled over her like a smothering lead X-ray apron. She should've known her self-imposed exile couldn't last. It had taken six years for the nightmare of her past to catch up with her. The Drakes had found her despite her changing names and relocating to another state.

Judging by his expression, Adam hadn't forgotten or forgiven what she'd done. She couldn't blame him. She couldn't forget or forgive her actions that night, either. She pressed a hand over the empty ache in her stomach—a sensation that never seemed to abate.

With a face as rigid as a granite mountainside, Adam glared at her from the top step. She didn't climb the treads to join him, and probably couldn't have even if she'd ordered her gelatinous legs to move. Her run home in the sweltering heat had taken a lot out of her, but not nearly as much as this man's presence. Her mouth was parched, her water bottle empty. She needed to rehydrate. But not so badly that she'd invite him inside her home.

"My father has lung cancer," Adam stated without preliminaries—typical of him. Andrew had been the charming twin.

The bald statement punched the air from her. She struggled to wheeze enough breath to respond. "I'm sorry."

"He wants you to run his practice while he undergoes treatment."

No! Fear and guilt collided, sending razor-sharp fragments of pain slicing through her. She couldn't let Danny Drake back into her life and her heart only to say goodbye to her father-in-law again. She'd already buried too many loved ones. Her parents. Her baby sister. Her husband. Her son.

She wanted to ask about Danny's prognosis, but couldn't handle knowing even that much. Distance, both emotional and geographical, was her ally. "I can't."

"You owe him."

"I have a practice here, Adam. People depend on me." Sweat snaked down her spine.

"In a backwater town this size you can't possibly have enough business to operate five days a week."

True. Quincey was a one-stoplight rural Southern township. But the slow pace gave her just enough time and money to work with her rescue animals. As if to reinforce that point, Bojangles's nicker pulled her attention to the pasture beside the house.

The bay gelding shifted his hooves and pushed his broad chest against the board fence as if sensing her distress and wanting to come to her aid. She and the horse had a lot in common—they'd both been left behind by the people they loved. She'd taken enough psychology courses to know that saving the horse had been a substitute for saving the baby she couldn't.

"I wish your father well, Adam. But I can't help. Give Danny and Helen my best. Goodbye."

He didn't take the hint to vacate her porch. Fine. She'd go around back. She pivoted.

"You owe him, Madison."

Her spine snapped straight under an icy deluge of guilt. Yes, she did owe the Drakes. They'd taken her in even before the tornado had killed her family. For years they'd been her surrogate parents, but then her mother-in-law had said things that still haunted Madison's dreams. Neither Adam nor his father had witnessed Helen's emotional explosion, but Madison had been shredded by the verbal shrapnel.

Reluctantly, Madison faced him again. Sweat-dampened hair clung to her forehead. She shoved it back with an unsteady hand. "Adam, you don't want me there."

"No. But I want my father alive. His wishes are the only reason I'm here."

"What does Helen say about this?"

A nerve in his jaw twitched. "My mother will do whatever it takes to convince Dad to undergo the most promising treatment protocol. We both will."

Hope that Madison hadn't realized she'd been harboring leeched from her, leaving her drained, aching and empty. They didn't want her back. She was a necessary evil, not a long-missed family member.

"I can't, Adam."

Disgust twisted his lips. "Andrew was right. You are a cold, selfish bitch."

Cold, selfish bitch. The words sliced her like a new scalpel, reopening the gaping wound left by the hateful argument that night when she'd learned the man she'd loved had sabotaged her carefully made plans. Plans *they* had discussed. Plans *they* had agreed upon.

But she would never tell Adam or his parents about those final, horrible moments before the accident. Their memories of Andrew were all they had left and she didn't want to spoil them.

Her nails bit into her palms. "Danny needs to find someone closer to Norcross. Quincey's a seven-hour drive away."

Adam descended the stairs and stopped a yard from her, bombarding her nerves in a dozen different ways. He looked so much like his brother—same dark hair, blue-green eyes, features and height. But he wasn't the husband she'd loved, the one who'd betrayed her, the one she'd buried because she'd lost her temper and made a mistake that she couldn't wash away no matter how many tears she cried or how many animals she saved.

Anger emanated from Adam. "*You* tell Dad to get someone else. I tried. He won't listen to me."

Although Adam's voice was firm and authoritative, for the first time since she'd met him fifteen years ago she saw naked fear in his eyes. He was afraid of losing his father. She understood that fear all too well, since she'd already walked that lonely path. But she couldn't allow herself to be vulnerable again. She might not make it out with her sanity intact this time.

She pushed away thoughts of the dark days after the wreck, of a cold, clammy hand and blood…so much blood.

"I'm sorry. I can't," she repeated and scrubbed her palm against her pants.

Tires crunched on the gravel driveway of her farm followed by the low rumble of a diesel engine pickup truck. Panic clawed up Madison's spine. June, her friend and tenant, was home, and knowing the curious deputy, as soon as she parked her vehicle by the cottage she rented from Madison, she'd come over to investigate the strange car beneath the pecan tree.

She had to get rid of Adam before the tight-knit community of Quincey found out about the atrocity Madison had committed. No one here knew about her unforgivable sin—and she wanted to keep it that way. Otherwise the townsfolk might turn against her and cast her out of the sanctuary she'd created for herself.

Maybe all Danny needed was someone outside the family to make him see reason. She could afford to drive down to Georgia *once*. Then she'd come home and life would return to normal.

"I'll come Saturday and talk to him."

Adam's gaze held her captive for several tense seconds, making her heart pound as she listened in dread for June's approaching footsteps.

"You reverted to your maiden name," Adam accused.

"Yes, I…" How could she explain that she'd wanted to erase everything about her marriage to his brother? She couldn't. "Look, I can't invite you in. I have plans this evening."

A plan to clean cages, but that wasn't how he interpreted it if the revulsion filling his eyes was any gauge. She didn't enlighten him.

"Make sure you show up. Here's the address and my number." He pulled a business card from his pocket and wrote on the back, then thrust it at her. He strode to the sedan and drove away just as June rounded the house.

Madison sagged in relief, but the damage had been done. The scab had been ripped away. All she wanted to do was crawl into the farmhouse and tend her wound. She didn't want to talk to anyone—not even a friend.

"Who's the hunk in the rental car?" the blond deputy asked.

"Rental?" Madison dodged the question.

"Sticker on the back bumper. Rental company license plate frame. Good-looking guy—where'd you find him? Not in Quincey, that's for sure."

Should she claim he was someone who'd gotten

lost and was asking for directions? No. She never lied to her friends. She just hadn't always shared the whole truth. But how much should she tell June? Only the basics—

"He's my ex-brother-in-law."

June's eyebrows lifted. "I didn't know you were divorced."

Again Madison hesitated, but she trusted June as much as she trusted anyone. "Widowed. A long time ago."

"Oh, I'm sorry, Madison. I didn't know. I haven't seen him around before."

"We haven't kept in touch."

Questions filled June's eyes, and Madison scrambled to keep her from asking them. "Are you going to help me feed up tonight?"

"Not a chance. I'm grabbing a quick shower, then heading over to babysit for Piper. What'd he want anyway?"

So much for a distraction. "A favor. I have to go out of town Saturday. Can you watch the menagerie?"

"Happy to. Not much else to do." June scanned the empty driveway. "Is your truck in the shop again?"

"Yes."

"You should've called me. I would've given you a ride home."

"I needed the exercise. It's only a couple miles."

"You ran in this scorching heat?" Madison nodded

and June's gaze sharpened. "You should be flushed and sweaty, but you're pale. Sure you're okay?"

Not even close to okay. "I'll be fine. It's been a long day. Mondays usually are."

And it was about to become an even longer week, knowing that at the end of it she would have to face the nightmare of her past.

SATURDAY MORNING MADISON steered her truck into the driveway of the unfamiliar address Adam had given her.

She parked and her doubts surrounded her like a pack of snarling wild dogs, paralyzing her. The cedar siding and river rock home was set on a heavily wooded lot that sloped gently down to a pond. The neighbors' houses were barely visible through the towering, dense pines, but the peaceful setting did nothing to soothe her jagged nerves.

Had Danny and Helen moved from the place where they'd raised their boys? Had the memories been too much to bear? While Madison could understand the need for a fresh start, the possibility they'd sold the home where the boys' growth had been marked on a door frame and by the trees they'd planted in the yard swamped her with a sense of loss that made leaving the truck very difficult.

She'd spent nearly every holiday, school break and weekend in the Drakes' sprawling ranch house from shortly after she'd met Andrew until her vet school graduation. But that fairy tale had been an illusion.

How could she have been so completely blinded by love that she hadn't seen Andrew's narcissistic streak until the final months of their marriage? She'd attributed the change in his personality to the stress of her accidentally becoming pregnant, and she'd blamed herself for messing up her birth control and their five-year plan. But thanks to the alcohol he'd consumed at her graduation celebration, she'd discovered how wrong she'd been.

How could she ever again trust her judgment when it came to men?

She couldn't. And because of that she'd vowed to remain single and limit herself to living with a menagerie of rejected pets. She wouldn't let anyone get too close again, and not even the two women she considered her best friends knew the whole sordid story. She couldn't risk them turning on her like the Drakes had.

Nervousness dampened her palms and quickened her pulse. She forced her fingers to release the steering wheel, then flexed them in an attempt to ease the stiffness.

The sooner you say your piece, the sooner you can go home.

Bracing herself, she climbed from the cab and pointed her feet toward the front door. Emotions warred within her, adhering her feet to the concrete.

Then she remembered she hadn't locked her truck. In Quincey no one locked their doors, but Norcross was a suburb of Atlanta. Unlocked doors, even in a neighborhood as nice as this one appeared to be, were an invitation. And she had a lot of valuable vet equipment in her truck that she couldn't risk losing. She pushed the pad on her key fob, and once that task was done she had no more excuses for stalling. But she still couldn't make herself move.

She inhaled so deeply she thought her lungs might explode, then slowly released the pent-up breath. She licked her dry lips, then she checked the buttons on her shirt and smoothed her hair. The strands clung to her damp palms.

Stop procrastinating, Madison.

The door opened and Danny Drake stepped out onto the long, covered porch stretching between the front gables. He descended the stairs and came toward her. Save a few more gray hairs, he'd barely changed. He was still tall and lean like Andrew, and his eyes, the same bluish-green as his sons', crinkled in a smile as he silently lifted his open arms. "Madison, it's so good to see you."

Confused by the familiar welcome when she'd expected hostility, Madison stumbled awkwardly into his embrace. He enfolded her, bringing the memories rushing back. She hadn't expected this and hadn't realized how much she'd missed Danny's bear hugs. Tears stung her eyes and a sob rose in her throat. She gulped down her response and hugged him back.

"Oooph." He bowed his back, a grimace of pain pleating his face.

"I'm sorry. Did I hurt you?"

"Long and boring story." Holding her at arm's length and assessing her, he shook his head. "You're skin and bones, Maddie."

"I finally took up distance running."

"Good way to clear the head, but hell on the knees. I had to give it up a couple years back. I'm riding a bike now instead. Guess we won't be running any races together the way Andrew had wanted."

A needle of pain slipped under her skin. "I guess not."

During school Madison had been too busy with her studies to accompany Andrew and Danny on their cross-country runs. She'd promised to join them after she graduated. Yet another plan that hadn't come to fruition.

Danny searched her face. "It's good to have you home. I've tried to be patient and let you grieve at your own pace. I knew you'd come back when you were ready, but I can't wait any longer. I need you now, Maddie." His voice cracked.

Her brain snagged on Danny's words. He knew she'd come back? He meant come back to visit, right?

Danny's gaze shifted past her shoulder and his eyes widened, then filled with approval. "You're still driving Andrew's truck?"

"Yes." The pickup was her albatross, a reminder of what she'd had and lost. It was also paid for. Her car had been totaled in the wreck and she hadn't wanted the burden of car payments. "It's reliable."

Well, most of the time, thanks to Quincey's genius mechanic and his love for his pack of hunting dogs.

"Come inside." He led her toward the house.

"This is a beautiful place."

"Isn't it? Helen has coffee ready. She suspected you'd be an early bird."

At the mention of her mother-in-law, Madison's stomach resumed churning. Was it a good sign that Helen remembered Madison's habits? Whenever Madison and Andrew had visited from university, Madison had risen early and driven in the predawn hours while Andrew slept in the passenger seat. They'd always arrived in time for breakfast to allow for a full day with his family, and Helen had never failed to greet them with an elaborate spread.

After Andrew had finished vet school, moved back to Norcross and joined his father's practice, Madison had remained near campus and continued the predawn drives, meeting Andrew at the Drakes' home to begin their weekends together. Funny how it wasn't until the blinders had been ripped away that she recalled the number of times Andrew had said she could give up the drives anytime she wanted if she moved home with him. But that would have meant quitting school. At the time she'd thought he was teasing, but in actuality, she'd been the living definition of blind and stupid. She quashed the memory.

Back then excitement over seeing her husband had kept her awake and urged her to start the drive early. This time dread had caused her insomnia. She hadn't been able to sleep, and at 1:00 a.m. she'd finally given up and decided to be productive rather than toss and turn. Fifteen minutes later she was on the road.

In the past, anticipation of the feast had made Madison's mouth water, but today her tongue was as desiccated as a hundred-year-old skeleton.

Adam waited inside the foyer. Madison's steps and heart stuttered. Each time she saw him it was like being slapped in the face with her highest and lowest moments simultaneously. "Hello, Adam."

"Mom's in the kitchen." He strode away without acknowledging her greeting.

"Ignore his rudeness. He's not taking my diagnosis well. I suspect his doctor friends have worried him unnecessarily with worst-case scenarios about cancer treatment." Danny gestured for her to follow Adam.

The arrogance of Adam taking the lead seemed out of character for the respectful man she'd once known. Andrew had been the irreverent one. But Adam's attitude was the least of her worries. She fell into step behind him, taking in the way his shoulders and biceps stretched the seams of his polo shirt, and then her eyes drifted down the inverted triangle of his back, across his firm butt and to his thighs.

When she realized where she was looking she jerked her gaze upward.

Her involuntary scrutiny was merely a casual comparison of the differences between him and his lanky twin—Adam had more muscles—that was all.

The bright, sunny kitchen at the back of the house resembled a spread from a cooking magazine. Golden oak cabinets with glossy gray granite countertops and top-of-the-line stainless steel appliances lined one wall. More cabinetry made up a crescent-shaped center island with barstools separating the kitchen from a large den with a river rock fireplace at the far end. French doors in each room emptied onto a screened-in porch overlooking the water.

Knowing how much Helen had loved cooking for her family, Madison could see how she'd be happy here, but her mother-in-law didn't look happy today. She stood by the glass-top stove, spatula in hand. She didn't relinquish the utensil or make any move in Madison's direction. Her flat brown eyes and tight, unsmiling mouth held no welcome.

While Danny barely showed signs of the passage of time, Helen had not aged well. She looked at least fifteen years older.

Madison forced a smile and felt her parched lips crack. This was the cold reception she'd expected. She wasn't surprised or disappointed. "Good morning, Helen."

The hateful words her mother-in-law had said six

years ago hung between them. A dozen tense, silent seconds ticked past.

"Madison." Helen hunched her shoulders, turned to the stove and flipped the pancakes.

Adam shoved a mug of coffee in Madison's direction. "Have a seat. Cream and sugar are on the table."

His barely civil tone brought a chill to the room. Danny pulled out a chair for her. Madison sat and wrapped her icy hands around the hot mug. She sipped and waited for someone to initiate conversation, but the uncomfortable lull stretched. Her pulse banged in her ears. Stalling wasn't going to get the job done *or* get her on the road.

"So, Danny...your wince outside? You said it was a long story...?"

He shrugged gingerly. "We're renovating the house. You know how I always need a project. I finally got around to tearing out that old paneling in the den and study like Helen always talked about. I fell off the ladder and cracked a rib. X-rays for that caught the spot on my lung."

Anxiety twined through her. "So you've not sold your home? Whose place is this?"

"It's Adam's."

She scanned the space again, seeing it from a different perspective. The furnishings had cleaner lines than the fussy, cluttered style Helen had preferred, but none of it resembled the oversize leather mancave furniture Andrew had chosen for the house he'd bought and furnished during Madison's last year of vet school.

You cold, selfish bitch. What kind of woman wouldn't want to stay in a nice home like this and raise her child? What's wrong with you?

Was there something wrong with her?

She blinked away the suffocating memory. "What's your prognosis, Danny?"

The words popped out before she could stop them, and then she cursed herself. She didn't want to know Danny's chances.

"The tumor's localized and appears to have clean edges. No sign of metastasizing into surrounding tissue."

"That's good." But cancer was still scary. Another awkward pall blanketed the room. A decade ago they would've been teasing, laughing and talking shop throughout the meal. Andrew would have found something humorous in the tense situation. But he wasn't here. And that was her fault.

Helen plopped a platter of pancakes, link sausages and hash browns onto the table with enough force that it was a wonder the cobalt stoneware didn't crack. No one made a move. In the past they would have dug in, good-naturedly fork fencing over the feast.

"When can you take over for me, Maddie?" Danny asked as he seated himself.

Madison gulped coffee and scalded the back of her throat, then she looked at Adam, who stood by the window, his arms folded, expression rigid. He'd obviously not relayed her answer to Danny.

Then she looked into the eyes of the man she'd respected more than any other, a man who'd shown her the practical side of veterinary medicine. He'd been a demanding but excellent teacher, better than any of her professors. She dredged her brain for the speech she'd practiced all the way down I-85.

"I can't, Danny. It's a seven-hour drive each way. You need to hire someone from the service that offers substitute veterinarians. It's a good group. They use only board-certified doctors. They'll find someone for you." She dug the sheet of paper from her pocket and smoothed it on the table in front of him. "I wrote down the contact information."

Danny's face turned mutinous—an expression she'd seen on Andrew's several times. He ignored the page. "I want *you,* Maddie. You know how I do things. I taught you my methods."

A boa constrictor of guilt wound around her. "I have a practice to run. People depend on me. I'm the only vet in a thirty-mile radius of Quincey."

"What happened to our plan to run the office together and for you to take over when I retired?"

He couldn't possibly be hanging on to that, could he? But then she recalled what he'd said outside about her coming back when she was ready. He hadn't meant for a visit.

"Andrew and I were going to take over Drake Veterinary." And her husband had made it clear on the night of the wreck that he had other plans for her. "That idea died with him. He was your flesh and blood. I'm not."

The Drakes had proved that point by staying at Andrew's bedside until he died two days after the accident—not once stopping by to check on Madison who'd been only two floors away. She'd grieved for her child and then her husband alone. Their absence had demonstrated where she stood with the Drakes.

"You're still a Drake," Danny insisted.

"No, Dad, she's not. Madison reverted to her maiden name."

Danny scowled at Adam, then refocused on Madison. "You're never coming back?"

"No, Danny. I've made a good place for myself in North Carolina."

He held her gaze and she had the sensation he was trying to compel her to change her mind—the way Andrew had whenever they'd disagreed. Back then she'd capitulated to her husband's wishes more often than not to keep the peace.

When she didn't fold, resignation settled across Danny's features. "Can't blame a man for asking. Pass the pancakes."

"But—" Helen protested. Danny cut her off with a sharp glance. Helen knotted her fingers and bit her lip. Madison passed the platter and waited to see if her mother-in-law would finish what she'd begun to say, but Helen remained mute, her distress evident in each fidgety weight shift and in the fingers that pleated the dish towel.

Madison looked at Adam and found him scowling at his father, then that arctic gaze shifted to her, freezing her clear to the bone. He hated her, and sitting in his kitchen, partaking of food he'd very likely paid for, suddenly seemed like an intrusion. Coming here had been a mistake.

She rose shakily. "I have a long drive back. I'd better get started." She took a step toward the door, eager to escape, then paused. "Danny, I'll be rooting for you. Call the veterinary service."

"Take care of yourself, girl. Don't be a stranger."

"Madison—"

"Helen, leave the girl be. You heard her. She can't do it. We'll be fine."

The three Drakes exchanged looks in a silent communication that excluded Madison. "Well… goodbye and good luck."

She bolted from the house, ignoring the rushed jumble of voices in the kitchen behind her. She didn't slow until she'd climbed into the cab and closed the door. With her heart still pounding she turned the key and the engine protested. "Not now. Come on."

She tried again. Crawling inside to ask for help was unpalatable. Bile crept up her throat. It took two more attempts before the motor caught. Eager to get down the road before she pulled over and emptied her stomach, she shoved the gear lever into Reverse.

A bang on the window scared her heart into a stall. Helen, her face without a smidgeon of color, stood outside the door. Desperation gleamed in her eyes. Madison gulped down her rising nausea and reluctantly hit the button to lower the glass.

"Danny made us promise not to say anything, but I can't let you drive away when your actions could mean the difference between his life and death. You have to help, Madison. He has a sixty percent better chance of beating the cancer if he has the tumor surgically removed, then follows up with chemo. He refuses to have the procedure unless you agree to run the practice while he's recuperating. He's more worried about what will happen to his patients without him than he is about what I'll do if he doesn't—" A sob choked off her words.

An urgent need to run crawled over Madison's flesh. "Helen, I can't."

Her former mother-in-law's cheeks flushed dark red and a white line formed around her lips. Fury filled her eyes. "I will not let you do this to me again. I refuse to sit by and watch someone else I love slip away from me because of your actions." Tears streamed down her cheeks and her breath came in snatched pants. Her entire body shook. "Can you live with another Drake death on your conscience? You have to come back for Danny. You owe us. You owe *me,* damn you, Madison Drake."

Monroe. Not Drake. Madison didn't correct her.

A chill started at Madison's core and splintered

outward like frost until even her fingers and toes felt frozen. She reached out a hand to console her mother-in-law, but Helen recoiled. "Don't touch me."

Madison winced at the fresh stab of pain. They'd once been so close.

Madison debated telling Helen the truth about Andrew. If she did, Helen would understand why Madison couldn't revisit the past and the office they had once shared. She opened her mouth, then her conscience slammed the door on her escape route.

Do no harm. It was more than a professional oath. It was a way of life.

She pressed her dry lips together, leaving the damning words unsaid. She couldn't destroy a mother's memories of her son by telling her what a manipulative, deceitful bastard he'd been.

Helen was right. Madison would never forgive herself if her actions caused another fatality. She owed the Drakes for the kindness they'd shown her. But mostly, she owed Danny for the practical, old-school lessons he'd taught her.

Resignation settled heavily on her chest, crushing her lungs. Head spinning, she gulped and battled for air and an alternative. None came.

"I'll do it."

But she'd come back on her terms.

Carefully setting boundaries was the only way to protect herself, her sanity and the practice that had become her life. She wouldn't get emotionally attached to this family a second time. And once she'd done her duty, she'd go home and try to find the peace in her life again.

CHAPTER TWO

"I'LL DO IT."

Adam whipped around from his position by the patio doors at the sound of Madison's voice. She stood in the doorway, her expression belligerent.

"But I'll only give you two days a week."

"Two days?" Danny protested. "But your practice is small and mine is—"

"I realize my rural office isn't up to your city standards, Dr. Drake, but I'm proud of it and I'm needed there."

Adam's father flinched at *doctor,* then sadness filled his eyes.

"I'll help you because you helped me. But once I get you through this, my debt is paid. I won't come back."

"Now, Maddie, let's not be that way," his father placated, the hurt quickly giving way to determination. "You're family, and families stick together."

"Mondays and Tuesdays," she continued as if he hadn't spoken. "I can't afford a hotel every week. You'll need to provide accommodations."

Her demands and her cold tone reinforced everything Andrew had said about her career-driven selfishness. Not that his father couldn't easily afford to provide a hotel room, and it would be best if his mother didn't have to worry about playing hostess, but Madison was making this all about herself. What *she* wanted. What *she* needed. When it should be about how she could best accommodate her mentor.

"For two months," she added in an irrefutable tone.

"Two—" his dad protested. "What if that's not enough time?"

"Then you'll call the service."

His father mulled over her words with a frown on his face. Adam waited for him to tell her where she could shove her selfish stipulations the way he had when Adam had announced his plan to pursue something other than a veterinary degree.

"I knew you'd come through for me, Maddie." The senior Drake crossed the kitchen and embraced the enemy.

Protests filled Adam's mouth. He bit his tongue. He'd learned long ago that trying to change his father's mind once he'd made a decision was a waste of time. Instead Adam focused on the success of achieving the desired outcome. With Madison's assistance they could pursue the most aggressive and successful treatment protocol. When she eventually let them down—and she would—his father would have already had the surgery. He'd be forced to call the service Madison mentioned.

The coldhearted witch kept her arms by her sides and her fists balled rather than return the hug. Adam studied her emotionless whiskey-brown eyes and tight face and his jaw tensed with irritation. Had she no compassion?

She detached herself from the embrace. "Let me know when you've arranged your surgery."

"I've tentatively scheduled the procedure for Monday."

Surprise ricocheted through Adam, mirroring the shock on Madison's face. Had his father been that certain she would agree?

"*This* Monday? You're only allowing me what's left of the weekend to make arrangements?"

"Wishful thinking on my part, I suppose, but I want to beat this disease, and the sooner we get started the better my chances," he said with just the right touch of earnestness. But his father had always been a master manipulator. "I called the surgeon as soon as Adam told me you were coming."

Adam watched the war wage in Madison's eyes, and he wouldn't have been surprised if she'd changed her mind.

"I'll be back tomorrow night. Let me know where I'm staying." She pivoted and stalked from the room, her slim figure as rigid as a steel beam. The front door snapped shut behind her.

Silence descended on the room. Moments later the sound of Andrew's truck engine struggling to turn over carried to them. It took three attempts before the ignition caught.

"That went well."

His father's smugness infuriated Adam. "I have to hand it to you, Dad. That took balls. What made you sure she'd agree?"

"I know Maddie."

It had always irritated Adam that he'd tried for years to win his father's approval, but from the moment Madison had waltzed into their lives she could do no wrong in Danny Drake's eyes.

Adam whipped out his cell phone. "I'll make the hotel arrangements."

"No hotel. Madison's family."

"The motor home only has one bedroom," Helen pointed out.

"That's why she'll stay here with Adam."

The words hit him like a sucker punch to the gut. "Me? Why?"

"I'm not putting her on the sofa bed in the motor home when I'll probably be up and down all night, and our house is far from being habitable—with walls ripped down and wires hanging everywhere. *You* have two empty bedrooms."

"I don't want that viper here."

"No talking about her like that. And Madison's going to need transportation. While I like that she's still sentimental enough to drive Andrew's truck, it doesn't sound as reliable as she claims it is."

"You're going to rent a car for her?"

"No. You're going to drive her to and from the office. We'll send Andrew's truck to my mechanic and have him take his time on the repairs."

Adam gaped at his father's audacity. "Are you out of your mind? I don't have time to babysit *or* play taxi. I have a job."

"You have that hospital running like a well-drilled army unit. It'll survive if its administrator cuts his days a little short while Madison's in town."

Was that the compliment he'd waited a lifetime to hear or just another form of manipulation? "Dad—"

He joined Adam by the window and clapped him on the shoulder. "Adam, I need you to make sure she gets to work on time each day. I can't lose patients over this health scare. The medical bills from this treatment are going to be astronomical even after my health insurance pays its part. I don't want to burn through my retirement paying them off. Your mother and I will need something to live on…if I make it through this."

Damn it. He *was* being manipulated. But his father's points were valid.

"We'll have dinner together every night Madison's here. Helen will cook all of our favorites. Just like old times."

Old times, his ass. Life would never be the same again. If his father believed otherwise, then he was in for a reality check. And it irritated Adam that his father, who'd never been late or left the office early a single day in his career, expected Adam to do so.

"You're asking too much."

"Fine. Call Madison. Tell her never mind. I'll cancel the surgery and take my chances with the chemo-radiation cocktail."

Once more Adam had underestimated his father. Danny Drake knew which buttons to press to get what he wanted.

"Fine. I'll handle it."

MADISON CRADLED THE phone, marked the last name off Tuesday's appointment roster then leaned back and massaged her throbbing temples. She was already beginning to regret her decision to help Dann—Dr. Drake.

He's not friend or family anymore. Keep it strictly business.

A key turned in the lock, and the front door of the clinic opened. Her assistant's blond head appeared in the gap. Piper stepped inside, scanned the empty waiting room with confusion puckering her forehead.

"Hi, boss. I saw your truck outside. Why are you here on a Sunday? Did we have an emergency? If we did, you should've called me." She came around the registration counter and into the workspace she usually occupied.

"It's not the kind of emergency that required me to pull you away from your family. I was going to call later and explain. There's going to be a change in our scheduling for the next couple months."

"Is something wrong? Are you okay?"

Physically, yes. Mentally, no. Madison sifted through the facts. Piper knew more about her past than anyone else. In a weak moment Madison had confided that her husband and unborn baby had died and that Madison had sworn off men and romantic entanglements forever. But that was all she'd shared, and she preferred to keep the rest on a need-to-know basis.

"I'm fine, but my former father-in-law has cancer. I've been shanghaied into substituting in his veterinary practice for him while he undergoes treatment."

Worry filled Piper's eyes. "What about our clients?"

And her job. Madison understood the concern. "I'm only subbing on Mondays and Tuesdays. We'll operate on our regular schedule the rest of the time."

"Where's his practice, and is your truck up to that many road trips?"

"Norcross, Georgia, and I'm keeping my fingers crossed about the truck."

Piper bit her lip and shifted on her feet. "Is he paying you?"

In the shock of the moment payment had never crossed her mind. "We didn't discuss that, but I suspect not. I'm actually repaying an old debt. He helped me with my internship."

"Madison, I don't mean to get into your business, but you see a lot of patients on the barter system. We don't make enough to cover that many hotel stays,

and with one of your two rental cottages vacant…
Can you afford to do this?"

"I can't afford to refuse. Dan—Dr. Drake will
take care of my accommodations. Piper, I'm going
to need your help *and* Josh's. Do you think your son
would be willing to check on my critters during the
day on Mondays and Tuesdays? I'll pay him. June
has me covered before and after she gets off work."

"I can't see why a preteen would turn down an opportunity to get paid for doing something he loves,
but I think you should consider trading his help for
horseback rides instead of cash. It's something Josh
really wants, and he's crazy about Bojangles."

"That would certainly help me financially, but I
don't want to short him." She checked her watch.
"I need to get on the road. I don't have time to meet
with Josh today. Would it be okay if he and I ham-
mered out the details when I get back?"

"Of course. This means you'll be missing our
Monday lunches. Do you promise to eat if I'm not
around to force-feed you?"

Madison grimaced. "And here I thought you loved
my company and my chicken salad."

Piper grinned. "That, too."

"I've rescheduled the appointments for this week,
but I'll need you to take care of subsequent weeks'
patients when you come in tomorrow."

"No problem. Are you sure you want to do this,
Madison? It's a big imposition, and I haven't seen

your in-laws in town or known you to visit them since you've lived here."

"We haven't kept in touch."

"You know…being married to Quincey's chief of police comes in handy. If you'd like, I can ask Roth to write something official banning you from leaving the state." Piper's blue eyes twinkled with mischief.

Madison laughed. "Thanks, Piper, but I don't think I want a probation officer monitoring my every move, even temporarily." She pushed to her feet. "I need to go home and pack. It's a long drive."

Her cell phone tweeted, signaling a text message from a number with a Georgia area code. The number on Adam's business card. Her stomach swooped.

Flight arranged. Be at your county airport at six tonight.

Surprise mingled with trepidation because the plan was moving forward. "What do you know? The Drakes bought me an airline ticket. I don't have to drive seven hours after all. That means I'll have time to negotiate with Josh."

"In that case, come to Sunday brunch and have some of Mom's awesome shrimp and grits. You can talk to Josh before he, his dad and grandfather head for their favorite catfish hole."

"Let's go, then," Madison said. She grabbed her purse and followed Piper out the door.

Flying would save her a lot of time and gas money, but it also meant she'd be stranded with the Drakes. If something went wrong she'd have no means of escape. But at the moment being without her truck was the lesser of two evils.

MADISON SCANNED THE terminal looking for a ticket counter or an electronic board listing flights, but saw neither. Although she'd never had a reason to stop by the local airport before, it was too small and too empty for her to have missed anything that important. She was the only person wandering around.

Shouldering her small duffel bag, she approached a desk occupied by a bored-looking fortysomething man reading a fishing magazine.

"Good evening, sir. I'm supposed to fly to Norcross, Georgia, tonight. Could you tell me where I can pick up my ticket and where my flight is boarding?"

The man looked at her over the wire rims of his glasses as if she'd spoken a foreign language. "We don't serve commercial carriers, miss. Lost our last one a few years back. We're strictly general aviation. All we get are private planes and the occasional corporate jet, and politician or military landing. Better verify your flight information. I got nothing for you."

How could she have misunderstood? "Thank you."

She pulled out her cell phone as she walked away

and reread Adam's text. No, it said exactly what she remembered. She'd have to text him for clarification. She dropped her bag at her feet.

"Madison," Adam's deep voice called as if she'd conjured him.

She looked up to see him striding toward her wearing faded jeans and a black polo. He had sunglasses perched on top of his head.

Her breath hitched. Had he always been this handsome? Of course he had. He looked just like Andrew, only with shorter hair, a broader build and a scowl that was somehow more attractive than his brother's charming, ingratiating grins.

Why was he here? What had happened to her airline ticket?

"This way," he said before she could ask and jerked his chin toward the end of the building from which he'd come. She bent to grab her bag. The heat of his hand covered hers on the strap as he did the same. The contact seared her. She snatched the burning extremity away.

Static electricity. That's all.

Who was she trying to fool? Warmth pooled low in her belly and a tingle worked its way through her veins, but that was simply Mother Nature talking, reminding Madison that she was too young to be put out to pasture. Her ovaries were still fully functional and wanted a workout.

She squashed that reaction and slowly straightened. Grasping the strap, he rose beside her, his gaze drilling hers through narrowed, suspicious eyes.

She carefully blanked her expression.

"Is this all you packed?"

"I'll only need a couple scrub suits. This isn't a pleasure trip."

His scowl deepened. He about-faced and headed for a pair of glass doors on the opposite side of the building from where she'd parked. The breath leaked from her lungs like a tire going flat. She shouldn't antagonize him, but for pity's sake, her skittish reaction would make one think she'd never been touched by a man before. Well, she hadn't in a long time. Years, actually. Still, celibacy was no excuse for her neglected hormones to start tap-dancing now—and for Andrew's brother no less.

Maybe her vow to live without sex had been a bad one, but pickings were slim in Quincey, and small-town people thrived on gossip. That made finding a local man she could like and respect, but who wouldn't demand more than a friends-with-benefits relationship, a difficult proposition. She wasn't the type to drive out of town for one-night stands, and her few experiences with dating websites had not been good ones. Only two of the guys ever made it past the initial screening phone call, and those dates had been a waste of time and gasoline.

No. That whole romantic fantasy of soul mates and forever was not for her. She'd never let herself be that vulnerable again.

The doors slid closed between them, kicking her into action. Why was Adam here, her brain nagged again. Had he decided to drive her to Norcross? If so, why hadn't he informed her of the change of plans? She hustled after him to get her answers.

Before Adam had surprised her at her house a few days ago, she'd never spent any time alone with him and didn't want to contemplate the long drive cooped up in a car with him now. She checked her watch. They'd arrive so late that she wouldn't get more than a few hours' sleep, and she'd be good for nothing in Dr. Drake's office tomorrow.

The doors slid open automatically, revealing an asphalt tarmac—*not* another parking lot. A half dozen planes were tethered in a row. Adam was already halfway to one small white aircraft with blue and silver stripes and three windows on the side. Her feet stalled. The cool air from the terminal swirled past her, blending with the warmth radiating from the pavement.

He opened a door on the side and shoved her bag through it. Her brain screamed in protest. He turned and then did a double take, as if he'd only now noticed she wasn't immediately behind him.

"Are you coming?" He folded his arms and waited with one leg bent, staring at her through the dark sunglasses he'd lowered over his eyes. He presented an all too appealing picture—like a cologne advertisement for an adventurous man or something. "Madison, we need to get in the air."

Dear heaven. She wasn't mistaken. They were traveling by plane. "I thought you and Andrew were deathly afraid of flying after that near-miss midair accident when you were kids."

"I don't run from my fears."

But Andrew had. Goose bumps danced across her skin as awareness drifted over her like a chilling mist. How could she have missed that when she'd been married to the man for five years? But the moment she heard Adam say the words she recognized the truth. Every vacation she and her husband had ever taken had been within driving distance. They'd either stayed in a hotel or the family's pop-up camper.

She looked at the tiny aircraft and apprehension tickled her spine. "*That* is our plane?"

"It's a Piper Seminole, a safe one. Fast, too."

She swiveled her head from side to side. There wasn't anyone else nearby. "Where's our pilot?"

"You're looking at him."

Her mouth dried and adrenaline raced through her veins. "You own a plane?"

"In partnership with several surgeons at the hospital."

He closed the distance between them, then pushed up the dark lenses. His steady gaze held hers. "Madison, I became a pilot so I could understand what happened that day and make sure it didn't happen to me again. You'll be safe with me—safer than on the interstate in Andrew's old truck. Once we get in the air you'll see some amazing scenery, and in a couple hours you'll be on the ground again."

She wasn't convinced.

He huffed an impatient breath. "Flying will save you ten hours of travel time round trip each week."

When he put it that way... "I'd be lying if I didn't admit I'm a little apprehensive. I've never flown before."

"Conquer your fears, Doc, or they'll conquer you. Trust me, you'll love it once we're airborne."

Trust a man who detested her? Tall order. She wasn't sure she'd love flying, but she ordered her feet forward, taking one step, two, on legs as weak and numb as they'd been after she'd finished her first half marathon. Was it fear? Or excitement?

Adam stepped in front of her. "I have to get in first since there's only one door, then you'll step up onto the wing and slide down into your seat. Watch where I put my feet."

Another bubble of nervousness rose in her throat. She hesitated, running her gaze over the aircraft and searching for loose seams or bolts or anything that didn't look...right. Not that she knew what she was looking for. But she hated the idea of climbing into that tin can and being trapped beside Adam for the length of the flight when her body was having fits of nostalgia for her missed sex life.

But Adam was not Andrew, and she was *not* going there with him.

Adam climbed aboard, then turned and offered

his hand to help her climb inside. The moment their palms met and his long fingers curled around hers a current of awareness flowed through her, and she realized she was in trouble because her body obviously did not know what was good for it.

A PRICKLE OF foreboding crept up Madison's spine when the headlights' beam landed on the brick pillars marking the entrance to Adam's neighborhood. Surely Helen and Danny weren't waiting for them? It was almost ten o'clock—too late for visiting.

Adam had said little during the flight, communicating more to the people on the other end of the radio headset than with her. He'd only spoken to Madison when pointing out pieces of interesting scenery—a winery and a lake and the tail end of the Appalachians. His silence had screamed louder than a crowd of rowdy teenagers at a rock concert that he didn't want her here. That made two of them.

But she had to admit, he'd been right. Other than twinges of anxiety during takeoff and landing, she'd enjoyed the flight.

The lack of conversation had been both a blessing and a curse. What could she say to someone who only tolerated her out of necessity? But the lack of interaction had given her time to worry about how she'd handle staying at the Drakes' home—a place where she'd once experienced so much love but which now held open hostility, at least from Helen.

Mostly she'd tried to prepare herself for sleeping in the bed she'd once shared with Andrew.

Adam steered the car into his driveway and hit the remote to open his garage door. Her sense of foreboding rose along with that door.

"Are your parents meeting us here?"

"No." He parked and turned off the ignition. The garage door lowered behind them with a hum of gears, sealing her inside.

A sinking sensation weighted her stomach. Adam left the car, opened the trunk and extracted her duffel bag. Her brain screamed in denial. She threw open her door and bolted to her feet. "I'm staying here? With you?"

"Yes." The bite in the word revealed his displeasure.

"Why not a hotel or at your parents' house?"

"They're living in a motor home parked in their driveway while the renovation is underway. There's no room for you."

No. No. No.

"This isn't going to work. Call Danny. I'm sure he'll make arrangements for a hotel."

"He's having surgery tomorrow. For cancer—a life-threatening disease. He has enough on his plate without worrying about your demands. Could you think about someone other than yourself for once?"

She gasped at the injustice of the statement. "I don't want to inconvenience you."

"Dad wants you here."

"How will I get to his office? Is he going to loan me his car?"

A bark of laughter severed her words. "No one drives Dad's Corvette except him."

"But—"

"Madison, he asked me to make sure you kept your promise. I'm to drive you to work each morning and pick you up each evening."

Adam was her babysitter. "He doesn't trust me?"

"Why should he? You've given him no reason to believe you won't cut and run when things get tough."

Madison gulped the panic welling within her. She was trapped. Trapped in hell with the spitting image of her dead husband. With no escape. No matter how bad things got. And she was too far from anywhere to pay what would no doubt be an exorbitant taxi fee.

Two nights under Adam's roof. She inhaled and exhaled, fighting for calm. Two nights, she repeated silently. She could get through them, but next week she'd insist on alternative accommodations.

CHAPTER THREE

ADAM MIGHT BE forced to house and chauffeur Madison, but he didn't have to befriend her. He planned to park her in her room, putting her out of sight and out of mind until tomorrow. And then he'd have seven more weekends to get through—if she kept her promise. He doubted she would. He expected her to bail long before September.

He dropped her suitcase inside the door of the bedroom on the opposite end of the house from his and stepped out of her way. "Guest room's here. Bathroom's next door. We leave at seven in the morning. Be ready."

Madison swept past him, trailing the barely perceptible fragrance of flowers that had taunted him in the cockpit during their flight. Her scent wasn't overpowering like some of the perfumes the women he encountered at work often wore. Instead, Madison's was just subtle enough to tease his nose and interfere with his concentration as he tried to identify the components.

A ridiculous waste of time. He turned to walk away. A gasp stopped him.

Madison stood by the bed, her body rigid, facing the shelf above the television holding Andrew's sports memorabilia. Individual protective glass boxes enclosed an autographed football from Andrew's favorite NFL player, a pyramid of signed baseballs they'd collected on a summer road trip when hitting as many major league ballparks as possible, and a golf glove from the Masters Tournament champion the year they'd both graduated high school.

"I'd forgotten about those." Madison's voice quivered slightly, as did her fingers when she tucked a dark lock of hair behind her ear. When she'd been married to Andrew she'd kept her hair cut to chin length. It hung to the center of her back now, with shorter strands sweeping her shoulders when she turned to look at him.

Something lurked in her eyes—something deep, dark and…painful? Adam dismissed the notion. If she'd thought about his brother or the Drake family at all since Andrew's death, Adam had seen no evidence of it.

He'd forgotten about the collection, too. He never came into this room. He'd been dating an interior designer when he'd built the house, and he'd given her free rein when she'd volunteered to do the decorating. But yes, he still remembered the shock the first time he'd seen what she'd dug out of the boxes in his attic.

Putting Madison in here with Andrew's prized possessions hadn't been intentional. He'd simply chosen the room farthest from his. But if seeing the collection served as penance, so be it. Why should she be able to walk away and forget when he couldn't?

"You abandoned them along with everything else in your house."

"Andrew's house. He bought it."

"To surprise you."

"The deed and loan were in his name. He chose all the furniture." Her resentful tone grated like the screech of a rusty hinge.

She ducked her head and tugged at her cuffs. "I left behind the things that meant something to you and your brother. He would've wanted you to have all this since you collected them together."

Andrew hadn't cared about the sentimental ties to the items. He'd considered them all investments—items he could sell later when the star's value went up.

"You left everything, Madison, creating an additional burden for those of us who had to clean up after you." *Him*. He'd been the one who'd had to parcel out his brother's belongings, deciding what to keep, sell or store. He'd had to list the house and sell it. His mom hadn't been up to the task, and his dad had been slammed at work trying to cover his and Andrew's patients.

"I'm sorry. I—I only took what I could carry in the truck, and the love of sports was something you and he shared before I came along."

She'd come between him and Andrew, breaking a bond he'd believed indestructible, and if he didn't do as his father requested and deliver her to the office each week she could drive a bigger wedge between him and his parents, too.

"You mailed us the house keys along with your power of attorney, relinquishing your share of everything but the life insurance and the pickup. You didn't even bother to call or say goodbye to my parents."

He caught her reflection in the mirror, saw her eyes close, fanning dark lashes against her pale skin. When her lids lifted, whatever emotion he thought he'd seen earlier had vanished.

"I said goodbye at the memorial service. Helen preferred it that way."

"Quit blaming your insensitivity on my mother. You bailed without any regard for the damage you'd left behind."

She flinched and opened her mouth. Seconds ticked past. Then she sealed her lips.

She faced him with one hand splayed across her upper chest. The action parted the neckline of her plaid cotton shirt and revealed the area above the scooped neck of the T-shirt she wore beneath it. The shape of her bones showed clearly beneath her skin. His father had remarked on Madison's thinness after she'd left yesterday. Adam hadn't noticed until now. She'd lost weight. Too much.

"I'll be ready by seven. Thank you for allowing

me to stay, Adam. I know this isn't your first choice, either. Next week I'd prefer a hotel."

His father would never agree to that, but he wasn't going to waste his breath. "Tell that to my father."

"I will."

He should leave, but his feet remained rooted. Madison had always been pretty, but as Andrew's girlfriend then his wife she'd been off-limits. Adam had never examined her that closely before, but he could have sworn the angles of her face had been softer six years ago, and he didn't remember her camouflaging her shape beneath layers of loose clothing then either. She looked…fragile.

Probably just another woman starving herself to fit into size-zero jeans. But he couldn't have her collapsing on the job. "Have you eaten dinner?"

"I had a big lunch."

"You know where the kitchen is. It's stocked. Help yourself. I won't wait on you."

He made his escape, passing through the back door, then the screened porch. He jogged down the steps to the slate patio below. Moonlight glimmered on the water, but his favorite view did nothing to soothe him tonight. He punched his father's number into his cell phone.

"She's here," he said the second his father connected.

"Good. I knew I could count on her. You'll get her to the office in the morning?" Worry tightened his voice, and worry was one thing his father didn't need right now.

"Why do you think I flew her in, Dad? Not because I wanted to spend time with her. Once I drop her off tomorrow she'll be stranded. Your idea of taking her truck to the shop was a good one, but it would have been a one-visit deal—we'd have had to think of something else next time. Flying her in covers every visit, and it saves her time, so she won't question my motives."

"It's expensive."

"It's cheaper than hiring a substitute doctor."

A chuckle hit his ear. "You're more like me than you're willing to admit, Adam. Now I can rest easy. Thanks."

No. He wasn't like his father at all. "I'll see you in preop, Dad."

"You don't need to come by the hospital in the morning. I'll see you after I get out. Take special care of our girl. You could even stop by the office and have lunch with her."

"You mean check up on her? Don't push it, Dad. I'll see you before they wheel you back."

"Madison's still your sister-in-law, Adam. She deserves respect."

"She's not my anything anymore. She severed those ties long ago. Tell Mom I'll be there in the morning. She'll need my support even if you don't."

"MADISON."

Madison jolted awake at the sound of a familiar voice. *Andrew?* No. Adam stood over her. They looked and sounded similar, but she'd always been able to tell them apart—a test she'd passed multiple times when Andrew had pulled his hijinks. "What?"

"I asked, what you're doing out here?"

She blinked and looked around. Then it came back to her. She'd barely slept—how could she in that shrine to her dead husband? Cold penetrated her skin, seeping down to her bones. Dawn illuminated the pond. How long had she been on the screened porch? Pushing back her hair, she straightened on the swing, tightened her grip on the blanket she'd wrapped herself in and banded her arms around the void in her middle.

"Did I oversleep?"

"You didn't answer my question."

And he hadn't answered hers. "I came out to listen to the bullfrogs. They reminded me of home."

Her dreams had been filled with the screech of metal against metal as her car had scraped against the guardrail, then the snap of it breaking through and rolling over and over. As always, the impact of the vehicle slamming into the tree and the pain of her stomach colliding with the steering wheel had jolted her awake. It was a familiar dream, one she'd had hundreds of times. But it still rattled her. Sometime this morning she'd trudged out here rather than risk a replay.

She gingerly eased to her feet. Her left foot was slightly numb from being tucked beneath her and made keeping her balance an iffy proposition. She grasped the swing's chain. The links were cold against her palm, but she would not ask Adam for help.

His hair was damp and his chin gleamed from a recent shave. The unbuttoned collar of his white dress shirt revealed a wedge of tanned skin. A navy-and-red unknotted necktie draped his shoulders. The combination of his cologne, menthol shaving cream and minty toothpaste filled her nose.

She'd forgotten the appeal of a freshly showered man first thing in the morning. Her heart raced like a rabbit's, and adrenaline gave her a burst of alertness. Certainly the intimacy of the situation was the only reason.

Yeah, right.

Adam looked good—even better than his brother had on his best day, mainly because he lacked Andrew's cocky you-know-you-want-me swagger. Adam had a harder take-me-or-leave-me edge, or maybe there was a maturity about him that Andrew, with his perpetual fraternity-boy persona, had lacked.

But her damned hormones couldn't tell the difference between the enemy and Andrew.

"Coffee's in the kitchen. I'm pulling out of the garage in thirty minutes."

The scent of coffee from the mug he held in his

hand penetrated her distracting thoughts. "I'll grab a cup and get dressed."

She ducked past him, ignoring him as best she could when he shadowed her inside. Ten minutes after she'd left Adam she was as ready as she was ever going to be to face him again, but neither the caffeine nor her quick, steaming shower had done anything to erase the pall of last night's nightmares. The uneasiness lingered in her mind. She hadn't had the dream in over a year, and she'd thought she'd finally banished the hellish mental movie. Apparently Adam's appearance had resurrected the reruns.

He pivoted sharply when she entered the kitchen, wearing his usual scowl. What had she done to irritate him this time? Breathe?

"Are you starving yourself on purpose?"

The attack took her aback. "What?"

"Did you eat anything last night or this morning?" He practically growled the question.

Why did he care?

"Don't bother lying, Madison. I buy the groceries. I know what's in my house."

"I told you I wasn't hungry last night."

Even if she'd been able to bring herself to rummage through his cupboards for a snack, she'd been too stressed to force down anything. The shrimp and grits lunch yesterday had been her last meal, and she was paying for that this morning with a noticeable lack of get-up-and-go.

"Dad's practice is a busy one. You'll be going nonstop, since you insist on cramming a week's worth of patients into two days. You'll need something substantial to get through the day."

Well, that explained everything. Adam wasn't concerned for her well-being. He was thinking of his father's practice.

"Could we stop somewhere on the way to the office?" A yogurt parfait might soothe her nervous stomach.

"Junk food's not the answer." He raided the fridge, tossing items onto the counter, then he broke four eggs into a large skillet, and efficiently whisked them with a fork. He added fresh spinach, cheese and herbs from a well-stocked array in the cabinet. Bustling around the room like a man on a mission, he dropped bread into a toaster and poured two glasses of orange juice, which he plopped on the table with a thump.

His swift, economical movements implied he'd prepared breakfast for guests before. *Women?* She crammed that thought back into her mental closet. Adam's social life was not her business.

But she couldn't help comparing him to his twin. Andrew's idea of cooking had been to microwave leftovers. A savory aroma filled the kitchen. Her mouth watered and her stomach growled enthusiastically.

With a flick of his wrist Adam folded and plated the omelet, once again surprising her with his competence. After dividing it, he slid half onto a second plate, then set it in front of her, adding a piece of toast. "Eat fast. We need to go."

"I— Thank you, Adam."

"Don't get used to it. I'm not your personal chef."

"I didn't ask you to cook for me."

"We both know I'm not doing this for you." He applied himself to his meal, and Madison did the same, choking down her resentment along with breakfast.

Once breakfast had been consumed Adam rose, grabbed their empty dishes and put them in the dishwasher. "You have five minutes."

"I'm ready."

His gaze searched her face, making her hyperconscious of the ghastly reflection she'd seen in the mirror. But makeup wasn't her thing, and even if she'd wanted to disguise her pallor or the dark circles beneath her eyes, she hadn't packed any concealer. Why worry? She had no one to impress.

"Dad's surgery's at noon. I won't leave the hospital during the procedure. You'll have to hitch a ride to lunch with one of the staff."

"I don't usually eat lunch." Unless Piper or June forced a midday meal on her.

A muscle in his jaw knotted. "I'll pick you up at six-thirty unless the surgery runs late." He rose and braced his fists on the table, leaning across it. "Madison, I don't have the time to babysit you. Do not become a liability."

She wasn't looking for any favors and didn't want

to be beholden to anyone. "I can take care of myself."

"Yeah, I can see that. You're doing a great job." His sarcasm stung like a whip. "You're ten pounds underweight and your clothes hang on you like a sack."

Her hackles rose. It was okay for her friends to nag her, but Adam had no right. "I lost weight when I took up running, and I have more important things to spend my money on than new clothes. I might be built more like a plank than an hourglass, but I'm in good shape—I have to be. It takes strength to manhandle heavy animals."

Adam looked unconvinced or, more likely, uninterested. Well, bully for him. His opinion didn't matter anyway.

ADAM STRODE TOWARD his father's office, eager to ditch Madison and get on with his day. He mentally scrolled through his task list, trying to find time to fit everything into his schedule.

Madison stopped on the front porch so abruptly in front of him that he almost barreled into her. He locked his muscles and shot out a hand to prevent a collision. His palms landed at her waist and his nose grazed the top of her ponytail. The scent of her hair filled his nostrils. The firmness of her hips registered a split second before the warmth of her body scorched his palms. He had the oddest urge to caress her unexpected curves.

What in the hell? He removed his hands and backed away. "Is there a problem?"

Her small breasts rose and fell, then her gaze ricocheted from the door to his face. Emotions chased through her eyes so rapidly he couldn't label any of them—but none were good. "Damn it, Madison, you're not backing out."

She swallowed, then licked her lips. His gaze locked on her sweeping pink tongue, and his brain took a seriously wrong turn. Her damp mouth was not alluring. Definitely not. He had no inclination to find out how she tasted. None. Despite his brother's boasts about his hot sex life, Madison was Andrew's wife. End of story.

Even thinking about touching her was perverted. If his pulse pounded double-time it was only because he didn't have time for this second-thoughts crap.

"Madison," he warned when she remained motionless and silent.

"I'm fine."

Liar. He knew it as well as he knew his own name. What was it about this office that repelled her? He didn't have the time nor the inclination to find out. "The staff's expecting you. They'll show you the ropes."

"I— Do I know any of them?"

What difference did it make? "How am I supposed to know? They'll do their job. Make sure you do yours."

He returned to his car.

He was not running, damn it. He had a jammed schedule and needed to get started. Madison was a grown woman, a trained veterinarian. She didn't need him to hold her hand and make introductions.

He checked his rearview mirror. She stood stiffly on the porch, her fists clenching and relaxing by her sides. Guilt and frustration needled him. He was on the verge of throwing the vehicle into Reverse and dragging her inside when she reached for the handle and opened the door. It closed behind her. He merged into traffic. He'd done his part and delivered her to the office. The next few hours were up to her.

Madison had ghosts to face. But she deserved to suffer through the experience alone. He'd been living with those damned ghosts for six years and no one had made it easy for him.

"LUNCHTIME," DR. DRAKE'S assistant, Lisa, said. "Princess Pug was our last patient this morning."

Madison heaved a sigh of relief and nodded. Adam hadn't been kidding when he predicted she and the staff would be busy. She hadn't had a minute to dwell on the past since she'd stepped through the door this morning and found a patient waiting— a fact she greatly appreciated. She wasn't looking forward to the lull ahead when the memories would crowd into the now empty halls and treatment rooms.

She trudged toward the private offices. She'd been

able to avoid the back of the building until now, but she hadn't packed a lunch and didn't want to force her company on the staff. She definitely wouldn't bum a ride to lunch as Adam had suggested.

Dread quickened her heartbeat as she approached the office she'd shared with Andrew. A lump the size of a Saint Bernard lodged in her throat. She wanted to duck her head and plow past, but she forced herself to stop outside the door.

C'mon. You can do it.

It took colossal effort to turn ninety degrees and face her past. She deliberately kept her gaze high, focusing on the wall behind Andrew's desk. She started at the long horizontal transom-style windows just below the roofline that allowed sunlight into the room. Then she let her gaze slide down. His mahogany-framed diploma occupied the same spot. It was flanked by the bookshelves he'd ordered custom-built in the same dark glossy finish as the frame. The textbooks and knickknacks he'd collected still cluttered the shelves.

Her heart thumped harder and her nails bit into her palms. Taking a bracing breath, she allowed her gaze to click incrementally down like the second hand on a clock to the high back of his chair and then to the surface of his desk. The leather blotter and desk set she'd given him as a graduation present remained in the center. The frame that had held their wedding photograph still occupied the front right corner. She inched forward on leaded feet, and slowly turned the rectangle around.

Seeing the two of them with their hands linked, love in their eyes and radiating from their smiles, crushed the breath from her like a horse pinning her against a stall wall with his haunch. They'd been so young, so idealistic and so certain of their future together. At least she had been.

Had Andrew been plotting even then to derail her plans? Had he ever intended for her to join his father's practice? Or had he always planned for her to be a stay-at-home mom like Helen?

She scanned the rest of the desk and a familiar emptiness yawned in her belly. She cradled the ache with both hands. Andrew had gloated that their son had been conceived during a quickie on this surface while the staff was at lunch. He'd thrown *that* in her face that horrible night.

And that was when she'd taken her eyes off the road.

A tremor racked her. She pried her gaze away and examined the rest of the space. Another shrine to Andrew. Nothing had changed since he'd left, and yet ironically, nothing in *her* life was the same.

With his drunken boast he'd crushed her faith not only in him but in herself. How could she have been so blind, so gullible, so stupid?

An undeniable urge to bolt swept through her. She raced down the hall into Dan—Dr. Drake's office and planted her palms on the edge of his desk.

It had been six years. She shouldn't still react this viscerally.

Out of habit, she gulped deep breaths and rammed the darkness into its hidey-hole by counting her blessings. Her health. Her home. Her practice. Her pets. Her friends. The peaceful town she'd grown to love.

Tilting her head back, she closed her eyes and tried to focus on something else—anything besides the grief gnawing away her hard-won peace. There had to be something positive in this horrible experience.

Her morning had been crammed with everything from avians to reptiles, testing her memory and her training to the limit. Not knowing what she'd find upon entering a treatment room had been both intimidating and exhilarating in ways Madison hadn't anticipated. She'd enjoyed being kept on her toes.

"You okay?" Lisa asked behind her.

Madison spun around. "Yes. I'd forgotten how exciting and varied Danny's patients could be. At home my most exotic patient is a ferret and once in a while an ornery donkey."

"Sounds dull. It's never that here. We're eating in the break room—I hope you like pizza. Better come and get yours before Jim scarfs it down."

Surprised to be included, Madison straightened. "You ordered delivery? I'll pay for my share."

"Adam covered it."

Adam. Her nerves twanged. For the first time

since she'd stepped into the office Madison glanced at the clock. Almost one o'clock. Danny would be in surgery. She'd been too busy this morning to keep track of time. A fresh wave of worry snaked through her. She wanted to call and check on Danny. But she wouldn't. If she intended to keep their relationship strictly business, then checking up on him was out of the question.

She followed Lisa down the hall. "Does Adam always send food?"

"No, not Adam, but Dr. Drake always orders take-out on the days we're slammed and don't have time to go out."

Madison had suggested that practice when she'd interned here. "Does that happen often?"

"Often enough—especially during shortened holiday weeks. Dr. Drake has more patients than he can handle, and he hates to turn anyone away. He definitely needs a partner."

Kay, the receptionist, Jim, the groomer, and Susie, the kennel manager, were seated when Madison and Lisa entered. Kay was older than her predecessor, a perky twentysomething who'd shamelessly flirted with Andrew even in Madison's presence.

"Madison, you did well this morning."

Warmth surrounded Madison. "Thank you, Kay."

"You hit the ground running and never missed a beat. Dr. Drake was right. You're one sharp cookie."

"Da—Dr. Drake said that?"

"He's talked about you for months."

Madison's heart jolted. *Months?* She hadn't agreed to come until Saturday, and yet he'd been discussing her with his staff?

"I have a practice in North Carolina."

Jim laughed. "We've heard all about your little practice and your farm."

The fine hairs on her body rose. Danny had known where she was all along? How much of her business—personal and professional—had he followed? Knowing he'd been spying disturbed her.

Lisa paused with her slice just shy of her lips. "He told us about the good ol' days when you shadowed him and his son, but he didn't tell us why you left."

The unspoken question decimated Madison's appetite. "I didn't feel comfortable here after Andrew died." She forced herself to take a bite. A full mouth gave her an excuse not to elaborate.

Kay nodded. "It must be hard coming back to the place where you worked with your husband. You were both so young—it's such a sad story."

What had Danny told them? The pizza turned to a cheesy, greasy paste in Madison's mouth. She chewed and chewed, then finally swallowed the wad. "Y'all have helped by keeping me busy."

Kay covered her hand. "I'm sorry, hon."

Madison's eyes stung at the unexpected show of sympathy. She'd needed this six years ago, but she couldn't handle it today when her nerves were already exposed and raw from seeing ghosts. She hadn't cried in years and wouldn't now in front of strangers.

"I noticed Miss Findley's and her dog's diets have failed," Jim said.

Madison shot him a grateful glance for his obvious attempt to head off an emotional display. She let the conversation about the morning's patients roll past her. She'd choke down her lunch if it killed her rather than let the others know how badly their revelations had disturbed her.

Bite. Chew. Swallow. Repeat.

Did Danny honestly believe she'd abandon her practice and return to Norcross? Everything she'd heard implied he'd been expecting her for longer than a few days' time. How far was he willing to go to get her back? Would he, like his son had, stoop to using underhanded tactics to get his way?

"Hernia surgeries are supposed to be a piece of cake. But you never know. Dr. Drake isn't young."

Kay's statement jerked Madison from her thoughts. "Hernia?"

Heads bobbed around the table.

Jim reached for a second slice. "Dr. Drake never mentioned any symptoms. He's been lifting big dogs like nothing bothered him. I had no idea. I could've helped."

"He told you he was having hernia surgery?" she repeated to make sure she hadn't misheard.

"Yeah, last month when he scheduled it."

A month. He'd told her he'd scheduled his *cancer*

surgery after Adam's visit to her *last week*. Which was correct?

Madison looked into the trusting faces and realized she was the only one in the room who knew the truth. Or was she the only one who didn't? Had Danny lied to his staff? Or had he lied to her as part of some master plot to get her back to Norcross?

But if he'd lied to her, then so had Adam and Helen. And exactly how long had this scheme been in the works?

Was there anyone here she could trust?

CHAPTER FOUR

A SCUFF OF sound brought Madison's head up from the stack of files on Dan—Dr. Drake's desk. Andrew stood in the doorway. A shock wave slammed her back in the chair.

No, not Andrew, she quickly corrected. Andrew was dead. She'd held his cold, limp hand until the paramedics had pried her fingers loose to put her in a separate ambulance, and that had been the last time she'd seen him alive. Despite being surrounded by memories of him today, he hadn't come back to haunt her in his old stomping grounds.

Shorter hair, a perpetual frown and a broader build gave away Adam's identity. Lines of stress and exhaustion bracketed his eyes and downturned mouth. "Are you ready?"

"How did you get in? I turned the dead bolt behind the staff."

"I have Dad's keys."

She had no keys, which meant she couldn't leave without explaining to Kay why she needed a set or risk leaving the office unlocked and unprotected, which she would never do since she knew how much each piece of equipment and bottle of medicine cost.

An intentional oversight? Most likely, given the way this trip had transpired.

"What procedure did they end up doing on Da— your father?"

"A lobe resection."

Lobe meant lung, not hernia. Danny hadn't lied to *her*. She should be relieved, but she wasn't.

"You should have warned me that he'd lied to his staff."

Dark eyebrows spiked upward. "About what?"

"He told them he was going in for a hernia operation."

She hated liars. That was ironic since her life back in Quincey was based on a lie—one of omission, one that hurt no one. But her story was still dishonest no matter how she justified it. When she'd first arrived in Quincey she'd let everyone believe that she was a recent vet school graduate who'd just happened to hear about Dr. Jones's practice upon graduation. No one knew she was running from a past that wouldn't quit pursuing her.

"Is it impossible for you to comprehend that Dad might not have wanted his employees to worry about their job security?"

"Trust is essential in any partnership—business or personal." A lesson she'd learned through Andrew's betrayal.

Frustrated by the whole messy situation, she

swiped a strand of hair off her face. Unless she wanted to alienate the people she was supposed to work with over the next eight weeks, she'd have to perpetuate the lie by not revealing their beloved boss's faults.

"I'll give him an opportunity to tell them the truth, but he needs to do it as soon as possible. I will not look them in the eye and lie to them. If they ask a direct question, I'll answer it truthfully."

"Tell him that when you visit him tonight."

Alarm splintered through her. "Visit him?"

"You're going to stand by his bedside and tell him everything is wonderful—even if it isn't."

"No." The idea revolted her so much she pushed away from the desk. If she never set foot in another hospital it would be too soon. Lying there after she'd lost her baby, seeing the sympathy on the doctors' and nurses' faces as they bustled into and out of her empty room and having no one to tell her what was going on with Andrew had pushed her to the brink of sanity. It was a doctor she'd never seen before who had informed her of Andrew's passing.

"I'm not going to the hospital, Adam."

"Yes, you are. Let's go." He turned and left.

She racked her brain for an excuse he would accept. "It's been a long day. I need to rest for tomorrow."

He held the front door open for her, his hard eyes bored into hers. "Your day has been nothing compared to what my mother and father have been through."

True, she admitted with a pinch of remorse. "Your father won't be ready for company."

Adam turned the key, locking her out of the building. She couldn't go back inside. "Your reassurances will quicken his recovery."

Another truth she didn't want to accept. Resignation settled heavily on her shoulders. "Can we at least stop somewhere so I can grab a sandwich?" Procrastination at its finest. "I appreciated the lunch, but it was a long time ago."

"And you only ate one slice of pizza."

Yet another unpleasant surprise. As if there hadn't been enough of them already. "You're checking up on me? What do you care if I eat?"

"I told you. This isn't about you. It's about my father's practice and your ability to hold it together until he returns. Frankly, I don't think you'll last. I think you'll bail at the first opportunity. But until you do, I'm going to do my part."

Indignation stiffened her spine. "I keep my promises."

"We'll see about that." He held open her car door, then closed it behind her, sealing her inside the silent compartment. *Trapped.* The word echoed through her brain and made her skin crawl. She'd never been prone to claustrophobia, but she suspected this need to claw her way out might be how it felt.

Anger steamed through her. Why had she come back? Why had she let herself be suckered into helping?

Because you want this debt behind you so you can finally find some peace.

Adam rounded the hood and slid behind the wheel. "Passing out due to low blood sugar won't get you out of helping. You can eat in the hospital cafeteria—our food is good. I need to check on Dad one more time before going home. When I left—"

He clamped his jaw shut and wrenched the key in the ignition. His Adam's apple bobbed. Witnessing his emotional response deflated her anger and dredged up a reciprocal concern she did not want or need.

"How is Danny?" She wished the words back the instant they escaped. She'd been fighting with herself all afternoon trying not to care, but that was easier said than done when she'd been treading the tiles she and Danny had walked together so often.

"Surgery went as well as could be expected."

He pulled out of the parking lot, turning the opposite direction from his house. Her nails dug into the armrest. She wanted to insist he take her back to his place. But judging by his hard face and white-knuckled grip on the steering wheel, arguing would be a waste of time. She was at Adam's mercy, dependent on him for food, shelter and transportation. She'd resolved after the crash to never let herself rely on anyone again, and yet here she was.

She should have brought the truck, but she worried every time she took a long trip that it wouldn't make it home. Then what would she do? She wouldn't be able to reach the livestock on surrounding farms.

The truck's starter was at the top of the list of expensive things needing repair. On the drive home from Georgia Saturday she'd been afraid to turn off the engine when she filled the gas tank for fear that the vehicle wouldn't restart, and then she'd have to pay for a tow from someone besides the mechanic who traded his skills for animal care. Working here instead of at home meant she wasn't earning the money she'd need to buy the parts.

But her debt to Danny was one that money couldn't repay. So if she had to go to the hospital then she would, but she wouldn't leave empty-handed. She had questions of her own for Danny, like why had he created the elaborate cover story? Why and for how long had he been spying on her? Did he honestly believe she'd throw away the life she'd fought so hard to build and return here to the place where she'd been betrayed?

Adam made the drive in silence, which suited her fine. Andrew would have filled the ride with chatter about his day, his patients, his brilliance, his skills.

She glanced again at the tense man beside her. The only thing she and Adam agreed on was that neither of them wanted her here. The hospital came into view and memories impaled her like shards of shattered glass. She fought to conceal her response to the sight of the big yellow-brick building. If Adam noticed the cold sweat beading her upper lip, he didn't mention it.

He passed the emergency entrance, then public parking, before turning into an employee lot where he had to swipe his ID in order for the gate arm to lift. He pulled into a space near the building with a sign marked Hospital Administrator. Adam had been the rule-following twin. He wouldn't squat on someone else's turf. That meant he'd found success outside his brother's and father's shadows.

"Have you worked here long?"

"A little over three years."

She followed him through an employee entrance, which also required the use of his card. A rainbow of scrub-garbed employees strode briskly through the halls. She checked her watch. It was close to the 7:00 p.m. shift change. Most people nodded or spoke to Adam as they passed. Apparently he was liked and respected here, which suggested he wasn't always the arrogant sourpuss he presented to her. A barrage of curious glances fired her way, but he didn't introduce her to anyone.

The staff elevator was packed when they entered, forcing her to stand too close to Adam. She turned her back and faced the doors like everybody else, but unlike the others, she was totally aware of the man behind her. His scent. His body heat. Her palms moistened and her pulse quickened. An anxiety reaction to the hospital? Yes, that was all it was.

The doors opened and four more people stepped

in, forcing her to squeeze even closer to Adam. He put a hand on her back to stop her and the impact hit her like a spark of static electricity. She prayed he didn't notice her jump.

"How's your dad?" one of the men asked.

"He came through surgery well. Thank you, Ted."

Adam's breath stirred her hair, sending a shiver skittering down her spine. No, she wasn't reacting to him, but to his twin, the one whose memory had been dogging her footsteps all day.

But it couldn't be a reaction to Andrew, she admitted reluctantly. Andrew had never made her insides quiver by simply breathing. But she couldn't—wouldn't—let it be because of Adam, either. It was likely just abstinence causing the chaos. Damn her deprived, confused hormones. They were soaking up Adam's maleness like a drought-ridden field did a summer rain.

She tried to think of something besides the man behind her. But her mind went blank. She focused on her breathing, then on feeling the floor beneath each of her toes. But no matter what she did, she couldn't dull her hypersensitivity to Adam's proximity.

The doors opened again. "This is our floor."

His hand touched her waist again, delivering another jolt. She bustled out as quickly as she could without knocking aside the others crammed into the box. She'd rather face Dr. Drake and the hospital room instead of this crazy hormonal imbalance.

The minute she cleared the crowd the smell hit her.

Antiseptic. Alcohol-based hand sanitizer. Scorched coffee. Leftover food from the rack of trays waiting to be picked up. Hospital smells were the kind you never forgot. Then the muffled sounds penetrated the pulse pounding her eardrums. Hushed voices. A distant cough. Someone moaning in pain. Televisions on different channels droning from multiple rooms. She hadn't forgotten the noises, either. When you lie in bed with nothing to think about except your misery, you searched for any distraction.

"He's at the end of the hall." Adam's long stride carried him away.

Her mouth dried. It wasn't the same floor, but the layout was identical. Different paint and tile colors didn't change the memories or the emotions this place evoked. She didn't want to be here, but she would get through it the same way she'd gotten through everything else life had thrown at her—by treating each difficult moment like the Iditarod, gritting her teeth and soldiering on step after step, mile after mile. The sooner she did this, the sooner Adam would take her home. No, not home—his house. Back to that shrine to Andrew. But even that was better than here.

She ordered her feet forward, then stopped outside the room, where Adam guarded the entrance. Through the open door she spotted Helen in the recliner by the bed. Her former mother-in-law hadn't noticed their arrival. She had her head bent over her wringing hands. Her shoulders drooped and lines creased her forehead. Worry had robbed her face of all color, save the shadows as dark as bruises beneath her eyes. Sympathy clutched Madison's insides.

Adam tapped on the door and Helen's head snapped up. She bolted to her feet, pasted on a forged smile for her son, then her gaze, filled with a cocktail of anger and loathing, focused on Madison.

"Good. You're here." Her cold tone held no welcome. Bitterness twisted her lips. "I need a breath of fresh air."

She barged past them. Only then did Madison look at the patient. A chest tube and a catheter drained into containers hanging from the bed. *Dann—Dr. Dra—* Who was she kidding? She couldn't keep her distance. Not when she'd been walking in his footsteps and handling his patients and instruments all day. She'd lost count of the number of clients who'd asked about him.

Danny's face was nearly as ashen as Helen's. His eyes were sunken and closed, his lips pale and dry.

Adam touched his shoulder. "Dad, Madison's here."

Danny's lids flickered open, revealing a blue-green gaze so like Adam's, but the irises looked faded and his gaze unfocused. "How's my girl? I've been waiting for you."

His weak voice tugged at something deep inside her. She'd never had a chance to say goodbye to *her* father. Was she saying goodbye to Danny now? No.

He'd only been out of surgery a few hours. He'd be back to his old self soon. She had to believe that.

The hand he lifted from the bed trembled. Madison tried to harden her heart, to block out the worry, but she couldn't. She did, however, ignore that hand. *Say your piece and get out.*

"We had a smooth day at the office. Your staff is wonderful. That's why I can't believe—"

He coughed and winced. The words died on her tongue. How could she condemn and interrogate him when he was in pain and still hung over from anesthesia?

She couldn't. Her questions could wait until next week. "I can't believe how efficient they are."

Adam's hard face relaxed slightly.

"They know…how I like…things done. You do, too. Well trained. Like you." His struggle for breath between words made Madison uncomfortable. The hand tethered to the blood oxygen meter gingerly covered his rib.

"They definitely know your methods."

"Dad, you need to rest." Adam pulled out his wallet and offered Madison some folded money. "Take Mom down to the cafeteria."

Appalled at the idea of one-on-one time with Helen, she tucked her hands behind her back. "I'm not hungry."

He caught her left wrist, pressed the money into her palm and folded her fingers around it. His hands were warm, slightly rough, inarguably firm, but not hurtful. Her senses rioted.

"Please, Madison. She hasn't left his side all day, and she insists on staying here tonight. She needs a break. See that she takes it."

When he put it that way, how could she refuse?

HELEN LEANED AGAINST the wall by the nurses' station, staring into the black sludge they called coffee. If she had the energy she'd teach them how to make it correctly, but every nerve in her body was raw and each muscle was so exhausted from fear and worry she wanted to crumple to the floor and cry. But, of course, she wouldn't.

Desperately needing the caffeine and the sugar she'd liberally poured into the cup, she forced herself to sip the vile brew. She had to be strong for Danny. She couldn't lose him. He was her life, and she'd do anything—even tolerate the woman who'd killed her son and grandchild—if it helped him beat this cancer.

But enduring Madison's presence wasn't easy. Every time Helen looked at her former daughter-in-law the agony started anew. She remembered the conversation she'd had with Andrew when he'd confessed Madison was making him look bad at the office and the glint in his eyes a few months later when they'd announced the surprise pregnancy.

What had Andrew done? Had he taken her motherly advice the wrong way? And had the car accident been partly her fault?

No. Madison had been driving. Andrew's and little Daniel's deaths were Madison's fault. She had to believe that. She *had* to or she'd lose her mind.

How could Danny "forgive and move on" so easily? Madison had told the police officer that she and Andrew had been arguing at the time of the crash, and she'd admitted to taking her eyes off the road. If that didn't make her guilty, then what did?

But Danny refused to listen. It was as if he'd closed the door on Andrew the day they'd walked away from his lifeless body here at this hospital. He refused to talk about their loss and got mad at her if she tried to. If not for the fact that he kept their son's office exactly as Andrew had left it, she'd think Danny had forgotten Andrew had ever existed. But now she was beginning to suspect he'd kept the office waiting for Madison's return.

"When Madison comes home..." had become a hated chorus in their house. Danny yammered about her as if she was a saint who could do no wrong, the resurrection of all their hopes and dreams, one who would make their lives whole again. But their lives would never be the same—not without Andrew. You'd think Danny would realize that. Madison had made her lack of appreciation for all they'd done for her clear at every turn.

"Mom."

She straightened at the sound of Adam's voice

and smoothed her expression as best she could before facing him. She didn't want him to worry and wouldn't let him know she clung to the cliff of her breaking point with splitting fingernails.

"Please show Madison where the cafeteria is located."

She flinched, sloshing the swill in her cup. He wanted *her* to take care of his brother's killer? It seemed like betrayal that he, too, expected her to forget Madison's part in ruining their lives. "It's in the basement and easy to find. There are signs to mark the way," she said to Adam, ignoring Madison, who stood behind him.

"I don't have time to look for her if she gets lost, Mom. Just make sure she gets there and gets back, and grab something for yourself while you're there. You haven't eaten today."

She stared into her son's implacable face. What he asked wasn't fair. It wasn't right. But he could be as hardheaded as his father sometimes, and she couldn't afford to offend Adam. If anything happened to Danny, Adam was all she had left.

The panicked sensation began to swell again, making it difficult to draw a breath. She punched her anxiety like rising dough, then dropped the almost full cup into the trash can and headed for the elevators. Madison fell into step beside her. Helen said nothing. Her grandmother had taught her that if she didn't have anything nice to say she shouldn't speak at all.

The wound Madison had inflicted was too deep to heal. Helen had never hated anyone in her life. The Bible said "forgive those who trespass against us," and she had tried. But she was weak and she couldn't find it in her heart to forgive Madison *Monroe*.

The crowded elevator saved her from having to make conversation. She wedged herself into the opposite corner. Once they reached the cafeteria, the smell of the food made her nauseous. Needing to escape but unable to bear the idea of going back upstairs and seeing Danny hooked to machines and looking like death, she pivoted toward a table by the window. All she needed was five minutes to regroup, then she'd return to her bedside vigil.

"Don't you want something?" Madison called.

"No."

She stared at the fountain in the walled courtyard outside. Her life was a lot like the koi's. More often than not she felt as if she was swimming in circles and getting nowhere. Her existence had no purpose or meaning anymore. Preparing dinner for the boys used to be the highlight of her day. Then after Adam left it was only Andrew and Danny. Now Danny worked all the time. He seemed to prefer the office to their home and his animals' and his staff's company to hers.

She'd been excited when Adam moved back to Norcross, but he had little time for his mother. Come to think of it, his avoidance of home had started soon after Madison and Andrew had become involved. On the rare times he had come home during a school vacation Adam had spent almost no time at the house. He'd preferred going out with his friends to hanging out with his brother—yet another reason to dislike the woman. She'd come between her sons, dissolving the closeness that only identical twins shared.

Helen closed her eyes, blocking out the voices around her. She tried to remember the good ol' days when she'd had all three Drake men sitting around her table. Three hungry males willing to try any recipe she served, and more often than not, she'd had a houseful of their friends, too. She'd been happy then.

What would she do if Danny didn't make it? The thought darted out of nowhere, catapulting her from her peaceful place.

Don't think that way.

But she couldn't help it. Other than lunches with the garden club every two months, Helen had nothing to entertain herself with except watching cooking shows on TV. When she experimented with new recipes, she usually ate them alone. Her labor-intensive meals had often turned into congealed messes by the time Danny got home.

Madison set a lidded cup and a handful of creamers and sweeteners in front of Helen, then lowered into the chair across from her. "I suspect the coffee here is slightly better than upstairs. It doesn't smell burned."

"I didn't ask for that." And she wouldn't drink it.

She didn't want to be beholden to this woman for anything more than her help with Danny.

"I know. But Adam gave me money and asked me to get you to eat. I didn't know what you wanted."

"I'm not hungry." Helen scanned Madison's tray. A grilled chicken and spinach salad and a bottle of some kind of vitamin-fortified water. How could Madison eat at a time like this? If the surgeon hadn't gotten everything, Danny could die. Even now there could be nasty cells floating around in his body looking for healthy tissue to attack.

"Are you sure you don't want something?"

She battled another wave of fear. "No."

Madison stabbed the salad with her fork and put some into her mouth. She chewed, but she looked as if she derived no pleasure from the food. It hadn't been that way when the two of them had shared the kitchen on weekends when Madison had come home from school. Bitterness welled inside Helen, burning the back of her throat like acid.

"Do you know what the first questions out of Danny's mouth were when he came out of anesthesia? 'Where's Madison? How's my practice?'" Helen couldn't keep the hostility and pain from her voice. She was no actress.

"Danny defines himself by his job. Most men do."

"Danny is more than a veterinarian. He's a husband and a father first. There's more to life than his damned animals."

She bit her tongue. She never swore. It wasn't ladylike. Her grandmother had raised her better. But to hear Madison defending Danny got on her last nerve. From what Andrew had said before he'd… passed, Madison was like Danny. Career obsessed and uninterested in mothering their child.

If Helen's fears were true and Andrew had done what she suspected he might have done, how angry would a career-driven woman be at having her plans derailed? Angry enough to wreck a car on purpose? Angry enough to cause an injury that might hurt the unborn child he claimed she hadn't wanted?

"I know he's more than a vet, Helen, but there are so many animals in need of help that sometimes when you get home you have nothing left to give." Surprise then regret filled Madison's eyes. She ducked her head as if she regretted her confession.

"Not in your tiny practice." *Not nice, Helen.* Shamed by her rudeness, she hid her face by drinking some of the coffee. It was better than the tar upstairs, but it could use improvement. And Adam had paid for it, so she wouldn't owe Madison anything if she drank it. She opened the lid and added cream and sugar.

"My practice may be small, but because it's in a rural area it's a dumping ground for abused or unwanted animals. It keeps me busy."

"Euthanizing the strays?"

"No." Madison sounded genuinely shocked by the question. She stirred her salad. "I should. But

I can't unless there's no chance for quality of life. My farm's full of them. I try to find homes for each one, but not every animal is adoptable."

Helen had always wanted a dog or cat, at first for the boys, then for herself when she discovered she couldn't have more children, but Danny said he got slobbered on by animals all day. He didn't want to have to deal with them when he came home.

After Madison's family had been killed, Andrew had called her "his little stray," and Helen had adopted her like the daughter or pet she never had. But Madison had bitten the hand that fed her, so to speak. Helen owed her no loyalty, especially if she'd—

No, don't think that. Surely a woman who couldn't euthanize every stray that crossed her path wouldn't deliberately wreck her car because she hadn't gotten her way. Or would she?

Madison's golden-brown eyes met hers. There was a hard glint to them that had not been there before Andrew's passing. "How long has Danny been spying on me?"

Affronted, Helen stiffened. "He is not spying. He's interested in your welfare. He invested a lot of time in you."

"Yes, he did. And that's why I'm here." Madison pushed the green leaves around in her bowl again. "He doesn't really believe I'll abandon my practice and move back to Norcross, does he?"

Helen wished she could say no with certainty,

but since his diagnosis, his comments suggesting otherwise had become so frequent she couldn't ignore them. She gulped more coffee, trying to wash down her worry.

What if Madison returned and Danny and Adam discovered Helen's part in the unwanted pregnancy? She'd lose their respect. She might even lose her husband and son.

"We both know you're not going to come back."

"No. I'm not. How long do you think it will be before your house is livable?"

"Danny insists on doing all the work, so not until he's healed enough to do it. Why?"

"I'd prefer not to inconvenience Adam."

"Isn't his house nice enough? Danny says your farmhouse is nothing impressive." The ugly words jumped from her mouth before she could stop them.

Madison flinched. "I'd prefer a hotel."

"I'll talk to Danny and see if we can get you a room, but don't get your hopes up. He's not sure he can trust you to keep your promise."

Madison laid down her fork and snapped the lid onto her half-eaten meal. "I'm well aware that none of you trust me, Helen. But unlike some people, I keep my promises."

Helen caught a glimpse of regret before Madison bolted to her feet. Trepidation trickled through her. "What are you implying?"

"Nothing. I'm just tired. We'd better get upstairs." And then she walked away.

What had Madison meant? She'd never been one to make unkind remarks. Or had she hidden her true nature well? Did she know about that mother-son conversation? Was she confirming that Andrew had done something he shouldn't have?

Digging for answers was like picking at a scab. It hurt. It made Helen's heart bleed. And she wasn't sure how much more grief she could handle. Best to let sleeping dogs lie before she learned something she couldn't live with.

CHAPTER FIVE

SHAKING HIS ARMS to ease the burn in his muscles, Adam walked away from the weight bench. One more set and maybe he could sleep. Working out this close to bedtime wasn't a good idea, but he was too wound up to lie on his back and stare at the shadows dancing across the ceiling, as he'd done last night.

A flash of movement outside caught his attention. He stepped closer to the window. Madison paced the screened porch on the opposite end of the house in the dark. The moonlight reflected off her white clothing.

It was almost eleven o'clock—too late for her to be up, considering she'd barely stayed awake during the car ride home from the hospital. Or had she been faking it when she'd had her head back against the headrest and her eyes closed?

He grabbed his towel, wiped the sweat from his face and headed down the hall to find out what was wrong.

In the den he simultaneously flipped on the light and thrust open the door, then stepped outside. Madison spun to face him. The cool night air chilling the sweat on his skin had beaded her nipples beneath her thin T-shirt. His heart thumped hard against his ribs. He yanked his gaze back to her face. "What are you doing out here?"

"Unwinding."

Every muscle in her long, bare legs was as tense as a bowstring, belying her answer. She bit her lip and folded her arms. The move hiked up the bottom of her shirt a few inches, revealing the hem of her shiny running shorts. At least she wasn't naked beneath the shirt. Her toes curled on the deck, and lust kicked him square in the gut. He punted it right back. There was nothing sexy about bare feet and unpainted toenails.

"You should be in bed. Tomorrow will be as busy as today."

"I'm not tired yet."

The shadows beneath her eyes told a different story. "You can't sleep out here, Madison. There's a perfectly good bed inside."

"I'm fine. Don't let me keep you from—" Her gaze traveled across his bare chest, then down to the waistband of his gym shorts—his only piece of clothing. His blood chased south right behind it. "Whatever you were doing."

Damn it. He would not get a boner in front of her. He crushed the towel in his fist and willed the response away, but that didn't stop him from rising to half-mast.

He caught a glimpse of her expanded pupils before she turned away. His skin warmed.

"Go to bed, Madison." Self-directed anger added gravel to his tone.

"There's no point in going until I can sleep," she replied without turning away from the moonlight-streaked pond.

And then it hit him. "You're avoiding the bedroom."

Her gasp and quick pivot confirmed his guess.

"I live with the reminder that Andrew is dead every time I look in the mirror at the face we shared. But *you* can't even handle sleeping with his old trophies." He shouldn't take pleasure in that, but he did. Petty of him.

"That's absurd. They're only inanimate objects."

He could see her false bravado in the hiking of her chin. The pinking of her cheeks contrasted with the white line of tension outlining her lips. "If you're not at the top of your game tomorrow, the staff will have to work harder to cover for you."

If her spine stiffened any more it would snap. "I never give less than one hundred percent at work."

She stalked back into the house and not a moment too soon. He'd never looked at Madison in any way other than as Andrew's girl. And come hell or high water, he wasn't going to change that now.

But despite her insistence that nothing was wrong, something seemed off, and he couldn't have her falling down on the job.

He followed her, but first detoured by the laundry room to don a T-shirt. No need to court trouble, and the way she'd looked at him could cause nothing but mayhem. He needed to call Ann, his longtime friend with benefits. A few uncomplicated hours with her and this unwanted awareness of Madison would not be an issue.

He found Madison in the hall outside the bedroom with her hand inches from the doorknob. Her fingers curled, relaxed then curled again, but she made no attempt to grasp the knob.

His conscience pricked him. Was she still mourning his brother? If so, putting her in that room was cruel. But no, Andrew had insisted Madison cared for nothing and no one besides her job—not even the baby she'd conceived. And thus far Adam had seen no evidence to the contrary.

"There's another guest room if you can't handle that one."

She lowered her hand and slowly turned. Her eyes locked on his face. "You don't think much of me, do you, Adam?"

"My opinion doesn't matter. Twenty-four more hours and you'll be at home and not my problem until next week."

"Twenty-*four*?"

"I'll fly you home after you visit the hospital tomorrow night."

Her eyes widened in obvious dismay. "Why do I have to go back?"

Selfish. "Because my dad needs to know he hasn't misplaced his faith in you even though I'm certain he has. You *will* let him down. It's just a matter of when."

"You're wrong, and I'm tired of you and your mother throwing that in my face. But only time will prove that *I* abide by my word." She entered the room and firmly closed the door.

Something about the way she'd stressed *I* hinted at deeper meaning. But he didn't have time to worry about that tonight. His chauffeur duties were cutting into his work time. That meant he had to be on his game and doubly effective when he was on the job. He needed sleep. And he would not let concerns about Madison rob that from him. She'd already taken too much.

THANKFUL FOR THE lunch break, Madison retreated to her office, sank into her well-worn chair and propped her elbows on her scarred desk. She dropped her head into her hands. The morning had been stupendously long.

It was good to be home, but she was beginning to wonder if she had PTSD from her trip to Georgia. Being back in Drake territory had been like walking barefoot across the kitchen floor after she'd dropped and shattered a glass. She never knew when she'd get stabbed by another shard of memory, or worse yet, a splinter of attraction for Andrew's clone.

Her second visit with Danny had been every bit

as touchy as her first. It couldn't be clearer that neither Adam nor Helen wanted her there, and tolerated her only out of necessity. Danny, on the other hand, hung on to her every word, making her feel doubly guilty that she was counting the days until she could leave Norcross and the Drakes behind for the last time.

Seven more weeks to go. How would she survive?

Had she been jumpy this morning? Yes. Distracted? Affirmative. A little short with the clients who'd grilled her about her absence? Absolutely. She'd caught Piper looking at her strangely several times, but thankfully, her assistant had not asked questions. She wished she could say the same about her clients. If the afternoon went like the morning, Madison would be lucky not to offend anyone.

"Lunchtime!"

At Piper's cry Madison lifted her head. Her assistant and June, her tenant, stood side by side in the doorway. Their up-to-something expressions did not bode well for Madison's downtime.

"What's up, ladies?" She hated to ask.

"It's time for chicken-salad sandwiches," Piper said.

"It's Wednesday."

"You weren't here on Monday."

Their chicken-salad-at-Madison's-on-Mondays habit was practically sacred. When June wasn't on duty or could carve a few minutes out of her schedule she joined them. "Sorry, but I haven't prepared the chicken salad."

Piper pulled a plastic container from behind her back. "Lucky for us, I begged a recipe from one of the church ladies. It's not as good as your grandmother's recipe, but it'll do."

"And I made brownies." June displayed another container. She opened the resealable plastic top, stepped forward and waved the dessert beneath Madison's nose. The scent of chocolate filled the air. Madison's mouth watered. "Nothing fixes stress like chocolate."

The deputy could bake. Madison had not bothered to learn—what was the point when it was just her? Homemade sweets were a treat. "Who said I'm stressed?"

Piper and June exchanged a hiked-eyebrow look.

"Why, bless your heart, dear," June drawled in a syrupy fake Southern accent that sounded remarkably like Madison's nosiest client—one who'd grilled her within an inch of her life an hour ago. "Just eat one of these. You'll feel better."

"I'm fine. But I will take one of your better-than-sex double-chocolate walnut brownies." She reached for a treat and took a big bite. The gooey, fudgy flavor filled her mouth. Heaven.

Piper shook her head. "Nothing is better than sex if you're doing it right."

June jabbed Piper with an elbow and stuck out

her tongue. "Not all of us are having newlywed sex. Quit rubbing it in."

Piper blushed and Madison smiled. Piper had recently managed to reunite with her old flame and her son's father. If Madison weren't so happy for Piper she'd be envious.

June's gaze swung to Madison. "I'm surprised you're not singing the same satisfied song after spending two nights with your sex-on-a-stick brother-in-law."

The brownie turned to mud in her mouth. Madison gulped. One of the walnuts raked down her throat like a jagged rock.

Piper perked up. "He's attractive?"

"Hot." June touched the air and hissed a sizzling sound.

"He's my brother-in-law."

"You're the one who said your husband died a long time ago. That makes Mr. Tight-Buns-and-Broad-Shoulders fair game. The man has swagger down to an art. I would love to frisk him. I might even use my handcuffs. Unless you want to?" She waggled her eyebrows at Madison, her eyes sparking with mischief.

Madison considered hiding behind her desk. "I'll pass."

"I see Madison's point. He *is* family," Piper agreed as she doled out paper plates. "But June's right, too, Madison. Your marriage ended years ago. If this guy trips your trigger—"

"He doesn't."

Something was tripping her trigger, but it wasn't Adam. It was hormones. And memories of a time in her life when she'd thought everything perfect.

June pulled up a chair and piled a sandwich and two brownies on Madison's plate. "Family is not just genetics. It's who you make it. You two are my family because I say so. And Hot Stuff has been out of your life for how long?"

"Six years, but—"

"So he's no longer related. He took himself out of that equation when he didn't contact you until he needed a favor. And as I might have mentioned, he's H. O. T. Hot."

So maybe Adam was attractive. She had to admit that though Andrew had been a devoted runner and in excellent shape, he had never lifted weights. Adam obviously did. His solid, well-defined and well-placed muscle was proof of that. Adam's pectorals with their tiny hard nipples, his biceps with their cording of thick veins and his washboard abs were a call to every dormant feminine atom in her body—a call she intended to ignore.

"You two are killing my appetite. But before you get too caught up in your fantasy, you need to know Adam and Andrew were identical twins."

"Ooh," the women chorused simultaneously.

The deputy shrugged. "That makes it tricky, but not illegal. He's still far better looking than anything you'll find around here, and his expensive clothing tells me he's successful at whatever he does. I wouldn't discard him too quickly—unless you're throwing him my way."

"He's an out-of-towner, June, and we all know you swore you'd never relocate again for a man."

"True. Burned once and all that. But you should take a good, long look at him. He's delicious."

"You are delusional, Deputy Jones, and strangely repetitive today. My practice and my home are *here,* and the Drakes are a complication I don't need. No, thanks."

They turned their attention to the food, but Piper and June's inquisitive gazes never strayed far from Madison. When she could stall no longer, Madison took her last bite and pushed her empty plate aside, then leaned back in her chair and waited.

"Are you going to make us drag it out of you? You know I have professional experience with interrogation." June said it with humor, but Madison saw the seriousness behind the smile.

"There's nothing to tell."

"Bull. Your former in-laws haven't visited once in all the years I've known you, and yet you dropped everything and ran the moment Handsome snapped his fingers. I've never known you to do anything that impulsive unless it involved an animal in distress. You don't have to help them if it's going to keep you up all night."

"What makes you think I'm not sleeping?"

"Because I saw your lights on in the house, then

in the barn, and I heard you talking to Bojangles around 3:00 a.m."

Madison winced. June had lost sleep watching out for her. "I'm sorry I kept you up."

"Make it up to me by starting with, 'I'm doing them this *huge* favor because...'" She waggled her fingers in a give-me-more gesture.

Madison poked at the crumbs on her plate, wishing she could ignore June's request. But June and Piper were picking up Madison's slack with the practice and the menagerie. They deserved to know at least part of her story.

"My family was killed by a tornado early in my junior year of college. The Drakes took me under their wing." She ignored their sympathetic awws and plowed on. If she stopped now she'd never get out the sordid story. "Andrew proposed on my twenty-first birthday. We married a year later when I graduated from the university. I practically lived with Andrew's family during school breaks and vacations, and during vet school I worked with Dr. Drake every chance I had. Danny, my father-in-law, taught me more about treating animals than any of my vet school professors.

"Andrew was three years older than me. He joined his father's practice when he graduated. I was supposed to do the same when I finished." Bombarded by memories and what-should-have-beens, Madison's words vanished.

"But you didn't?" June prompted.

"No. I..." How much could she tell without risking them hating her? "Andrew and the baby I was carrying were fatally injured in a car accident on the way home from my graduation party. I couldn't face the Drakes after that. It was better for me to leave."

"Better for whom? I can't believe you didn't need their love and support in your time of grief," Piper said. "Don't think I'm judging. I've made a few tough choices of my own and cut people I loved out of my life. And I know that unless someone's walked in your shoes they can't fully understand your struggle."

"Andrew's mother said I was a constant reminder of what she'd lost and that looking at me made her sick."

"The bitch." June jumped to Madison's defense without hesitation. "She turned you away when you needed her most, and you're helping them now—why?"

Madison's palms moistened and her pulse drummed in her ears. These women were her friends. She didn't know what she'd do without them. But she couldn't live with herself if she lied when asked a direct question. "I was driving the car."

Like synchronized swimmers their expressions went from curious to understanding then empathetic. Piper circled the desk, perched on the armrest of Madison's chair and put an arm around her shoulders. "I'm so sorry, Madison. What happened?"

"I hit black ice and we plunged down an embankment. The car rolled. Andrew had been partying and refused to wear his seat belt. His head hit the windshield. My stomach impacted with the steering wheel, snapping my son's spine. He—Daniel was stillborn fourteen hours later."

The confession left her throat as raw as if she'd coughed up razor blades. Being told her son had not survived, then enduring an induced labor *alone* and praying the whole time that the doctors were wrong had been absolute hell. Then they'd placed his tiny, lifeless body on her chest and her hopes had been crushed. She battled to hold back the tears burning her eyes and clogging her throat, because if she started, she didn't know if she could stop.

"Had you been drinking?" June probed gently.

Leave it to June to get to the facts. "No. I didn't plan my pregnancy, but I never would have done anything to endanger my baby."

Tears welled in Piper's eyes. "I can't imagine losing Josh. And to lose Roth at the same time… I think it would destroy me." She pressed fingers to her lips.

Afraid of losing control, Madison turned away from Piper's emotional response and focused on June's calm face.

"Madison, do you know how many accident calls I get during winter months? This is eastern North Carolina. Neither our drivers nor our maintenance crews know how to handle slick roads. Georgia is well south of us and usually warmer. I suspect they're less equipped than our state."

Madison's nails bit into her elbows. It was only then she realized she'd been hugging herself while she talked. "Andrew and I were arguing. I took my eyes off the road."

There. She'd said it. Confessed her sin. Or at least most of it.

June shook her head. "We all take our eyes off the road, and the problem with black ice is that you usually don't see it even when you're looking directly at it. And I suspect all couples argue, although that is not my area of expertise."

"We do," Piper chimed in. "I love Roth to death, but that doesn't mean I don't sometimes want to strangle him."

Another wave of emotion swelled in Madison's chest until she thought she might burst. She should have known these two would stand by her. But would they if they knew that seconds before hitting the ice she'd screamed at Andrew that she wished she'd never married him, never gotten pregnant, and that she couldn't stay married to a man she couldn't trust? After the crash, after she dialed 911, she'd tried and tried to take back the hateful words, but Andrew had never opened his eyes to acknowledge hearing her apologies.

"How's your mother-in-law treating you now?" June's question pulled her from the dark memory.

"She barely looks at me, and when she does…"

Madison shuddered. "When she does there's only hatred in her eyes."

June's expression turned militant. "I wouldn't go back."

"I have to. I owe Danny. He put me years ahead of my peers with his help. Without him I wouldn't have been prepared to run your grandfather's practice without first serving an internship somewhere else."

Piper rose and paced the office. "For what it's worth, I agree with June. You owe them nothing. But let's put this into perspective. You're doing this because you feel you owe your father-in-law. So in a sense, you're doing this to fulfill a personal debt, to make yourself feel better, and once you do you'll be free and the satisfaction will be yours. Focus on that, Madison. Focus on getting this burden off your back. Forget the old hag. Do what you need to do for you."

"And if you happen to find a little fun in your brother-in-law's arms—"

"No," Madison interrupted June. "I can't look at him without remembering Andrew." And everything that had gone wrong with her marriage. "If I feel anything sexual toward Adam it's only because he's a carbon copy of his brother, and Andrew and I had a good sex life."

And that was the only reason the thought of finding herself in Adam's arms made her skin burn and gave her the jitters. It had nothing, absolutely nothing, to do with the man himself.

"AND YOU'RE SURE the same veterinarian is available for the entire period no matter how long we need him? My husband wouldn't like it if his patients didn't have continuity of care," Helen asked late Friday afternoon. She'd put off the call as long as she could because Danny wasn't going to like it.

"Yes, Mrs. Drake."

"And you promise the doctor will listen to Danny and do things his way? My husband is very particular."

"Yes, ma'am."

"Okay then, I—" The bedroom door opened. Danny stood in the hall. "I'll have to call you back." She snapped her cell phone closed and popped to her feet. "You shouldn't be up. If you needed something you should have called me."

Temper slashed red streaks across his pale face. "What are you doing?"

"Chatting with one of the girls."

"Don't lie to me, Helen. These doors are thin."

Her insides shook. She and Danny rarely argued—primarily because in nearly thirty-eight years of marriage she'd learned to avoid his temper. "I called the service Madison recommended. They can have a vet here Monday morning, and they've promised you'll have the same substitute for as long as you need him and for as many days as you need—not the miserly two Madison is giving you."

"I don't need the service. I have Madison."

"*If* she comes back."

"She will."

Sometimes she wanted to shake him for his stubbornness. "Why are you so determined to believe the best of her after what she did?"

"Because she came when I asked her."

She hated to disillusion him, but she had to make him see he'd misplaced his faith in Madison *Monroe*. "No, Danny, she came when *I* asked her."

"What are you talking about, woman?"

"I chased her down the driveway after she refused your request and persuaded her to change her mind."

Anger flared his nostrils. She braced herself for the explosion. "I forbade you and Adam to speak to her. I told you to let me handle it."

"We gave you a chance. It didn't work out. So I... helped. Neither Adam nor I think she'll return. She hasn't even answered his text. He expects her to be a no-show Sunday night."

"He does, does he?"

"Why do you want her back? She barely spoke to you Tuesday night other than to say, 'We had a good day, Dr. Drake.' *Doctor.* As if we hadn't taken her in and treated her like our own."

"She's family." His pallor worsened and he swayed, then braced himself on the doorjamb.

Alarm kicked through Helen's system. "You need to sit down before you fall over."

"I'm fine," he snapped.

"The doctor warned you not to overdo it on your

first day home. Please let me help you to bed, where you're supposed to be."

"I've been in bed for a week. That's the last place I want to be."

Sometimes he acted as childish as her boys once had. "You only had surgery five days ago, Danny."

"How dare you go against my wishes and speak to Madison?"

The lack of bite in his anger worried her. "You know I love you, and I'll always do what's best for you. So just this once I had to bend the rules a little. What if I hadn't? She wouldn't have come."

"She would have. All she needed was time to think it over. She would've done the right thing. Madison always did. And you need to be nicer to her. If something happens to me, who'll take care of you?"

The possibility chilled her to the bone. "Don't say that. You're going to get through this. Your oncologist said so."

"Yes, he did. And I hope he's right. But this was a wake-up call. If cancer doesn't get me, something else will. You'll need someone to look after you."

He was beginning to sound like Madison had all those years ago. Helen hadn't liked the gloomy speech then and she liked it even less now. "Don't go borrowing trouble. Adam will be here if anything happens."

"Adam's very good at his job. He didn't graduate cum laude from the best hospital administration program in the country just to come home and stagnate in a small suburban hospital. To be promoted in his field he'll have to move to a larger facility. And one day he's going to accept one of those job offers that keep coming his way."

"He's been getting job offers?" She pressed a hand over her irregularly beating heart. Adam hadn't mentioned being courted by other hospitals.

"Yes."

"He'll stay close by. Saint Joseph's was a good school, but he's a Southern boy. He didn't like all the snow up north."

"The South covers a lot of geography. And when he marries, you'll be lucky if you like his wife half as much as you loved Madison. You need her, Helen. You used to say she was the daughter you wished you'd had—the one I failed to give you."

They had covered this topic before, but not in years. She'd thought he'd forgotten and moved on. "Getting the mumps was not your fault."

Danny's case of adult mumps had resulted in the rare side effect of sterility and had killed her dream of having a large family.

Back then she'd been furious with him for risking his health by volunteering to treat animals in the projects, knowing many of the immigrant owners hadn't been vaccinated. But Danny had been confident he'd be fine—after all, he'd had his immunizations. They couldn't have known they'd fail.

"You gave me two wonderful sons, and one day

Adam will give us grandchildren. We'll have them to love."

Her heart ached at the reminder of the grandson she'd lost, but she tried to placate Danny because she never lost sight of the fact that he had been a good provider. She'd never had to work outside their home. He'd allowed her to be a full-time mother to their boys, and she'd loved every second of it. He and her twins had been the center of her universe.

How would she manage if something happened to him? She wasn't trained for any job. Madison's old words came back to haunt her.

Don't think like that. He'll be fine.

Danny's trembling increased and as a result, so did her anxiety. His knuckles turned white against the door frame.

"Adam will be here soon. You don't want him to see you looking like you're going to keel over. Let's get you settled in bed. I'll get the veterinary magazines that came while you were in the hospital. That way you can read and keep up-to-date."

"My recliner. Not the bed."

He shot her one of his don't-argue-with-me glares and she bit her tongue. Hardheaded man. "Yes, dear."

She gingerly ducked under his good arm. He shifted his weight to her, and her knees nearly folded under the burden. His wince of pain kept her from complaining. They shuffled one slow step at a time through the narrow hall of the motor home that wasn't meant for two to pass side by side. Her hip connected repeatedly with the wall, but she kept her whimpers to herself. She would have bruises tomorrow.

Maybe Adam could talk his father into bed and help him there. She wasn't sure she could manage on her own. If only Danny didn't have too much pride to accept Adam's offer of a room. They'd have been much more comfortable in the house than here. But Madison would have been there, and seeing her every evening was difficult enough without throwing mornings into the mix.

She eased Danny into the chair. His gasp of pain pierced her. "I'm sorry. Let me get you another pain pill."

"Not time yet."

"But you're hurting."

"Pain is to be expected. I'm wired up like a turkey. I want to be clearheaded when Adam gets here. My journals?"

"I'll get them." She hurried from the motor home to the house, her steps slowing as she traversed the walk. There were so many memories under that roof. They'd bought the house shortly after she'd become pregnant, and from the day she'd brought Andrew and Adam home from the hospital until the day they'd gone off to college these walls had been filled with noise, love and boyish messes. Without them their home had felt completely empty, as it did most days now.

Adam, always the most independent, had gone to school in Pennsylvania and immediately found a part-time job and rented an apartment.

But Andrew... Thank God Andrew had chosen a school closer to home. He'd had a few months' independence, then he'd started coming home on weekends. She'd been happy to do his laundry, cook his meals and prepare goody baskets for him to take back to school. And then he'd brought Madison into their lives, and Helen had taken her into the fold.

Back then Madison had been a sweet farm-raised girl who'd loved to help Helen take care of her men. Madison had been smart, resourceful and a joy to be around. She and Helen had had things in common like difficult relationships with their mothers and love for Andrew. Not that Madison had ever complained about her mom, but Helen had picked up a few of the comments she'd let slip, and having lived a similar strained life, recognized the patterns.

The problems had started when Madison began to outshine Andrew in his father's practice. Madison's mother should have taught her better. A girl never made her man look bad. As far as Danny was concerned, Madison could do no wrong, but Andrew hadn't liked being second best. He'd always been... competitive. Helen pushed back that thought and quickened her steps.

Now all she had left were Adam and Danny. She had to focus on them. She didn't want or need Madison in her life. She couldn't risk her returning for good and causing problems with Adam the way she had Andrew.

Helen grabbed the tall stack of mail that had accumulated while they were at the hospital and put Danny's magazines on top. She had more important things to think about than the past and what might have been.

CHAPTER SIX

ADAM PUSHED OPEN the door to Ann's town house Saturday night, then laid her keys into her palm. Where was the desire and anticipation he should have been experiencing as he followed her inside?

He'd taken her to their favorite restaurant, where they'd consumed a very good meal and shared a nice bottle of wine. The conversation had never lagged. Ann was an ambitious and successful fund-raiser. He liked and respected her. They'd shared many similar evenings in the past, ending in mutual sexual satisfaction before he went home. The arrangement worked because neither of them was ready for marriage.

He watched her as she moved around her living room, lighting the candles that littered practically every flat surface. Her movements were slow, deliberate and sensual. She had a great figure and dressed to accentuate her petite curves. The candlelight glinted on her short, spiky blond hair. A pixie cut, she called it. Boyishly short, but totally feminine at the same time. Diamonds twinkled in her ears and a solitaire dangled between her breasts. Numerous rings sparkled on her fingers, and her nails were painted to match her fuchsia dress.

He removed his suit coat, draped it over a nearby chair, then sat in his usual spot on the sofa, trying to rouse his absentee enthusiasm. She crossed the room, then eased down on the cushion beside him. Her spicy perfume penetrated his nostrils. He didn't remember it being this strong. Perhaps she'd accidentally put on too much?

He stroked her soft cheek, traced her jaw and still…nothing south of the border. "I've never seen you looking more beautiful than you do tonight, Ann."

One golden eyebrow arched. She tilted her face away from his touch. "And yet…"

"What do you mean?"

"What's bugging you, Adam? Besides worrying about your father."

He lowered his hand. "Nothing."

"We've been *close* for almost two years—too long for me to believe *that*."

"It's nothing except that I've been trying to cram more work into fewer hours, and I've had to stop by the hospital every night this week to give my mother a break and to make sure she eats something. Now that my dad's home that stress should let up—except while my sister-in-law's here."

"Your sister-in-law? You haven't mentioned her before."

And he shouldn't have now, but what was done

was done. "Nothing to say. She's been gone since Andrew died."

"Why did she come back now?"

"Dad asked her to fill in for him while he's out."

"She's a veterinarian like your brother was?"

"Yes."

"But how does that affect you?"

"I'm responsible for her while she's in town."

A frown puckered Ann's brow. "Responsible how?"

"I fly her in and make sure she gets to the office."

"How old is she?"

"Thirty-three."

"And she can't get herself where she needs to be?"

The muscles in the back of his neck knotted. "None of us trust her to do what she's promised."

"And what exactly has she promised?"

This was beginning to sound more like an interrogation than general curiosity. "To run Dad's practice two days a week for eight weeks."

"Why not hire someone dependable?"

"Dad trained Madison. He refuses to consider anyone else."

"He's close to her?"

"He used to be." Ann had met his parents only once. It hadn't gone well.

She rose and crossed to the window. "Is she pretty?"

He recoiled and stared at her rigid spine. "Ann, she's Andrew's widow."

Ann turned. "But is she pretty?"

An image of Madison flashed into his head. With her dark brown hair scraped back, her face pale and her unflattering, ill-fitting clothing, his answer should be an unequivocal no. She made no effort to enhance her looks the way Ann did. But then he had to acknowledge that while Madison's hair—straight and parted down the middle—probably lacked style by Ann's standards, the strands were glossy and thick. Madison's ivory skin was flawless, save a few freckles on her nose. Her lips were full and naturally dusky red, and her eyes the shade of good whiskey.

He shrugged. "I suppose she is, in a granola-crunching, tree-hugging way."

"So she's a natural beauty. Where's she staying?"

He didn't like the direction this was headed. "In my guest room." Ann's eyes rounded. "At my father's insistence. 'She's family,' he says."

Ann said nothing, but her folding arms communicated her objections loud and clear.

"There's nothing going on between us, but there is something between her and my mother that I can't figure out and Mom refuses to discuss."

"Like…?"

"I don't know. Before the accident they were close—so close that sometimes when I went home for the holidays I felt Madison fit into my family better than I did. Then after the memorial service she bailed. She left town without a word, a forwarding address or even a phone number. I guess my mom hasn't gotten past that betrayal."

"And you?"

"Have I forgiven her? I lost my brother to a car accident. She was driving and she was cited, and then she dumped settling Andrew's estate on me. So do I hold a grudge? Yes. In the months before Andrew died he said some things about her that make me wonder if they'd still be married today if he were still alive."

"If they weren't, would you be interested in her?"

Where had the levelheaded woman he'd known gone? "No. Even if they weren't together, she'd still be Andrew's wife."

"You sure about that? Because I've never heard you get this worked up about anyone before. Don't get me wrong, Adam. I'm not jealous. I don't have the right to be. You and I never promised each other exclusivity. And I don't hang out with your family. So if you and she—"

The idea made his skin feel two sizes too small. He bolted to his feet. "Ann, it's not like that."

She studied him with her head tilted and her lips pursed. "Even if it's not, I don't think you should be with me when she's occupying so much space in your head. Call me in eight weeks—if you're still available."

Women. Their logic escaped him. "I will be. Without a doubt. But you're right. I'm not good company tonight. I'll talk to you soon."

He grabbed his coat and let himself out her door,

wondering why he wasn't disappointed that the evening hadn't ended the way it usually did.

THE WOMAN STRIDING toward Adam in the airport looked like a different person. As she had last time, Madison wore jeans, laced-up leather work boots and a plaid button-up shirt untucked over a cotton shirt. Again she'd made no attempt to impress with her clothing, and if she wore makeup he saw no evidence of it. Her mink-brown hair draped over her shoulders to the tips of her breasts without even a trace of curl.

Unlike last time, Madison's brisk pace carried a sense of purpose and her expression was one of determination. She looked more like a professional, confident in her abilities, than the wounded, wary victim she'd portrayed last week. Her self-assured stride caught the attention of the three other men in the echoing, otherwise empty terminal.

Madison nodded to the man behind the desk when he glanced up as she passed. He sat up straighter, then stumbled to his feet. "Evening, miss. Need help?"

"No, thanks." She flashed a smile at the airport employee.

That smile took Adam aback. It was the first glimpse he'd seen of the woman who'd married his brother. During his trips home prior to Andrew's accident, Madison had been bubbly, outgoing and always smiling. Her sparkle had lit up the room. Those traits had been noticeably absent last week.

"Are you sure, miss? You're juggling quite a bit."

"I'm sure."

It was only then that Adam registered the plastic wheeled cooler she dragged behind her topped with a larger duffel bag as well as a smaller canvas bag slung over her shoulder. Her gaze met his, and the remnants of her smile faded. He'd been so caught up in his father's battle that he hadn't noticed how much she'd changed beyond her clothing size.

Her demeanor was more reserved, making her seem older and wiser, and because of the mental mileage she'd accumulated, more attractive than she'd been as a naive college coed.

No. Not attractive, he rejected instantly.

Liar.

The pretty girl had become a beautiful woman. And while she was too slender in his opinion, she didn't look unhealthy. Too bad Andrew wasn't here to benefit from Madison's maturity. Or would they have divorced if he'd survived the crash? Andrew hadn't sounded happy during their last conversation the week before he'd died, and Adam hadn't attended Madison's graduation party. He'd been new at his job and had chosen to save his vacation days for Christmas. He should have gone to see his brother one last time.

Adam waited for Madison to reach him. "You didn't answer my text."

"I didn't think 'Same time, same airport' required a response."

"What is all this?" He gestured to her bags.

"My food, my suitcase and my exercise gear."

"I didn't feed you well enough last time?"

"You told me to take care of myself. This time I came prepared to do so. I will not be a liability or dependent on you or your father's staff for my meals." She met his gaze head-on while throwing his words in his face.

A knife of discomfort pricked his ribs. He'd been an ass last week. He would never treat a hospital employee—even one he disliked—the way he'd treated Madison. Admitting that grated.

"Let's go." He held out a hand, carefully waiting this time for her to relinquish the cooler's extended handle. Touching her had an effect on him that he didn't like, couldn't control and wouldn't repeat.

"Have a good flight, miss," the man called after her, earning him another smile from Madison.

Attractive women always garnered attention, and Madison had the kind of bone structure that made her eye-catching even without the makeup most women couldn't live without. *A natural beauty,* Ann had said, and he guessed it fit.

But his lack of sexual interest in Ann had nothing to do with the woman beside him and everything to do with the extra stress, obligations and concerns his father's diagnosis and surgery had put on him.

He loaded Madison's gear, then climbed aboard

and turned to help her into the plane. The current flowing from her palm to his as she slid into her seat was unwanted and best ignored. "Buckle up."

He started his preflight checklist.

"Did your father talk to his employees yet?"

"I haven't had an opportunity to broach the subject. You'll have to ask him tomorrow evening."

"You didn't talk to him? All week?"

"Not about that. Either my mother was present or Dad was too weak. It isn't urgent."

"It is to me. I have to face those people tomorrow. And why couldn't your mother be part of that conversation? You don't want her to know he lied?"

She dug out her cell phone and offered it to him. "Call him."

"He goes to bed right after dinner. He still lacks the stamina to do anything else, and he won't have the energy to call each of his employees tonight."

Not what she wanted to hear if the downward curve of her mouth was an indicator.

"Want to get out, Madison? Prove me right? Demonstrate that you don't have any consideration for anyone but yourself?"

Her scowl deepened, and her golden-brown eyes sparked like flint. "Just get the plane in the air."

She pulled a music player from her back pocket and inserted the ear buds rather than don the noise-cancelling headphones under her seat. The gesture made it very clear she didn't want to talk to him during the flight. That suited him fine.

MADISON KEPT HER mouth shut during the drive from the airport. She was peeved. She couldn't believe that in six days Adam couldn't have found one moment to talk to Danny. Her integrity with Danny's employees didn't matter to him.

Adam turned the car onto a familiar road and her irritation escalated. "You didn't get a hotel room?"

She hated to be greedy, but she knew the Drakes could afford it.

"No. Dad insists you stay with me."

Great. She resigned herself to more sleepless nights in the shrine. She'd survived worse. She'd shove Andrew's junk in the closet. No, on second thought, she wouldn't give Adam that satisfaction.

They passed through the pillars and his house came into view. The garage door opened, then shut behind them, filling her with a sense of suffocation. She climbed out, took a breath and circled to the trunk. Adam had already picked up both bags and her cooler.

She followed him inside and marched toward the guest room, determined to treat it like an impersonal hotel room. She wasn't going to let Andrew's possessions spook her. But regardless of her vow, as she approached the closed door her feet slowed against her will.

But Adam entered a different room on the back side of the house. "You're in here tonight. I have the air-conditioning on, but if you need to hear the bullfrogs to sleep you can open the windows."

Dumbfounded, she blinked. His consideration surprised her. She could have sworn he'd taken pleasure in forcing her to face Andrew's mementos. Why was he being nice? She didn't trust his motives.

THE MOTOR HOME parked in the Drakes' driveway was a far cry from the old pop-up camper Madison remembered from her trips with Andrew. This model was as big as a bus and had walls that extended out on either side. Like a tour bus, the door was near the front. Someone, likely Helen, had flanked the entrance with pots containing red and white geraniums and petunias, and added a welcome mat.

The door flew open before Adam's fist could connect. Helen wore a scowl. Her pallor and the tension carving lines in her face shocked Madison. She looked even worse today than she had last week.

"Why are you knocking?" Helen had her purse strap hooked over her forearm and keys in her hand.

"Hello, Mother."

"I need groceries." Helen barged down the steps before they could ascend. "Dinner's in the kitchen. Your father has already eaten. Please keep an eye on him and convince him to get in bed if you can."

Helen directed her comments toward Adam and didn't even acknowledge Madison as she passed.

Adam, concern clear in his eyes, took a step after his mother. Madison grabbed his forearm. "Let her go. She probably needs a break."

His muscles tensed beneath her fingertips, then

his head slowly turned her way. She saw concern in his blue-green eyes before he lowered his gaze to her hand, making her aware of her instinctive trespass. She shouldn't have touched him.

Withdrawing her hand, she wished she could attribute her skyrocketing pulse to Helen's snub, but the tingling sensation that traveled up her arm before raining down like hot ash into her belly made the truth undeniable.

The slam of the car door was a welcome distraction. Madison watched Helen back her sedan out of the driveway and disappear around the corner.

"Don't just stand there. Bring my girl inside," Danny called out from the bus.

"After you." Adam swept a hand, indicating Madison precede him.

Grateful that she wouldn't have to visit Danny in the house that held so many memories or worse yet, the hospital, she climbed the stairs and found herself standing between the leather driver and passenger's seats. A large living room as wide as her den at home lay in front of her. Danny was stretched out in a leather recliner beside a fireplace.

A fireplace in a motor home? Above that, a big-screen TV hung on the wall and a long leather sofa occupied the opposite wall. She had no experience with this method of travel, and the luxuriousness of the house on wheels overwhelmed her.

"Maddie, come in and have a seat."

She crossed the tile floor, stopping in front of

Danny with an awkwardness she couldn't suppress. He extended one arm, demanding a hug. She quickly and gingerly embraced him, then stepped back. She would not let herself come to depend on such demonstrations again.

"You have more color in your face than the last time I saw you," she observed with her best clinical detachment.

"Hospitals drain the life out of you."

His words brought a quick jab of pain. She caught herself pressing a hand to her stomach and lowered it to her side. "Yes, they do."

She averted her face and caught Adam watching her.

"Are you hungry?" he asked.

"Yes." She wasn't, but she'd rather Adam believe that than know about the grief that still took bites out of her at unexpected moments.

He passed her, heading toward the galley kitchen. Were those granite countertops? He piled food on two plates. Having him serve her was unsettling in ways she couldn't even begin to explain. It made her feel cared for.... And that couldn't be further from the truth. She was a necessary evil to the Drakes—except for Danny—and she'd best not forget that.

She perched on the edge of the sofa, deliberately angling away from Adam, but her ears were attuned to his every move.

"How did it go at the office today?" The hunger in Danny's eyes plucked her sympathy strings. He'd lived for two things when she'd known him—his practice and his Corvette.

"We had a good day. Busy, but your crew is top-notch even without their captain. Why did you lie to them about your cancer, Danny?"

"Madison—" Adam rebuked.

Danny sliced a silencing hand. "It's a valid question, son."

"I told her you didn't want to worry your employees about their job security."

"That's part of it. Primarily I didn't want my clients deserting me like rats do a sinking ship. Cancer is a death sentence to a private practice. If people believed there was a small chance I wouldn't make it, they'd start looking for a new vet. And if the doctors are wrong and I can't return to work, I'll have to sell out. I want the business to have as much value as possible. Your mother has become accustomed to things like this." His gesture encompassed the motor home. "I want her to continue to have them."

That made sense, but it left Madison in a difficult position. "You expect me to keep lying for you."

"It would be best. For now."

"No." Danny opened his mouth again, but she cut him off. "I won't volunteer the truth, but I will not lie for you. You won't be sidelined for long—I know you better than that. You might not feel up to it this week or next, but soon you'll want to get out of this RV and exercise your brain. You'll have days when you'll be strong enough to go into the office for a few hours even if all you do is sit at your desk and review files. And when you do, you won't be able to hide the toll that chemo will take on your body. You'll need your staff's support until you're back to one hundred percent. You won't get that by lying to them."

"It'll be a while before he's ready to return to the office," Adam said as he put a plate in the microwave.

"You never know. The meds affect people differently. Some have it rough. Some have few side effects."

"And you know this how?" Adam asked.

"I've seen a lot of patients and their pets through cancer treatment." Madison turned her attention to Danny. "There's one more thing I don't understand. You told me you scheduled your surgery the Monday after I agreed to come, yet your staff knew about an upcoming surgery for a month."

Adam's head whipped around. "What? How long have you known, Dad?"

Danny shifted, his expression turning guarded. "About three months," he admitted grudgingly.

"And you said nothing?" Anger tinged Adam's voice. "Why?"

"I needed time to come to terms with the diagnosis, to investigate my options and get my ducks in a row."

"You should've told me, Dad."

"And you would have told your mother. What difference do a few months make?" Danny's serious expression morphed into a smile. "You and I practicing side by side again. I'm looking forward to that day, Maddie."

"As long as you remember it will be temporary. I'm not coming back permanently, Danny. You need to accept that, and stop encouraging your staff to expect it. I'm happy with my little rural practice."

"You can't be. You're too smart to stagnate in some backwater town."

"I'm not stagnating." Was she? "I get to treat large and small animals there—like I wanted to do back when I started college, before I met Andrew and you asked me to join your small animal practice."

"I may not treat horses or cattle, but I get more variety than you."

"True. But I love helping people make a living and that's what tending livestock does. Remember, I'm a farm girl at heart, and I see a lot of patients on the barter system. Just because someone doesn't have money doesn't mean they couldn't benefit from loving a pet."

"The risk of getting hurt is higher with large animals. You're too fragile—"

"I'm stronger than I look, and it's a chance I'm willing to take. Which brings up another concern. Why have you been spying on me, Danny? And for how long?"

"You call watching out for you spying? Is it wrong to care how you're doing? You're family, Madison. I gave you the space you needed to process your grief, but I needed to know you were okay."

He cared. Emotion squeezed her throat. She gulped it down—she was not family. "I'm better than okay. Jim tells me you've finished restoring your Corvette."

Danny beamed. "Yes. Why do you think I had time to start on the house renovations?"

"I need a car while I'm here, Danny. I don't like being stranded or taking Adam out of his way, and your practice is on the opposite side of town from the hospital. Since you're not driving yours…"

Out of the corner of her eye she saw Adam's head snap up, proving he'd been listening.

"Maddie, I love you, but I'm not loaning you the 'Vette. She's too temperamental."

"And too valuable," Adam added.

She ignored Adam. "Then loan me your bicycle. I can bike to work each morning. I brought my helmet and riding shoes."

"Bike to work in Norcross? It's not safe. As much as I love this town, the drivers are too aggressive."

"But—"

"You and Adam end up here every evening anyway, so it's only a few miles out of the way in the mornings."

The microwave beeped. She ignored it. "Then how about a rental car?"

"I'm afraid to spend the money when you're only

bringing in a fraction of my usual income and my medical bills are piling up."

She'd bet the motor home cost more than her entire farm. This wasn't about the money. "You like me dependent on Adam."

Danny shrugged and winced. "I like him seeing to your safety. You were raised in a small town, and you've been living in one long enough to forget what goes on in a metropolitan area."

Another valid argument, but she knew she was being played. "I'm not that naive. It's what Adam said. You don't trust me to fulfill my promise. Danny, if I wanted to cause trouble I could do more damage to your practice by wreaking havoc with your patients. Either you trust me. Or you don't."

"Of course I trust you, Maddie. If I didn't, you wouldn't be here. Now, who did you treat today?"

Stymied, she bit her tongue and let him change the subject. She wasn't getting anywhere. "You want a rundown of everyone who came through the door?"

"Each one you can remember."

"You're obviously feeling better, Dad, if you want to talk shop," Adam said.

He settled on the sofa beside her and offered her a plate. She took the dish and their fingers brushed. Her mouth watered and her heart quickened. But that was only her appetite making an enthusiastic appearance because she'd spotted Helen's fried chicken and homemade macaroni and cheese—her favorite foods.

"Dad, if you want Madison to have the stamina to run your practice, let her eat."

"But—"

"You can talk after dinner."

The frustration on Danny's face was clear, but so was his exhaustion. For a man who lived for his work, it had to be horrible being kept from it. Another wave of empathy washed through her. As he'd said, being a sole provider came with risks that a larger, multidoctor office did not. If something happened to her, she, like Danny, had no one to cover her caseload. But for her it wouldn't be financially feasible to use the substitute service. Danny, on the other hand, had enough clients to cover the substantial fee.

June's grandfather had passed away a year before Madison had bought the practice. The area animals had gone without routine care during that period and only dire circumstances had been enough to warrant a long drive to another facility. Madison felt guilty for not being there now. But this was a temporary measure. A means to an end that would bring her peace of mind. Eventually.

She pushed the worry aside and focused on Danny's tired face. "Tomorrow I'll bring you the patients' files. You can review my treatment protocol and tell me if you approve. If necessary, I'll make follow-up calls next week."

In her peripheral vision she saw Adam's head swivel her way. She resisted as long as she could before looking at him. The approval in those eyes meant far more than it should. And when he mouthed a silent "Thank you," her insides went warm.

She tamped down the reaction. His opinion of her should not—*did not*—matter.

CHAPTER SEVEN

HELEN TURNED INTO the driveway as the summer sun slid toward the horizon. It was almost eight. Had Adam been able to keep his father awake or would Danny have fallen asleep in his recliner the way he'd done every night since she'd brought him home?

She sat in her car in the driveway, twisting her wedding rings around her finger. The two-carat diamond sparkled, reminding her that she'd shirked her duty. But looking at Madison was too painful. Hearing Danny sing her praises was doubly so. He'd been "Madison this" and "Madison that" all afternoon until Helen had been ready to throw her cast-iron skillet at him. And he'd cut her off every time she mentioned Andrew. In the end, she'd made enough noise while preparing dinner to make talking impossible, then escaped the minute Adam arrived with *her*.

The RV taking up so much space embodied everything that had gone wrong in her life. Danny loved it. To him the ostentatious home on wheels, like the huge diamond he'd given her for their thirty-fifth wedding anniversary, symbolized his success.

She'd give it all up without hesitation if only she could have Andrew back and the promise that Danny would be with her for thirty-five more years.

Camping, if you could call it that, in this luxurious "monster home" wasn't how she had envisioned herself at fifty-nine. She'd expected to be vacationing at family campgrounds with a newer, larger version of their old pop-up, swatting mosquitos and frying corn bread and the fish that her boys had caught on a camp stove the way they had when Andrew and Adam had been younger. Only she'd have been doing it with little Daniel.

But Madison had robbed Helen of that opportunity. Helen should have been sharing pictures and tales of traveling and her grandchildren instead of listening enviously to her friends and having nothing to contribute. If only Adam would marry…

Her cell phone beeped, reminding her that it was time for Danny's medication. Her reprieve was over. She didn't want to go back inside. But she had no choice. Her feet dragged as she made her way across the concrete and up the stairs. At least Danny and Adam would be here to carry the conversation, if Danny was awake. She wouldn't be trapped alone with Madison as she'd been that day in the cafeteria.

Juggling the groceries, she opened the door and climbed inside. The living room and Danny's chair were empty. Panic hit Helen hard. Then she spotted Madison in the kitchen.

"Where's Danny? Did Adam talk him into going to bed?"

"Adam helped him to the bathroom. I don't think you'll get Danny into bed for a while. He says lying flat hurts his wired rib. Let me give you a hand with those."

Stung that Danny hadn't told *her* about the bed being uncomfortable, Helen shifted the bags out of reach. "I can manage a few groceries."

She dodged past her unwanted guest and carried her load to the galley. The sink and drying rack were empty, the dish towel neatly folded on the counter. The cast-iron skillet looked as if it had been cleaned and rubbed down with vegetable oil—the way it should be. Neither Adam nor Danny knew to do that. That left Madison.

"I would've done the dishes." Her grandmother would have rapped her knuckles for her ungracious tone.

"You cooked. Washing up was the least I could do. Dinner was delicious, Helen. Thank you." Madison hovered nearby like an unwelcome storm cloud.

"Don't thank me. Thank Danny. He's the one who insisted I cook all of your favorites."

"But you did the work and you did it well. You didn't have to."

No. She could have intentionally botched the meal. It would have been so easy to overcook the chicken or add a little too much of one ingredient or another. But she wouldn't do that to Danny and

Adam. She'd never serve them anything less than her best effort.

"This is a nice RV. If Danny takes as long on the house renovations as he did rebuilding the Corvette, you shouldn't suffer too much."

Helen stiffened. Danny took forever with his little projects, but Madison had no business insulting him even if her observation was right on the money. "The car wouldn't have taken fifteen years if Andrew had been here to help."

Silence ticked for a dozen heartbeats, making her feel like a bi—witch. Madison wrapped her arms around her middle, and Helen felt a twinge of shame for being rude. But how could Madison stand there and chat like nothing was wrong? As if one careless act on her part hadn't ruined both their worlds? Or had it ruined Madison's? Had she achieved her desired outcome when she'd lost the baby?

"Did you know Andrew hated working on that car? He only did it to spend time with Danny."

Blindsided, Helen stared at her adversary. "Andrew would never have said any such thing."

Madison's lips twisted in something that bore no resemblance whatsoever to the easy smiles that used to make people happy just to be around her. "He liked pleasing Danny."

Helen searched Madison's face. If what she'd said wasn't the truth, Madison certainly believed it was.

Male voices rumbled in the bedroom. Her men

were returning. "Don't tell Danny. He loved his time with Andrew."

"It'll be our secret, Helen."

Not their only one. Helen went rigid. Was that a threat to reveal their other conversation?

If you have any decency at all, you'll leave Norcross and never come back. The sight of you makes me sick to my stomach.

What would Danny say if he knew Helen had told his precious protégé to get out of their lives forever? She didn't want to find out.

Danny, walking gingerly with Adam one step behind him, entered the kitchen. Pain flickered across his face with every step—pain Helen wished she could take away. She felt helpless. Useless. Scared.

"Oh, good. You're awake. It's time for your medicine."

"I already took it. Where've you been? How long does it take to go to one store?"

She excused his grumpiness. He was never sick, and he didn't have the faintest clue how to be a good patient.

"I stopped by Shady Lawn on the way home." She heard Madison's gasp and ignored it. "I wanted to make sure the grounds were being tended and the flowers fresh. I do that the first of every month, and I haven't had time—"

"We pay someone to do that," Danny groused.

"Have you ever seen the mausoleum, Madison?" she asked.

"No." Madison's voice was little more than a whisper. Helen enjoyed the grief in her eyes. Was it mean of her to be happy to know Madison suffered, too? But Helen worked hard to keep Andrew and little Daniel's final resting place attractive. She planted flowers, picked weeds and decorated for the holidays. Madison had done nothing.

"It turned out beautifully. Adam can drive you by your husband and son's gravesite on the way home. If you leave now you'll make it before dark."

"I prefer my memories of them to be here." Madison placed a hand over her heart.

"It's hard to believe Daniel would have been five, and that this summer would have been his last grand adventure before he started school this fall. We could have—"

"Damn it, Helen," Danny snapped. "Quit living in the past. Move on. You're never going to heal if you keep tearing open the sutures."

Helen flinched and glanced at Adam for support, but her son's gaze was trained on Madison whose face had about as much color as a hospital bedsheet. Then Adam turned his attention to his father, not once looking Helen's way.

Why did they all want to forget Andrew and little Daniel?

"Dad, let me get you settled in your chair. It's time for us to go."

"Already?"

"Yes. You're dead on your feet, whether you want

to admit it or not. We'll be back tomorrow night."
Adam dusted a kiss on Helen's cheek. "Thanks for
dinner, Mom."

She hated for him to leave. But if he stayed, so
did Madison. "Tomorrow I'll cook your favorites."

"Sounds good." Adam hustled Madison out the
door, acting as if he couldn't wait to leave. That hurt.

One good thing had come from Danny's illness—
she got to see her oldest every day. Prior to the diagnosis she'd only seen Adam a couple times a month.
He worked too hard. If he'd settle down with a good
woman—not that Ann character—and give her
grandchildren things would change. She winced at
the thought. It was too similar to what she'd said to
Andrew.

"Helen, I need Madison here. Do you understand?"

Apprehension inched up her spine like a spider.
"Of course, Danny. I'm doing my best."

"Do *not* run her off. I want her back. Permanently.
I did not bust my tail to build my business only to
sell it to some clueless, snot-nosed, fresh-out-of-vet-
school kid who'll mistreat and mismanage my patients and may run it into the ground before he can
pay me for it.

"I taught Madison how to run it right. I want to
retire in five years so we can do all that traveling you
used to yammer about, but I can't without her here."

Vacations she'd wanted to share with her grandchildren.

As much as she wanted Madison gone, she would

have to suffer the agony of her presence in silence until Danny was better. But she'd be dam—darned if she'd have that woman back in their lives permanently.

Once Danny was on the mend, she'd work on changing his mind about Madison Monroe.

A STRANGE, HIGH-PITCHED chirp stopped Adam midpress. He lowered the barbell to the weight bench rack and went to investigate.

Seeing Madison bent over in the foyer stopped him in his tracks. His eyes involuntarily traced the long line of her legs left bare by her running shorts. Her thigh and calf muscles were nicely developed, smooth and feminine. And attractive.

He squashed that unwanted observation, but not fast enough to kill the spark of awareness prickling through his veins.

It took a moment to figure out she was stretching her hamstrings. She shifted her feet and her neon orange shoe squeaked on the floor. That was the sound he'd heard. She must have seen him, because she froze midstretch, her gaze fixed on his foot. She slowly straightened, her golden-brown eyes making the climb up his body as she did. His pulse thumped faster.

A white tank top clung to her torso, outlining her small breasts and displaying deltoids and biceps as nicely shaped as her legs. He'd been wrong. She wasn't too thin. Though she could stand to carry a few more pounds, she was long and lean and in great shape—the way he liked his women.

Another thought to crush. "What are you doing?"

"Getting ready for a run."

"It's dark."

"I came prepared." She touched the reflective belt around her hips. "I have LED head and arm bands, too."

"My neighborhood doesn't have streetlights, and the curvy roads and dense trees mean someone will be right on top of you before they can see and avoid you. It's not safe to run after dark."

She rolled to her toes, then sank back on her heels, flexing her calves. Her anxiety was practically tangible. "I'll be careful."

He searched her face, noting the tension around her eyes and mouth—tension that had started at his parents'. "Why did the idea of visiting the gravesite bother you?"

Her lashes descended briefly. A shaky breath rattled her breas—chest, then she met his gaze. "I don't like the idea of him lying there in a cold, granite box."

"Which him? Andrew or your son?"

Her hands fisted, then relaxed, then curled again—a habit he'd noticed more than once. "Both."

"If you didn't want a mausoleum, then you should have planned the funeral instead of leaving it to my father." Another duty she'd dodged.

"Having a tangible reminder of Andrew seemed

important to Danny. At the time it didn't matter to me where they were buried. They were gone. And that was all that mattered." The sorrow in her eyes was unmistakable.

"What's going on between you and my mother?"

The angst turned to wariness. "Nothing."

"She's uncomfortable around you."

"She's worried about your father."

"It's more than that."

"She blames me for the accident."

"You were driving."

She bowed her head. "Yes. I was."

There. She'd admitted it. Where was the satisfaction her confession should have given him?

"If you insist on running tonight, use the treadmill in my home gym."

She glanced at the front door as if wanting to escape, then back at him. Caramel eyes flicked over him again with that same prickly, skin-tightening result. "I don't want to interrupt your workout."

"Madison, you can't run your practice or my father's if you get injured. The gym's big enough for both of us."

White teeth pinched her pink bottom lip. "If you're sure."

"This way." He pivoted and led the way to the room adjacent to his bedroom. The original house plan had called for this to be a nursery, but he had a more practical use for it.

She entered, her gaze roving over his equipment, the

flat-screen TV on the wall tuned to CNN and the towel draped across the incline bench. He saw the exact second she noticed his bedroom through the open door. "I should probably wait and run in the morning."

"Will you be able to sleep if you don't work off some of your tension?"

She shifted her weight between her feet and shook out her hands like a runner on an adrenaline high before a race—answer enough. "I don't want to bother you."

"I'm almost done." Sharing the space with her wasn't his best idea. Pressure built low in his gut. Arousal. For Madison. His brother's wife. No.

With obvious reluctance, she crossed to the treadmill, mounted and turned on the machine. He returned to the weight bench, wrapped his fingers around the bar and lifted.

She set her speed, her feet slapping at a quick pace that his damned heart seemed determined to match. He'd never wasted time watching a woman work out, but he couldn't pry his gaze from her reflection, the flex of her arm and leg muscles, or the soft bounce of her breasts as she ran.

The unexpected shift of the heavy weight nearly dislocated his elbow. He checked his form in the mirror and found it dangerously wrong. His inability to concentrate was going to get him hurt, and his thoughts... They were wide off the mark.

He forced himself to do another five so he wouldn't

look like he was running, then racked the weight and rose. "See you in the morning."

Exiting to his bedroom, he shut the door, but the muffled hum of the treadmill and the slap of her feet penetrated the wood. He twisted the lock and headed for the shower, where the water would drown out the sound. But he couldn't escape his thoughts.

Andrew had accused Madison of being a self-centered glory hound, but the time she'd spent patiently replaying case after case with his father tonight, answering endless questions and not once boasting or bragging about her skills didn't sound like a woman demanding adulation.

He'd believed her to be heartless, but her tension tonight and her pallor when his mother mentioned Shady Lawn couldn't be faked. Perhaps she wasn't as unaffected by Andrew's death as he'd thought.

Had he misread her? Had Andrew been wrong about her?

No. If she'd cared about his family, she wouldn't have abandoned them when they needed her the most.

But something didn't add up. And he wasn't going to be satisfied until he figured out what was off.

"THAT WAS OUR last one?" Madison asked Kay.

Nodding, Kay took the folder and slid it into the box of files she'd gathered for Madison to take home to Danny. "Adam called to say he's running about thirty minutes late."

Good. That gave her extra time to prepare for his arrival. Seeing him in his workout gear last night had been yet another wake-up call to her dormant hormones. Maybe she needed to buy a vibrator and take care of business when she got home. But the idea of waltzing into one of those stores to purchase a sex toy set her face on fire. She couldn't imagine actually doing it. Maybe mail order.... No. Her rural route carrier might see the company's return address on the box, and word would get around.

"Should I stay until he gets here?" Kay interrupted.

"No. Go home to your husband. It's been a long day." The building's ghosts weren't haunting her as badly this week. Yes, unexpected memories of Andrew still ambushed her at odd moments, and the fact that he was the one who should have been covering for his father was never far from Madison's mind. But the ache was manageable for the most part, and the enjoyment of being run off her feet with patients kept her from wallowing in the past.

She walked to the kennel to check on the momma cat and the two kittens that had been left in the clinic's safe-surrender cage over the weekend.

The drop box had been Madison's idea when she'd still been in vet school—she'd been pleasantly surprised to discover Danny had kept it. The cages gave people who found strays, or who no longer wanted their pet or couldn't afford to keep them a safe, anonymous place to relinquish them. Pets surrendered in a vet's office had a better chance of surviving and/or being adopted than those dumped on the roadside or left at the animal shelter.

Madison opened the cage, lifted the pewter-colored cat and stroked her soft coat. The kittens mewed for their momma. "Susie's going to try to find you a home tomorrow. I can't take you with me, but I won't let them turn you over to the pound, either. You're a pretty girl and such a loving mommy."

The cat nuzzled Madison's chin and purred. She'd been malnourished and without a collar, but otherwise healthy. Thanks to the staff she'd been cleaned, deflead and thoroughly checked over. She'd make someone a good pet and in four weeks or so they could wean the kittens and find homes for them.

"Help! Help me," a thready female voice called from the front of the building. "Dr. Drake!"

Madison raced to the foyer. A diminutive woman who looked to be in her eighties stood by the counter. Her blue eyes were red-rimmed and filled with desperation. She held a tiny apricot-colored ball of curly fur in her arms.

"May I help you?"

"I need Dr. Drake."

"He's not here. I'm Dr. Monroe. I'm filling in for him. Who do you have there?"

"Peaches. She won't wake up. Please help her. She's all I have." Sobs shook the frail woman.

Madison moved closer, wrapping an arm around the woman's shoulder to get a better look at Peaches.

Then the smell hit her and she knew it was too late to help the dog. Organ failure created a scent like no other. But that didn't mean she couldn't help the teacup toy poodle's owner during this difficult time.

"Let's get Peaches back to an exam room."

ADAM HATED BEING late for anything—even something as onerous as picking up Madison. But the hospital had needed him, and averting a potential nursing strike was critical. The thirty-minute delay had stretched into almost an hour. And if Madison held true to the other women he'd known, she'd throw a tantrum over being kept waiting.

He parked beside a small older-model sedan, then strode toward the clinic entrance. He didn't recognize the car as one belonging to the staff. The waiting room was empty. Light streamed from his father's office. He headed down the hall. The sound of low voices slowed his steps. Who could Madison be entertaining after hours?

"Peaches was my daughter's dog," an unfamiliar quivery female voice said. "Marie was my only child. She had Down syndrome. My husband left us when she was diagnosed. He couldn't handle a special-needs child. When Marie died five years ago, Peaches became mine. Having Marie's dog kept her close somehow. I just wasn't ready to let her g-go."

"It's never easy to say goodbye. Do you have someone who can stay with you tonight, Mrs. Woods?"

Adam's pulse misfired when he identified Madison's huskier-than-normal voice.

"No. Taking care of Marie took up most of my free time, and I never bothered to try to make friends after she passed. People just don't understand the void left by losing a child."

"No. They don't."

Adam stopped short of the door and observed the scene via the mirror his father had hung so that he could see anyone coming down the hall. Madison sat on his father's leather sofa with one arm around a white-haired lady. The other hand covered both of the woman's. If Madison looked up she'd see his reflection, but she remained focused on her visitor.

There were dark spots all over Madison's light blue scrub suit that hadn't been there this morning. She wiped her face with the back of her hand, and it dawned on him that the spots were fallen tears.

"Do you like cats, Mrs. Woods?" she asked.

"I haven't had one since I was a child. But I liked them then. Why?"

"I'm going to take care of Peaches the way I promised. But I have a huge favor to ask."

"Anything. As good as you were to my Peaches—" Another sob cut off the words. Madison held her until she regained control.

"We have a momma cat with two kittens someone abandoned in our kennel. She'll be safe and warm here overnight, but if you want company, I'm sure she'd rather go home with you. Just for a few days."

"A momma with kittens? And someone put her out?"

"It happens all too often. She's a sweetie and a real snuggler. She purrs as loud as a lawn mower when you scratch under her chin. The kittens are adorable. Their eyes just opened. I can give you the litter box, food and everything you'll need. It might keep your house from feeling empty tonight."

The old woman blotted her face with a lace-edged handkerchief. "Company might be nice."

"Would you like to meet her before you decide?"

"I—I— Yes, I believe would."

Madison rose, then helped the older woman to her feet. "We haven't named her yet. Maybe you can help me think of something that suits her. She's a really good momma."

Adam backed into Andrew's office to give them privacy. His thoughts twisted like a roller-coaster ride. From the gist of the conversation he guessed the woman had lost her pet, and she and Madison were sharing tears.

Madison had to have put down numerous animals in six years of practice. Compassion wasn't something he would have expected from her. To find her crying over the death of someone else's dog contradicted what Andrew had said about her.

Which was true? Andrew's version or what Adam had just witnessed? Maybe Madison had mellowed over the years? But if she had, why had he and his mother needed to coerce her into helping his father? Maybe she was a damned good actress.

Without turning on the overhead lights Adam scanned his brother's office. The setting sun outside the high windows illuminated the room with a murky glow. Nothing had changed since Andrew had worked here. Everything on the desk looked the same as it had when Andrew was alive.

He saw the picture of his brother and sister-in-law beaming at the camera. The picture brought back memories of a happier time when he and Andrew had competed over everything. Grades. Sports. Their father's attention. Scoring with girls. Andrew had rubbed it in too many times to count that he'd found a woman worth keeping before Adam had. Adam had been happy for his brother, but a little jealous, too.

Not that he'd coveted Madison. He hadn't. But she and his brother had forged a connection that Adam had yet to experience. He'd seen his brother try to be a better man for Madison, no longer always putting himself first.

Returning to the present, Adam double-checked the desk, shelves and frames on the wall. The light coating of dust told him Madison hadn't been using this office.

Footsteps approached from the rear. "Are you sure you don't want me to drive you home and help you get her into the house? Dr. Drake's son will be here soon. He can follow us and pick me up."

"No, dear. I may be old, but I can manage."

Adam stayed in the shadows and assured himself he wasn't spying. He was simply allowing the woman her grief without the embarrassment of a stranger witnessing it. When they passed, Madison had a cat carrier in one hand and bags of food and cat litter in the other. The woman carried an empty litter tray.

"You'll be sure to tell the crematorium about my wishes for Peaches?"

"They're closed now, but I'll personally take care of the arrangements in the morning, and I'll get her ready for them before I leave tonight."

He remained in Andrew's office until he heard the front door close, and then he waited for Madison in the reception area. She'd know he was here as soon as she spotted his car. Moments later the door opened again and Madison entered.

"How long have you been here?" Her cool composure contradicted the emotional display he'd witnessed and the redness of her eyes.

"Not long."

"Thank you for not interrupting."

"Who was that?"

"One of your father's patients. I need a few minutes to finish up, but if you want to load up the box of files for Danny, they're in a crate behind the reception counter. I have one more to add to it, but I'll bring it when I come out."

No complaints about his tardiness? "We're already late for dinner."

"Send your mother my apologies, but this can't wait." She briskly walked to the back of the building.

Adam texted his mom about the delay, carried the files to the car and returned to cool his heels in the waiting room. Ten minutes passed and Madison hadn't returned. They needed to get on the road.

He went looking for her and found her in the back, placing a towel-wrapped object in a box. Then she set the box in the large refrigeration unit and peeled off her gloves. He opened his mouth to tell her to hurry up, but a quiet whimper stopped him.

She crossed to the sink, washed her hands then bent and splashed her face. She stayed hunched over, gripping the sides of the washbasin. Her shuddery breathing and her white knuckles on the tub were unmistakably those of someone fighting for control.

Madison crying? It didn't mesh with the image he'd held in his head for the past six years. Every cell in him screamed *run*.

He gave her a full minute to pull herself together. She didn't. "Madison."

She started, but didn't turn. "Five more minutes."

Her tear-choked tone tightened like an invisible noose around his throat.

Go. But he couldn't. Damn it.

"Are you all right?" he forced out.

"Yes. Just finishing up."

A lie. He knew it as well as he knew his own name.

He was a fixer, a problem solver, a dispute settler. He could juggle a thousand details and get down to the heart of the matter. And these details didn't add up. He didn't want to do it, but he closed the distance and cupped her shoulder. "Madison—"

She gasped, then tried to shrug off his hand, but he held on. "Please, Adam…just go. I'm almost d-done."

He wished he could do as she asked. Pushing gently, he forced her to turn, noting the strength of the muscles beneath his palm when she resisted. She wasn't a pretty crier. Her face was blotchy and her eyes and nose were as red as a drunk's on a two-day bender. But her grief came through loud and clear. And genuine.

She mashed her lips together in an effort to control the tremor of her mouth and tilted her head back to contain the tears pooling in her eyes. Her struggle unsettled him in a way bawling never could.

"Why are you crying over a stranger's dog?"

"Peaches was the only family she ha-had." A tear escaped and rolled down. Madison dashed it away as if trying to hide evidence, but another drop immediately leaked from the opposite eye.

He'd never seen this vulnerable side of her. He lifted his hand and stroked a thumb across her damp cheek. Her skin was soft and warm. Her lips parted and her breath caught. An odd current raced through him, making him hyperaware of each spiky, wet lash, each shuddery inhalation and the slight tremor of her frame as she fought to contain her emotions.

She hit him with a beseeching look. Asking him to leave? Asking him to help? He didn't know. Then as if someone had flipped a switch, the mood changed from one of comfort to something else. Her eyes went from wounded to wary to wanting. Reciprocal desire coiled hot and sinuous in his gut. He tried to put a lid on it, but it wouldn't be contained.

Cupping her face with both hands, he skimmed over the wet trails. A droplet clung to her lower lashes. His gaze fixed on it and he couldn't look away.

"Adam." Her near whisper carried a note of caution.

He heard it, but failed to heed it. Her scent rose up to meet him, undermining his rationality even more. Against his will he lowered his head. A fraction of an inch from her face he applied the mental brakes and ordered himself to back away, but then her warm, stuttered exhalation buffeted his chin, and his willpower dissolved. He sipped up that lone tear. Saltiness hit his tongue and hunger blindsided him. Even though he knew he shouldn't, he covered her mouth with his.

Her body went rigid and her hands splayed on his waist. Her *mmmph* of protest filled his lungs. But instead of pushing him away, after one shocked moment her fingers fisted in his shirt, holding him close. Her soft lips parted and he had to taste her. She met his tongue with hers, stroking a slick stream of fire that incited him to pull her closer.

He skimmed his palms down her arms and around her back, pulling her slender form against his. Big mistake. He knew it the second her curves conformed to him. But he couldn't stop himself from kneading her flesh and deepening the kiss. His heart slammed against his rib cage. His body burned. He cradled her waist, caressed her back. It wasn't enough. Desire unlike any he'd ever experienced consumed him. He wound her ponytail around his hand and tugged gently, angling her head for better access.

Then suddenly she yanked free, pressing her fingers over her mouth and backing, wide-eyed, away from him. "What are you doing?"

Damned if he knew.

"Adam, you can't— I— We—" She hugged her middle. "No. That shouldn't have happened. It can't happen again."

Shocked and disgusted by his loss of control and his hunger for his brother's wife, Adam rummaged the wasteland of his brain for words. Remorse and shame pelted him like hail. What had he been thinking?

He'd cheated on Andrew.

"It won't. I won't be a stand-in for my brother." She flinched. "I didn't ask you to."

No. And he wasn't proud that *he* had reached for *her,* kissed *her.* But she had kissed him back.

Two wrongs, and yet holding her had felt so right. But it wasn't. "Dinner's waiting."

"Can we skip it? I just want to go home. You can take the files to Danny tomorrow."

An odd feeling coiled in his gut. He wasn't disappointed that the selfishness he'd expected had returned—it helped quench his lingering desire.

"This isn't about you. You promised my father files. You'll deliver them."

For several seconds she stared at him as if debating arguing, then without a word, she swept past him.

But it was too late to put distance between them. He'd crossed a line he never should have broached. He had never stolen anything from Andrew before. God help him, he didn't know how he was going to forget that he'd betrayed his brother tonight.

Worse, he wasn't going to be able to forget how Madison had felt in his arms. How she tasted.

But it wasn't a mistake he'd repeat.

CHAPTER EIGHT

MADISON'S HANDS AND insides quivered like gelatin, but she did everything in her power to mask her anxiety from the others in the room.

Adam didn't kiss like Andrew.

Don't think about it.

"You sent Mrs. Woods home with a stray cat?" Danny's question snatched her back from her wayward thoughts.

"Yes." She tried to ignore the man seated beside her at the motor home's compact kitchen table.

Helen had positioned them so that they both faced Danny's recliner. Madison was hemmed between Adam and the wall, and every time he moved she caught a glimpse in her peripheral vision of the hands that had held and caressed her. Occasionally his elbow bumped hers, catapulting her pulse rate into triple digits. If that weren't distraction enough, she'd swear Adam's aftershave clung to her upper lip, and she smelled him every time she inhaled.

He didn't kiss like his brother. The thought bounced around inside her skull again like a ball in a pinball machine rebounding off the paddles.

How had she let the kiss happen? She'd seen it coming and done nothing to avoid it. Her only guess was that the combination of being bombarded by memories of Andrew and Daniel, then Mrs. Woods losing her pet and telling the story of her daughter, had pushed Madison back into that deep, dark well of agony after she'd lost her husband and baby. When she'd realized she could depend on no one but herself. But unlike Mrs. Woods, Madison had nothing to remember her baby by except a few sketchy ultrasound pictures.

She'd been weak in the office's back room. Needy. Desperate for someone to hold. And Adam had been there. But that was a poor excuse.

"Why the cats?" Danny asked.

Adam tossed his napkin on the table and turned his head to scowl at her. "The cat will probably outlive her, and then what will you do?"

Her pulse hiccupped at his aggression. How could he look at her as if he hated her when an hour ago he'd been kissing her into oblivion? She blinked, then concentrated on Danny—the less threatening companion.

"Mrs. Woods needed company tonight and a distraction when she went back into her house and saw all of Peaches's things. She has no family. The cat is a low-maintenance companion. She can keep it or return it. But I wanted her to have something to focus on to help her get beyond her initial grief."

"I know about transference, Madison. I wasn't aware you did. I never taught you."

"It's something I picked up."

Understatement of the year, as her menagerie of strays illustrated. She collected the unwanted, the unloved.

"I'd like to see how much more you've learned on your own."

She could still feel Adam's scrutiny. He'd watched her on and off throughout the meal, and each time those blue-green eyes had connected with hers a bolus of adrenaline had jetted through her veins. She laced her fingers in her lap, giving up any pretense of eating.

Why him? It wasn't fair that her body awoke for the one man she dare not have.

She dreaded being cooped up with Adam on the flight back home. She'd been fortunate that a cell phone call—business from the sounds of it—had captured his attention before they'd left the office parking lot. The call hadn't ended until they turned into the driveway.

"I'm glad you were there for her, Maddie, and proud that you were willing to stay after-hours."

Focus on the things within your control. "Pet emergencies don't limit themselves to office hours."

Danny nodded. "Not everyone understands that."

She caught sight of Helen going rigid in her peripheral vision and assumed that was a dig Helen had heard before.

"Peaches has been on the decline for almost a year. I warned Mrs. Woods repeatedly about what was ahead of her, but she wasn't ready to hear it. I'm not sure what she would've done if you'd refused to see her. For what it's worth, I would never have thought of sending the cats with her, but then you were always more empathetic and intuitive than Andrew and I put together. That's why you would have been such an asset to the practice."

The compliment flushed Madison with pleasure until she saw Helen's scowl deepen and the disbelief on Adam's face. "I'll call the crematorium first thing tomorrow and relay her wishes."

"The girls at the office will handle it."

"No. I promised Mrs. Woods I'd do it. But I'll need someone on your staff to meet the crematorium guys for the pickup. Peaches is ready for them. And since the grooming and kennel operations are operating while you're out, someone should be there. I'll just need you to follow up. The staff would like to hear from you anyway."

"Consider it done."

"Thank you." Madison checked her watch. "If you don't mind, I'd really like to go home."

"I wish you would stay, Maddie."

She knew he did. Discomfort pricked her like a bed of cactus needles. Danny had so much to worry about and nothing to distract him except her. He'd grilled her about today's cases over dinner, and even though he drooped with fatigue, he hungered for more.

"I have my own patients tomorrow, Danny."

"Adam could always fly you back early in the morning. You could get a good night's sleep and—"

Adam rose. "Dad, I have to work tomorrow. Madison's right. We need to go. There's a storm front approaching, and I need to get ahead of it."

At least Adam agreed that her staying overnight was a bad idea. She shot him a grateful glance. His gaze met hers, jolting her with an electric charge, and she couldn't look away. She saw latent anger melding with desire in his blue eyes. There was no way tonight's mishap could yield anything but trouble. She knew it and so did he. The knowledge sat like a hot brick in her belly.

It shamed her to admit Adam's kiss had thrilled her in ways Andrew's never had. She'd tingled from head to toe as if someone had given her an IV of champagne. That alien feeling had scared her into breaking the embrace. If it hadn't…

She sprung to her feet and gathered her dishes. Dear heaven, she didn't even want to contemplate what would have happened if she hadn't had that flash of sanity. Neglected hormones had poisoned her brain, and she clearly wasn't in control of her senses.

She needed distance and a week to regroup, to bolster her defenses and to remember that the Drakes had betrayed her before.

She carried her plate to the sink. Helen took the dish from her, frowning at the barely touched meal. "You used to love my Cajun-chicken pasta."

The creamy sauce blended with broccoli, asparagus and red peppers probably tasted as good as it looked—if one's taste buds hadn't been hijacked by an ill-conceived kiss. Although she'd forced down part of the meal, she hadn't tasted a bite. "I apologize for my lack of appetite. It's been a long day."

"Danny hardly gave you a minute to eat with all his questions." After a stabbing glance at her husband, Helen scraped the remainder into the trash.

"I don't mind." Madison didn't have the energy to keep being nice in the face of so much hostility. She headed for the door. "I'll wait outside."

She made it to the driveway. The car was locked. She couldn't hide herself away in the darkened compartment. She studied the scattered clouds racing across the sky. The dense, warm, humid night air enveloped her. It was almost ten. It would be midnight by the time they landed and two o'clock before Adam returned to Norcross. If they didn't beat the approaching storm, courtesy demanded she offer him a place to stay and let him fly back early in the morning. She prayed it wouldn't come to that.

The motor home door opened and closed. Madison's muscles seized up. She wasn't ready to face Adam or the chaos he'd created inside her. Not yet. Maybe she never would be.

Why him? Was her body trying to replace what

she'd lost? Was it looking for another peg of the exact size and shape as the hole Andrew's death had left behind? It seemed most likely that the chemical attraction had nothing to do with the man and everything to do with someone familiar.

"Thank you," Helen spoke behind her.

Surprised, Madison spun around, and for the first time she didn't see loathing in Helen's eyes. Hope swelled in her chest—hope she tried to squash, because she couldn't afford to get attached to this family again. "For what?"

"For coming even though you've already had a long day, and for being patient with Danny's endless questions. He enjoys your visits. He was on pins and needles when Adam texted to say you might not make it. Your late arrival kept him from falling asleep after dinner, and he was more animated tonight than he's been since this started."

Sympathy wound through Madison like a rampant kudzu vine, mingling with shame, because if she'd had her way she would have skipped dinner and been home by now.

"Your Mrs. Woods wasn't the only one who needed a distraction tonight. We met with the doctors today to discuss beginning chemotherapy next week. Danny's worried, even if he won't admit it."

And so was Helen, if the strain around her eyes was an indicator. "He'll get through this, Helen. You both will."

"Yes, well..." Helen scanned the leaves blow-ing across the yard. An awkward silence tested the strength of the tentative truce between them before she faced Madison again, her expression inflexible.

"If he's sick and needs my attention after the infusion, don't expect me to ignore him and cook for you," she blurted, then pivoted abruptly and returned to the RV, leaving Madison rattled. She should have known the break in hostilities wouldn't last.

The door opened before Helen reached it. Adam held it for his mother, then descended the stairs. Madison's nerves snarled into one big knot in her belly. He carried his suit coat draped over his forearm. Moonlight peaked intermittently through the clouds to gleam off his white dress shirt like a lighthouse beacon blinking to mark a hazard.

She'd have had to have been dead not to have noticed how firm and hot he'd been pressed against her earlier. And no matter how many times she might have wished in the months following the accident that she hadn't survived the wreck, she definitely was not dead. Every cell in her body was alive and craving attention—a man's attention.

"Let's go." His low voice rumbled through her.

She followed him to the car and after he opened her door, slid into the seat. Her heart bumped heavily as he rounded the hood, then settled behind the wheel.

Two hours of one-on-one. How would she endure?

His strained expression said he had something to say—something she probably didn't want to hear.

He twisted the key and the engine purred smoothly. "About what happened earlier—"

Alarm skittered through her. She didn't want to have this conversation. "Must we have a postmortem? It happened. It was a mistake and we both know it. It won't happen again."

"No. It won't. But—"

"Adam, *please.* Just let it go." She wished the overhead light would go out. She'd never felt more exposed. Her face burned with mortification.

"Do you always run from your problems, Madison?"

Her shoulders snapped back at the unexpected attack. "I don't run from anything."

"What do you call passing on the burden of the funeral arrangements and settling your husband's estate and abandoning my family the day after the service?"

She'd wanted to avoid this confrontation, but was doing so proving his point? "My leaving was for the best."

"For whom?"

The horrible scene with Helen replayed in her mind and emotion threatened to choke her.

"Your family."

He braced his forearm on the wheel and faced her. "Are you kidding me? That's the most egotistical thing I've heard you say. My mother needed you and you turned your back after all she'd done for you. She treated you like the daughter she never ha—"

"Your mother told me the sight of me made her nauseous." The words erupted before she could stop them. She didn't want him to think less of Helen, but she was tired of his barbed comments.

Hiked eyebrows and parted lips revealed his incredulity. "She would never—"

"She did. Ask her."

"When are you alleging this happened?"

His snide tone set her teeth on edge. "Right after the memorial service. She cornered me in the funeral home's garden."

Icy, disgust-filled eyes roved her face. "You're lying. My mother is never confrontational."

She didn't have the energy for this. "Believe what you want, Adam. I don't care."

She dug her iPod out of her bag, inserted the earphones and cranked up the volume to her favorite running playlist. The driving beat kept her from thinking about that cold day she'd realized she could count on no one but herself.

THE STORM HAD broken overnight with a fury that had matched Madison's inner turmoil. Wind and rain had lashed her windows, and thunder had shaken her small farmhouse, making it impossible to sleep. She'd spent most of the night pacing her kitchen in the dark, because she hadn't wanted to alert June to her wakefulness by turning on lights.

Had Adam made it back safely? She should have asked him to text her, but that seemed...like she cared. And she didn't. One ill-conceived kiss did not make a relationship.

The turbulence during their flight had rattled her teeth and made her stomach swoop with each drop in altitude. She hated to contemplate what Adam had endured on the return trip and hated even worse that she couldn't stop worrying about him.

She glanced at her cell phone on the table, then deliberately turned away. She would *not* call Danny on the pretext of reminding him about Mrs. Woods's Peaches, then casually dig for updates on Adam.

Adam was not her problem. But she couldn't endure the thought of being responsible for another Drake death.

She grabbed her phone, stomped into her rubber boots and headed outside to see if the storm had caused any damage. The heavy dawn air promised a muggy day ahead, but at least it didn't carry the panicked cry of a critter in need of rescue. The massive old oak and pecan trees surrounding the house were notorious for dropping branches, birds' nests and baby squirrels. It had only taken her a couple summer thunderstorms to discover why the former vet who had owned the farm had also owned a very tall ladder and a collection of incubators.

Bojangles nickered. She made her way to his enclosure, cataloging the debris on the ground. Nothing major, but enough that she'd have to find an hour this evening to clean up.

"Morning, buddy. You and Josh getting along?"

The gelding leaned across the fence for his scratch. She stared into his big brown eyes and fought for calm when what she yearned to do was jump on his back and ride like the wind away from this whole situation. But that would only confirm Adam's accusation that she ran from her problems.

Ned, her Nigerian Dwarf goat, bleated and jumped from the roof of his doghouse, then hopped and skipped across the yard toward the barn. His limp was barely visible now that he'd healed. He reminded her of the goats her family had kept on their farm in Lafayette to keep the fence lines clean.

The chickens scratched in their coop, tilting their heads as if to ask, "What's the holdup?" Madison picked up her pace. Three cats raced toward her. Prissy immediately started her figure eight through Madison's feet. Bossy and Cleo strolled beside her as she maneuvered to the barn without tripping. Even before she got there she heard Wilbur, her guinea pig, whistling from his cage inside the barn. Wilbur's racket roused Buster, the de-scented, domesticated skunk she'd adopted when his owner had threatened to release him into the wild after getting tired of his high-maintenance antics. She'd exiled him to an elaborate cage in the barn after the rascal had stolen and hoarded too many items to count.

Everybody was hungry except her, but she vowed to eat a yogurt-and-fruit smoothie before going to work rather than listen to Piper lecture. She bent over the food barrel to scoop out grain, and the cell phone in her pocket thumped against the steel. Instantly thoughts of Adam jumped to the forefront of her brain. She debated texting him, but suppressed the urge. He was fine. She'd checked the news online this morning and there had been no stories of plane crashes. If a hospital executive had gone missing, someone would have noticed.

She fed the indoor critters first, then turned her attention to the outside pets. After delivering Bojangles's oats, she fed Ned and scattered cracked corn for the chickens before releasing them from the coop. Coyotes had become a problem lately, requiring her to secure the hens at night. The birds filed out. Bug control at its best. There were only a few eggs in their nests. She carefully placed each one in her basket. Either Josh or June must have been collecting them during her absence.

She finished the remainder of her chores by rote, but her routine failed to soothe her as it usually did. The phone in her pocket kept distracting and tempting her. She headed to the house and encountered June in the backyard with a pair of coffee mugs in hand.

"Morning, Madison. You don't look like a woman who got her groove on with a handsome man. In fact, you look worse than you did before you left."

"Thanks, I missed you, too," she responded with a touch of sarcasm and accepted the dark brew. June made coffee like she did brownies—strong, dark and sweet. Heaven in a cup. She took a fortifying sip. "Mmm. Good. The storm kept me up."

"It was a doozy. I heard a big crash behind the vacant cottage sometime around four."

"I'll check it out before I head to the office."

"I'm off today. I'll do it and let you know if there's any damage when I swing by for lunch."

"We're doing lunch again?"

"Wednesday is your new Monday. Works for me 'cause it means I get a free lunch." June tilted her head. "Are you losing more weight?"

Madison braced herself for a speech. "I'm run off my feet in Norcross, but they feed me, so take off your mother-hen suit."

"Don't try to snowball me. I know stress kills your appetite. If you'd unwind a little with Adam—"

Madison held up a hand. "Not going to happen."

"You're the one who always said you wanted a man from out of town for a scorching encounter."

"That was the margaritas talking. Remind me to never attend another bachelorette party with you and Piper." They had partied a little too hard at Piper's.

June grinned. "Your brother-in-law fits your no-strings affair description perfectly unless you don't feel any attraction toward him."

The memory of Adam's mouth elicited a rush of desire so potent she missed a step. Shame scorched Madison's cheeks, and unfortunately, the deputy's narrowing eyes said she hadn't missed the reaction.

"Ah…not the case. Well, Doc, you have six more weeks to wise up and take advantage of him. And you have the added benefit of knowing he's not going to turn into a psycho stalker afterward. Can't say that for the guys we've met elsewhere."

"Adam can't stand the sight of me."

So why had he kissed her? That question had done more to keep her awake than the thunderstorm. She didn't have an answer.

The few times she'd cried in front of Andrew, her husband had developed an urgent need to be elsewhere—as if she'd become contagious. He'd never held her or gently stroked away her tears. And Andrew had never kissed her as if he didn't want to but couldn't help himself.

Adam had. Thoroughly. She'd felt his arousal against her leg and—

Oh, boy. Don't go there.

Too late. She shuddered.

Why had he done it? He hated her. He'd called her a liar and selfish. He resented her helping his father, though she didn't know his reasons.

The only way to protect herself from being sucked into the Drakes' world was to find out and then fortify herself against them.

"Madison?"

She jerked to the present. "Wow. Look how late it is. I'd better get moving. Thanks for the coffee. See you later."

And she bolted—exactly what Adam had accused her of doing. But June was too adept at questioning, and if Madison wasn't careful she'd get information that Madison wasn't ready to share.

"DID YOU SAY it?" Adam repeated when his mother ducked her head and developed a sudden, intense interest in stirring her marinara sauce.

"Did *she* tell you that?"

The mortified flush streaking her cheeks gave him the confirmation he needed. Madison hadn't lied. But had Madison's motives for abandoning them been a genuine wish to spare his mother's feelings or something more egocentric?

"Does Dad know you ran off his star pupil?"

His mom darted a look over her shoulder. "Shush."

Negative, then. "He's in the bathroom with the exhaust fan running. He can't hear us. Why, Mom? I've never known you to be malicious before."

She flinched. "She killed my son and grandson! I was distraught. And it was the truth. You know it was. Looking at her makes my stomach churn. You can't tell me you don't feel the same way."

What would she say if she knew he'd kissed Andrew's wife? He certainly had no way to explain it to her. Hell, he couldn't even explain it to himself. One moment he'd been impatient to get Madison out the door, to his parents, then on the plane and out of his way. And the next...

He'd screwed up.

He had zero experience with crying women, unlike Andrew, who'd broken hearts regularly before Madison had come along. He didn't know how to handle tears or the agony that Madison had fought so hard to hide from him.

But the offense wouldn't be repeated.

His mother wrung her hands. "Adam, I don't want Madison moving to Norcross. I know she's good with your father, but we have to find a way to convince him she's not the saint he thinks she is. I couldn't stand it if he persuaded her to return to the practice and I had to cook her meals and pretend nothing happened. Please tell me you agree."

"I do. But let her get Dad through the worst of his treatment. Morale is an important component of his recovery. Right now he thinks he needs her, but Madison will reveal her true nature eventually. Then if he still needs help, we'll convince him to hire the substitute service until he's back on his feet."

"It's good to know I'm not alone. It's just that sometimes…" Her eyes closed and she went pale.

"What?"

She shifted, and when she lifted her lids the turmoil in her eyes made his heart contract. "Madison and Andrew were arguing before they left her graduation party. She was angrier than I've ever seen her. I've never seen that look of fury and desperation in her eyes before. Sometimes I wonder… if she wrecked the car on purpose."

He gaped. "That's a serious accusation, Mom. You'd better have facts to back it up."

"I don't. I just have a…feeling, a mother's intuition that the marriage was in trouble."

"Are you saying Madison was suicidal and she tried to take them all out?"

"No. But she hated the car and the house he bought her, and she resented the baby. Andrew said she didn't want children getting in the way of her career."

All things Andrew had told him in the months prior to his death. But wrecking deliberately? If she wasn't suicidal that seemed unlikely, given Madison couldn't have controlled the outcome. And the report had said black ice.

"If she felt that strongly about not having children, she could have had an abortion."

"Andrew would never have agreed to that." She ducked her head and stirred.

His mother could sometimes be dramatic, and he wanted to dismiss the wild allegation. But the seed had been planted. Andrew had always been closer to her than Adam had, and his brother had confided in her. If Andrew's marriage had been less than perfect, there was a good chance their mother knew more about the difficulties than anyone else.

But if there had been the slightest chance Madison had wrecked the car on purpose, the cops would have charged her with a more serious offense than driving too fast for conditions, wouldn't they?

CHAPTER NINE

PIPER BREEZED INTO the office Friday morning like a woman on a mission. "Roth has an old marine buddy coming to visit this weekend. We need you to even the numbers at dinner tonight."

The way her assistant busied herself and refused to look Madison's way set alarm bells off in Madison's head. "You're trying to set me up on a blind date? Again?"

Piper hesitated. "Not exactly."

"You know I hate it when you do that."

"He's Roth's best friend. He used to be his spotter in the marine corps."

Roth had been a sniper. That had been a big bone of contention between him and Piper in the early days. "Not a good idea. If something happened then fizzled it would put you in the middle."

"Nothing has to happen."

"But you're hoping it will."

Piper's cheeks pinked. "Sam is a really good guy. He's the only man I've ever heard Roth say he trusted with his life."

"You're my closest friend. He's your husband's.

Anything less than happily ever after is going to cause problems. And you know I don't believe in fairy tales."

"Exactly. You'd readily accept that there could never be anything long-term between you and Sam. He's a lifer who plans to die with his boots on. He will never leave the corps voluntarily, and you won't leave your practice. But he's recovering from some kind of eye surgery and he needs a distraction."

She wished she could do it—pick up a man and have wild sex with no expectations. It would be nice to give her excess estrogen an outlet and get her hormones back under control. But she couldn't. She'd tried it once years ago when she'd desperately needed to prove to herself that she hadn't died with Andrew and Daniel. The night had been a disaster from the first hello to that final awkward, painful goodbye. She'd hated herself afterward, and it had taken ages to forgive herself. It wasn't going to happen again.

"Ask June."

"She's working."

"Piper, I've never had a good blind date."

"You need to do something to get your mind off Norcross. You've been jumpy all week, and you only remember to eat when June or I feed you."

"The summer heat's killing my appetite." Her toes curled inside her sneakers. It was a partial truth. This had been a record-breaking hot and humid July.

"You're running more and eating less. You can't keep going like this."

"I promise I'll be fine."

"You need some TLC, boss. Come and enjoy a dinner you don't have to prepare. The men are grilling. We'll drink margaritas and watch them flex their muscles."

She sighed. "There's no way you're going to let me out of this, is there?"

"Not a chance."

"Just dinner. No margaritas or man dessert for me."

Piper grinned. "Deal. I won't push for more, but—"

"See that you don't." She didn't plan to pursue a relationship with Roth's friend, but she had to admit her male-female social skills had dipped below rusty a long time ago. They could use a little polish. And she could use a night of someone's company besides her own.

SHE HATED BLIND dates. *Hated them.* Madison refused to dress up—if she was going to be tortured, she would at least be comfortable.

The smell of meat on the grill greeted her when she climbed from her truck, and her stomach rumbled. Her sandals scraped up the walk, reluctance weighting her steps. The side gate flew open and Piper's son, Josh, raced toward her with Sarg, the dog Madison had patched back together, by his side.

The abandoned mutt had been one of her successful adoption stories.

"Dr. Madison, we're out back." He eyeballed the fruit trifle in her hands. It was the fanciest summer dessert she had in her limited repertoire. "Want me to carry that?"

She surrendered the dish and petted the dog. "Thanks, Josh. How are you and Bojangles making out?"

"Great. Mom's giving me some pointers. I jogged him this week for the first time. It's kind of bumpy."

"You'll get the hang of it. I'm sure he loves your company."

"I'm trying to convince Mom to let me get a skunk. Buster's so cool."

"Not a good idea. Skunks steal and hide your things. Before I moved him outside, Buster swiped so much of my stuff that I'm still finding stashes of his ill-gotten goods."

"Oh. Maybe a guinea pig, then."

"A safer choice, for sure."

They reached the privacy fence that surrounded the backyard and nerves clutched her stomach. Showtime. Even if the meeting tonight wasn't going anywhere, she hadn't dated in a l-o-n-g time. Josh and Sarg raced ahead toward the table already loaded with food.

The buff blond marine stood just inside the fence. He also wore jeans and a T-shirt, making her glad she hadn't dressed up. Dark sunglasses covered his eyes. He had a longneck bottle in his hand. With-out waiting for Piper or Roth, he crossed the grass to meet her. "Hi, I'm Sam."

His greeting was cool, polite. Nothing more. Nothing less. Definitely not flirtatious. Good.

"I'm Madison. And I'm sorry about this. I tried to talk Piper out of the setup, but she's deaf when she wants to be."

His grin should have been lethal, but her hor-mones kept snoozing. "About as deaf as her husband, I suspect. No offense, but my life's a little unsettled now. I wouldn't put that on a woman."

"Understood. And ditto for me."

"Piper said I should get you a margarita as soon as you arrived. She's inside making them now. Want me to track her down?"

"No, thanks. Piper's trying to get me in trouble. I'll stick with sweet tea."

"Can't handle tequila?"

"Apparently not—a lesson I learned the hard way at her bachelorette party."

"Copy that. Roth has enough beer in the cooler for a platoon. Tea's this way."

She waved at Roth, who stood by the grill, and walked beside Sam across the lawn to the food table—it felt like the right thing to do. No pres-sure. No awkwardness. He was here under protest and so was she. Both duly noted.

He filled a glass and passed it to her. Their fin-gers brushed. No tingle, no fizz, no skipping heart.

Nada. Not his fault, because he was definitely gorgeous and well built.

"So you're a veterinarian. I've done a little work with military working dogs. They're a nice taste of home when you're deployed."

"And dogs are more loyal than any human you'll ever meet."

And so the night went. Sam was charming and interesting company, but he'd elicited nothing from her in the feminine department. She hadn't even noticed the passing hours until a lightning bug flashed in front of her.

"Wow. I'd better get going."

"I'll walk you to your car," he offered and Piper's eyes sparkled with interest in the flickering torch-lights.

"Thanks."

Madison's heartbeat quickened—not out of interest or excitement, but out of dread that she might have to head off an unwanted embrace. Sam stopped by her truck and offered his hand.

"It was good meeting you, Madison. Thank you for tonight and for being a good sport."

Surprised, Madison put hers in his. "It was good meeting you, too, Sam. You're good company. I hope you get the desired result at your checkup next week."

She'd learned the marine scout sniper had suffered a detached retina from an explosion. He was optimistic that the surgical repairs would allow him to return to the field.

The handshake was brief and without fireworks. She climbed into her cab with no exchange of phone numbers or mention of getting together again. Then she glanced toward the house and saw the poorly concealed disappointment on Piper's face before the curtain dropped.

But as far as Madison was concerned, the night had been a success of sorts. She'd passed an enjoyable evening in male company and she hadn't acted stupid.

All she had to do was keep up that winning streak when she returned to Georgia.

ADAM HAD SURVIVED the storm. That had been Madison's first thought when she read the text message Sunday morning.

Can't get away. Rental car paid for. Pick it up and get yourself here. Do not disappoint Dad.

The address of the rental car agency and the reservation number had followed.

She hadn't been happy about the relief rushing through her when she'd read his message. But she hadn't heard from him since he'd dropped her off after their white-knuckle flight until this morning's text and she'd been worried.

She turned into his driveway Sunday evening

just shy of bedtime. She'd delayed leaving home because she wanted to avoid one-on-one time with him. Climbing from the car, she stretched her stiff muscles. In an attempt to block the memory of the kiss from her mind she'd spent five days working herself to near exhaustion, first in the office and then in her yard after yet another summer storm. She'd succeeded. Mostly.

Then Adam opened his front door. His gaze hit her with the impact of a charging bull and every sensation came stampeding back. Her stupid heart sprinted just as fast as it had when he'd held her. Her palms moistened and her short, shallow breaths resembled an excited dog's panting.

So much for her lucky streak.

She yearned to turn and run the opposite direction. But she wouldn't, because no matter what he thought of her, she wasn't a coward.

He looked tired. Tension furrowed his brow and bracketed his mouth. His hair looked like he'd raked his hand through it a time or five. Compassion that she didn't want to feel kicked in. "Rough week?"

"The nurses are threatening a strike."

Don't look at his mouth. Or his wide shoulders.

"How's Danny?"

"His labs are where they need to be for him to have his first chemo treatment."

"Good. And Helen?"

"Holding it together."

His eyes narrowed on her face. She wished he

wouldn't look at her that way—it reminded her of the moment in the prep room when she'd realized what he was about to do and done nothing to prevent it.

"Come in. You know the way to your room." He took her cooler and opened the door wider.

She shouldered her bags and bustled past him, hyperconscious of him shadowing her down the hall. When they reached the bedroom her nervousness ratcheted up several notches. Stopping just inside the door she shifted on her feet and searched for something to say.

"I'm surprised you moved back to Norcross."

His lifted eyebrow told her the unexpected question had caught him off guard. "Why?"

"Andrew always said you couldn't wait to fly the coop and that once you left you'd never come back."

His lips compressed. "Priorities change."

"Why did you come back?"

"I had an opportunity and my parents needed help. Your point?"

"I don't have one. I was just curious." She'd spent far too much time wondering how much of what Andrew had told her had been a lie.

"Can I trust you to get yourself to the office on time?"

Insulted, she straightened. "I'm here, aren't I?"

"Get some sleep. Tomorrow's going to be a long day. I'll meet you at my parents' after work."

He turned on his heel and left.

Tension drained from her. What had she expected? For him to kiss her again? Of course not. And she didn't want him to.

Madison needed to work harder on distancing herself from the Drakes. Adam in particular. Because if she didn't, disaster was pretty much guaranteed. Maybe once this weekend was through they'd trust her enough to keep renting her a car and the intimate flights would no longer be necessary.

HELEN PUSHED OPEN the bathroom door. Danny was on his hands and knees in front of the toilet. "Are you okay?"

He clutched the bowl and vomited, then sank back on his haunches. "Does it sound like I'm okay?"

She bustled to the sink and dampened a washcloth for him. "What can I do?"

He snatched the cloth from her hand and mopped his pasty face. "Stop hovering, Helen. Can't a man puke in peace? I had the door closed for a reason. Get out."

It wasn't like Danny to be nasty, but he'd had his first chemo today, and he had a right to be testy. The chemo nurse had warned them that some medicines might make him sick, and it looked like this was going to be one of those meds.

"Can I get you anything?"

"Privacy. You've been in my armpit all day. Go buy yourself something pretty."

She tried not to take offense. The day had been

long and arduous—for both of them. "I don't need things, Danny. I just need you to be okay."

"I will be." He contradicted the statement by heaving again.

She felt helpless—just as she had each time one of the boys had been ill with something she couldn't fix. But at least they'd let her tend to them instead of being cranky. Well...Andrew more than Adam. Her firstborn had always been the more independent one.

Speaking of Adam... "I'll call Adam and tell him you're not up for Madison's visit tonight."

"No. I want to hear how she's managing." He bent back over the bowl, retching until he had nothing left.

"Danny, you can't handle—"

"Don't tell me what I can't handle. I'll be fine in a few minutes. *If* you leave me alone."

What if he wasn't? What if it only got worse from here? What if she had to watch him waste away like some of the others they'd met in the infusion room today? There had been some who she'd been convinced would not be there next week or next month or— She severed the thought.

What if Danny lost his hair or his fingernails, or... Once more she tried to squash her fears. She couldn't afford any negative thoughts. She needed to hold him, to tell him she loved him and have him repeat the words to her.

But he wasn't going to do that tonight. Danny was pushing her away, but he wanted to see Madison.

Helen couldn't help the twinge of jealousy needling her. And that was petty of her.

Was this how Andrew had felt when his father had praised Madison over his own son?

It had been during one of her heart-to-hearts with Andrew that Helen had said the words she wished she could take back. *Madison's priorities will change once the babies come. Her career won't be nearly as important as spending time with her child. Just be patient.*

"Helen, Madison and Adam will be hungry when they arrive. Go fix dinner."

She left Danny alone, but she couldn't cook tonight. Her heart wasn't in it, and Danny probably wouldn't be able to eat what she'd planned anyway. Yesterday she'd bought pork chops, intending to fry them for tonight's dinner. But the pamphlets she'd read today while he had his infusion warned that the smell of frying foods might make him nauseous. He was already sick, and she wouldn't do anything to make him feel worse.

She glanced at the clock. It was too late to concoct an alternate menu. Madison and Adam would have to feed themselves after they left. No matter what Danny said, she didn't believe for one minute that he'd be up for company within the next half hour.

Maybe he'd like a glass of water.

A knock on the door brought her up short of the cabinet. Adam, already? But she'd told Adam not to knock. She glanced out the windshield as she crossed the den, but she didn't recognize the small sedan parked out front. She pushed open the door. Madison waited on the mat.

Not who she wanted to see. Helen looked past her. "Where's Adam?"

"He told me to meet him here."

"Danny's sick to his stomach. I'm not cooking."

Helen didn't move aside and Madison made no attempt to climb the stairs. "Do you have the right foods in the house?"

"What right foods?"

"You should have received a list of things Danny might be able to eat and things to avoid."

"I didn't get that until today, and Danny was in no shape to go shopping. I haven't had time to go to the store since we returned home. The infusion took longer than I expected. All day, in fact." She hated the defensiveness in her voice, but Madison's questions made her feel incompetent.

"I'll be back." Madison returned to her car and left.

"Who was that?" Danny asked behind her. Helen spun around guiltily. He looked terrible and unsteady on his feet.

"Madison. You need to lie down."

"I don't want to lie down. I told you I wanted to see her."

"I didn't tell her to leave."

"Damn it, Helen, I needed her tonight. I have

to have something to think about other than how I feel."

He stomped back to the bedroom and slammed the door. A tangle of emotions twined through her. She wanted to make him happy, to do everything right.

But she was glad Madison was showing her true colors, and she'd be amazed if she actually did come back. The sooner Danny realized what Madison was really like, the sooner he'd let her go and hire the professional substitutes. That day couldn't come soon enough.

"WHEN I TOLD her I wasn't cooking she left without coming inside," Adam's mother said.

"That's not like her," his father added from his recliner.

Fury coiled inside Adam like a copperhead waiting to strike.

"How long ago did she leave?" He would track her down and drag her back.

"Thirty or forty minutes ago."

A flash of movement through the windshield of the motor home caught his eye. Madison's rental car pulled in and parked beside his. He crossed to the front door and shoved it open with enough force to make the hinges protest.

"Where've you been?"

She pulled plastic bags from the backseat. "Getting groceries. Your mom didn't have time to pick up chemo-friendly foods. I told Helen I'd be back."

Madison climbed the stairs, then paused beside him, her caramel gaze searching his face suspiciously. "Where did you think I went? Home?"

His anger deflated. He took a cleansing breath and her scent filled his nostrils—the same fragrance that lingered in his house long after she returned to North Carolina.

"You could've texted to let me know your plans."

"So you could keep tabs on me? Maybe have someone at the market call and report on my progress like you do at the office? Yeah, I know about the daily check-ins. You spy—just like your father."

The dig struck a nerve. She stood toe-to-toe with him, bristling with insult and challenging him to admit he'd misjudged her. When he kept his mouth shut she brushed past him, her shoulder bumping his chest with an electrical charge.

"Hey, Danny. Rough day, huh? I hope I found something to tempt your taste buds. It's normal for them to be out of whack after a treatment, so it might take some experimentation to find something that appeals. I got a little bit of everything to cover the bases."

"I knew you'd be back, Maddie."

That made one of them, Adam conceded. She carried her bags to the kitchen and set them down, then reached into a cabinet, retrieved a glass, filled it with ice and then the ginger ale she'd brought.

"Have you taken your antinausea meds?" She waited for him to nod, then offered him the glass. "Try sipping on this. Ginger's supposed to soothe your stomach. If it does, I bought some ginger root for Helen to incorporate into your foods."

He grasped her hand. "Thank you, sweetheart."

She didn't pull away. "You're welcome."

Madison had made it clear at every turn that she didn't want to be here, but there was no evidence of that in the kind way she treated his father. Adam glanced at his mother and caught her watching the scenario play out with downturned lips.

Madison returned to unloading the bags, filling the compact counter with yogurt, bananas, applesauce, Jell-O, fruit juice popsicles, canned soups and stews, a rotisserie chicken, a loaf of bread and sandwich meat.

"Helen, I don't know where this stuff goes. Do you mind if I leave it for you to put away?"

"No."

His father perked up. "I would love one of those strawberry popsicles, Maddie."

"Yes, sir." Madison opened the box and delivered. "Go slow. Everybody's different, but these are the foods I've heard are recommended."

"You shouldn't have had to do this. Helen should have—"

"Helen was busy taking care of you today." She squeezed his shoulder.

Madison coming to his mother's defense took

Adam aback. This was not the woman his brother had described.

"How did you know which foods to buy?" Adam asked.

"From parents of my patients. I have a tendency to pick up strays. Pets. People…" She shrugged as if it was no big deal that from the moment she'd walked in the door tonight she'd made him question everything his brother had told him about her.

His mother hustled to her purse and extracted her wallet. "Thank you. How much did you spend? I'll reimburse you."

"Don't worry about it, Helen."

His mother looked insulted. "I can afford to buy my own groceries."

"I know you can. But you've fed me countless times and will likely continue doing so while I'm here. Please let me return the favor. I didn't spend much, really."

His mother's expression wavered between humiliated, angry and about to cry. Adam decided to head off all three.

"Mom, have a seat. Would you prefer a chicken or ham sandwich?"

"I—I need to go to the ladies' room." She fled.

He turned to Madison. "I apologize."

"For?"

"Assuming the worst."

"How many times do I have to tell you I keep my word?"

It was time for him to start forming his own opinions of Madison instead of relying on his brother's. Either she had changed dramatically or Andrew had lied, and he was beginning to suspect the latter might be the case.

"That'll be the last time."

As soon as Adam unlocked his front door Madison ducked her head and tried to scoot past him and into the safety of the guest room. Something had changed between them tonight. Something that could spell trouble.

"Madison."

She stopped, and with dread swirling in her stomach, faced him. Proximity was not her friend at the moment. They'd become a team working toward the same goal when he'd helped her prepare dinner, and teamwork with him made keeping her distance and forgetting that kiss a difficult proposition.

"Thanks for what you did tonight. Dad's in bad shape and Mom's a wreck. But you stepped up to the plate and hit the ball out of the park before I could even assess the situation."

His praise filled her with warmth. Not a good thing. She'd prefer to have a polar ice cap wedged between them. "I'm happy I could help. Good night."

"What happened between you and Andrew?"

The question halted her escape. She did not want to have this conversation. Not now. Not ever. She'd already disillusioned him about his mother. She didn't want to corrupt his memories of his twin. "What do you mean?"

"He told me some things in those last few months, and I want to know if any of it was true. I wasn't there to see firsthand and judge for myself."

Uneasiness trickled down her spine like a melting ice cube. "What did he tell you?"

"That you didn't want the baby."

She reeled back a step in horrified disbelief, her hands covering her stomach. "Of course I wanted my baby. The pregnancy was—" She wasn't about to burden him with the whole sordid truth. "Finding out I was expecting was…a surprise. But from moment I learned I was carrying Daniel I loved him, and I started making plans for his birth. Andrew knew that."

"Even though the timing would have derailed your career plans?"

"Not by much, though. Sure, I'd have had to take a few months off, but I'd already talked to Helen. She offered to provide childcare."

His eyes widened. "Neither Mom nor Andrew mentioned that."

She yearned to escape, but she had to know the rest. "What else did he tell you?"

Adam's jaw shifted. "That he didn't know what or *who* you were doing to garner all the accolades in school. He implied the baby might not be his."

Dizziness assailed her. She staggered to the nearest door frame and gripped it to stay upright. *The bastard.* Just when she'd thought Andrew couldn't stoop any lower...

"He accused me of cheating on him?" A tension headache banded her skull. Her ponytail suddenly felt too tight, as if it were pinching her brain. She ripped the elastic band free and massaged her nape. "No wonder you all hate me."

"He didn't accuse. He implied it might be possible. Did you have an affair?"

"*No!* Adam, from the moment I met your brother I was too besotted to even look twice at another man. As for those accolades, I worked my ass off in school and took every extra assignment I could to earn the credentials I needed to take my place alongside Andrew and your father. I had no life beyond my classes, my textbooks and those projects, except for weekends and holidays at your parents'. I barely had time to eat or shower, and I certainly didn't have the time or energy to screw around."

He didn't look convinced.

"When did Andrew tell you all this?"

"After the ultrasound. He called to say you were having a boy and then told me the rest."

Their celebratory lunch right after the procedure had turned into their first argument about her future. Andrew had informed her he wanted her to delay starting work—at least until Daniel started school. And she'd told him she wasn't going to throw away years of education.

Why had he tried to turn Adam against her?

"Was the wreck an accident?"

Another shocking question. She blinked and silently repeated Adam's words, but no matter how many times she tried to reprocess his query, she came up with the same horrible conclusion.

"Are you asking me if I ran off the road, drove through a guardrail and down an embankment in an attempt to kill my husband and son on purpose?"

"You couldn't have known the outcome. Mom said you were angrier than she'd ever seen you when you left the party."

Because Andrew had spilled most of his diabolical plan before they'd left. He'd shared the rest in the car. "I was angry. But I am not a murderer."

"I didn't say you were."

"But you're suggesting it. Adam, I can barely stand to euthanize a suffering pet. How dare you suggest I'd intentionally hurt my husband and child. You are way off base. If you'd read the police report, then you know it said I hit black ice."

"And that you were driving too fast for conditions."

The words stabbed her like an ice pick. This nice little conversation had taken care of any camaraderie or sexual tension there might have been between them. Right now she never wanted to see him again. Anger and angst boiled in her veins.

"I won't stand here and argue with you all night. I have to work tomorrow." Not that she expected to sleep.

She turned and fled before she said something she shouldn't, closing and locking the door behind her. If Adam wanted to censure her for running from her problems tonight, then he could have at it. But she couldn't handle any more of his inquisition.

CHAPTER TEN

MADISON PERCHED ON the edge of her chair, last night's conversation with Adam still ricocheting around in her brain, the way it had been all day. Helen flitted about the kitchen like a nervous hummingbird. No wonder her ex-mother-in-law couldn't stand to look at her—Andrew had filled their heads with lies. But informing Helen that her precious son had been a liar was hardly what the woman needed to hear right now.

A mouthwatering fragrance filled the motor home, but the idea of eating made Madison queasy. Danny looked pale and drawn. "You should be in bed instead of entertaining me."

"I'm sick of that bed. I've been there all day."

"I didn't come to stay. I just wanted to drop off today's files before I headed north."

"Leave the rental car at the depot here and let Adam fly you home after dinner," Danny implored.

Adam… She'd avoided him this morning by slipping out of his house while he was in the shower. And if she had her way she'd be out of Norcross before he arrived at his parents' tonight. She checked her watch. She needed to hit the road now.

"Thanks, but no. I don't mind the drive. It gives me time to get my thoughts together for the week ahead."

"If you take the car you won't get back until 2:00 a.m."

"That's one of the reasons I need to leave now. Tomorrow will be a long day playing catch-up. I feel bad enough that I left my assistant to do all the setup for our week ahead."

"You could live better if you charged more for your services, Maddie."

"But I couldn't live with myself. I work in a rural farming community. Folks back home are doing everything they can to make ends meet. My clientele is very different from yours."

"It hurts me to see you wasting your talents. You're better than this."

"I don't want anything bigger or better or different. I love my farm and my practice." She pushed to her feet. "I forgot to tell you, I checked in with Mrs. Woods this morning. She wants to keep that momma cat, which she has named Silver Lining. I promised we'd help her find homes for the kittens in a few weeks, and that I'd spay Silver after the kittens are weaned. Anyway, rest up, Danny, and good luck with your second chemo on Friday. I'll see you next week."

He held out a hand. She placed hers in it. He squeezed weakly and tugged her down for a hug. "Take care, Maddie. I'll be waiting until you come again. I might need you to spring me from this joint. I love you, girl."

Madison heart skipped a beat. *Love you, girl.* The phrase he'd used so often in the past rocked her, scattering her composure. She struggled to regain it.

"Behave, Danny. Don't give Helen a hard time. Goodbye, Helen."

Her ex-mother-in-law paused in wiping the counter, her face an emotionless mask. "Thank you for the groceries."

Then she resumed her task. Madison assured herself she wasn't disappointed by the lackluster response.

"You're welcome." She hustled out the door. Adam's car turning into the drive dropped an anchor of dismay in her stomach. So much for a clean getaway. He climbed from the vehicle. The brisk evening breeze stirred his hair and flattened his shirt against his lean abdomen. Her mouth dried.

"Where're you going?" he asked as he closed the distance between them.

"Home."

"You're not visiting Dad?"

"I already did. He needs to be in bed and he won't go if I'm here."

Scowling, Adam reached into his pocket, then offered her a roll of bills. She kept her hands by her sides. "What's that?"

"Money to cover the food you purchased and gas for the trip."

"I don't need your money." Her momma had always said pride would be her downfall. That thought unearthed another can of worms that she refused to open.

"You need to fill up the rental before you return it or they'll charge the fuel to my card. I'll pay for it either way. It's cheaper if you do it on your own."

That was true. She swallowed her pride, took the wad and counted the twenties. "This is two hundred dollars. I won't need that much."

He heaved an exasperated breath. "Then give me the change next week, Madison. I'm not going to argue over a few bucks with you. Text me when you arrive."

"It'll be the middle of the night."

"Do it anyway. Do you have a ride from the agency or do you need to keep the car and turn it in tomorrow?"

"I left my truck parked in their lot." As long as Ol' Blue started she'd be good to go. If not, she'd sleep in the camper shell. It wouldn't be the first time.

He stared into her eyes until she was ready to climb out of her skin. Her pulse fluttered irregularly. She blinked to break the connection.

"See if you can get your dad to bed. He's wiped out."

Adam nodded, then headed for the motor home. Tension drained from Madison. She'd survived another week. Only five more to go. Then Adam paused at the top of the stairs and looked back. Their gazes met and her hormones shot off like a Fourth of July fireworks display gone haywire.

What was wrong with her?

She was going to need the long ride to get her head on straight, because despite everything she'd learned this weekend about Andrew's underhandedness, her hormones were apparently still nostalgic for the past. For another Drake. One who was exactly like her husband and yet different in every way.

MAYBE MADISON'S EARLY departure hadn't been as selfish as Adam had believed. His father looked bad—his face and even his lips were colorless. And as Madison had said, he should be in bed.

Adam scanned the living area. The smells permeating the air made his stomach growl in anticipation. He'd been in hostile negotiations all day and had skipped lunch. But there was no sign of his mother. "Where's Mom?"

Before Danny could answer, the bedroom door opened, and Helen came out wearing her walking clothes and sneakers. She looked almost as rough as his dad.

"Hello, dear." She dusted a kiss across Adam's cheek without meeting his gaze. "Go ahead and eat. It's roasted pork chops with vegetables—full of the nutrients your father needs. Make *him* eat if you can. I'll be back in a while." She let herself out the door.

Him? If her snide tone hadn't clued Adam in that something was wrong between his parents, her frozen expression would have. He hadn't seen that numb look since Andrew's funeral. But he didn't follow her out to ask what was bothering her. He and his mom had never had the confidant type of relationship.

He turned to his father. "Should I ask what that was about?"

"She's been hovering. Practically worrying me to death. I can't even vomit without an audience." He looked at his hands. "I might've upset her when I told her to get out of the bathroom."

"Cut her some slack. She's scared."

"You think I'm not?" his father snapped. Then instantly his face filled with regret.

That was the first time his father had admitted to fear. Prior to this he'd acted as if having lung cancer was no more serious than getting a cavity filled.

"I know you are, Dad. But we'll get you through this. You have the best oncology team in the area. I did the research and made damned sure of that."

His father stared into the unlit fireplace. The creases on his forehead and around his mouth cut deeper than ever. But as rough as he looked, his hair had been combed. His dad was vain about his thick salt-and-pepper hair and had been seeing the same overpriced stylist for decades. How would he handle losing it? Odds were it would start coming out soon.

"What if I don't make it, son?" Adam stiffened in apprehension. Did his father know something he didn't? "Will you look after your mother? All she does is shop and cook. She has no clue how to manage our finances or—"

"That's not going to be an issue."

"But what if it is? Don't hide your head in the sand, Adam. What if I'm one of the ones who doesn't come through this?"

"You only had one tumor, Dad, and it was less than three centimeters in diameter. Your survival rate after surgery should be close to one hundred percent unless the doctors have told you something they haven't told me."

"They haven't. Their fancy scans haven't identified any more tumors. Yet. You know surgery increases the likelihood of spreading the bad cells?"

"Your team is hitting hard and fast with the chemo to ensure that doesn't happen."

"Bronchioloalveolar carcinoma is the one cancer that hasn't been proved to respond to chemo."

"It's better to take the precaution."

"Damn it, it's not fair. I never smoked."

"I'm sure they told you BAC is more common in nonsmokers. The good news is that means your lungs aren't already compromised by years of smoking."

"I don't know if I can take six weeks of this."

Anxiety clenched Adam's gut. What choice did his father have if he wanted to survive? "The first day after chemo is the toughest. You'll feel better tomorrow and even more so on Thursday."

"Then they'll hit me with another treatment on

Friday and I'll feel like death all weekend. I'm going to ask them to move Monday's chemo treatments to Tuesdays—at least then I'll have one good day with Madison before they hit me again."

Unfortunately, true, if they stuck to the prescribed regimen. "I'm sorry, Dad. I know it's hard. But it's a short-term misery for a long-term goal. Focus on that if you can." Wanting to change the subject Adam crossed to the kitchen. "Dinner smells good. Want me to fix you a plate?"

"It probably won't stay down." Hearing the defeat in his father's voice was hard. Danny Drake had never been short on ego or confidence. He couldn't give up now or—

No. He couldn't give up. End of subject.

"Try some food. You need to keep up your strength." Adam served the meal his mother had left on the stovetop. He set the plate and a glass of ginger ale on a TV tray in front of his father, but Danny made no attempt to pick up his fork or glass.

"The infusion center really shook up Helen. There were a lot of sick people there. I don't know if she can handle going back."

It didn't sound like his mother was the only one who'd been rattled by the visit. "She's a caretaker. She'll want to be with you. Mom's pretty tough."

He shook his head. "Not anymore. Since Andrew died she's been clingy, morose and stuck in the past. Some days he's all she talks about. You missed most of that when you were living out of state, and you don't come around often enough now to see past the act she puts on for you. But Andrew was here almost every day—to get a free meal, to get his laundry done. She loved that."

Guilt took a bite out of Adam. "I've been coming every day lately. But I do my own laundry, and I don't need to be waited on. Have you talked to her about seeing someone?"

"I tried. She gets too emotional, and she's beyond listening to reason. She's been downright rude to Madison, and we need Madison here. I can't afford to have your mother run her off."

A week ago Adam would have insisted they could do fine without Madison, but after seeing the way she handled his father... Maybe they did need her. "Mom's been through a lot, and it sounds like Andrew might not have been completely honest with us."

Danny's eyes snapped up. He searched Adam's face. "It's about damned time someone got Madison's side of the story."

"Are you confirming Andrew lied?"

"Adam, I loved your brother, but loving him doesn't mean I didn't see his faults and didn't know that he always put number one first. Madison was the best choice he ever made. She was strong where he was weak, and ambitious when he was apathetic. He was a better man when she was around. But she raised the bar around here, and he couldn't keep being lazy and meet her standards.

"Andrew could be pretty convincing when he wanted something, and I always suspected he might've embellished the truth. How much remains to be seen. I never once believed Madison capable of having an affair—no matter what Andrew said. I saw the results of the extra hours she put in. But he had your mother convinced that Madison was as shallow as a petri dish."

And him, Adam admitted. He had a lot of research ahead to filter fact from fiction. But that would have to wait until the crises at work and with his father had passed. By then what Andrew had done wouldn't matter, because Madison would be long gone. And that moment couldn't come too soon.

Whether Andrew had told the truth or not was irrelevant. Madison would always be his brother's wife. He would not fill his brother's shoes. And he definitely would not fill his brother's bed.

RESENTMENT BURNED IN Helen's belly. "I love you, girl," she mimicked Danny's words to Madison and then glanced around to make sure no one had overheard her talking to herself. But the professionally tended yards around her were empty.

She couldn't remember the last time Danny had told her he loved her. Not in years. And she was honest enough to admit she resented Madison sweeping in like a savior, running the practice, buying groceries and entertaining Danny. By doing so Madison had managed to make Helen feel unprepared, neglectful and inadequate in her own home. The same way Madison had made Andrew feel.

Helen knew she should've gotten the shopping list sooner, but… She kicked a piece of gravel. It rolled and bounced along the asphalt, finally coming to rest on the edge of an emerald-green lawn.

Part of not preparing for Danny's care after chemo had been denial, she admitted to herself reluctantly. She hadn't wanted to believe Danny's reaction to the medicines would be this bad. She'd hoped he'd be one of the patients who went on as usual with few to no side effects. Instead, he looked far worse than she'd ever seen him. And it terrified her. The man was rarely ever sick, and even when he had been, he'd never missed a day of work. Seeing him struggle today to lift a glass to his lips tore her apart.

She rounded the curve and spotted three of her neighbors coming her way. She'd dubbed them the supercilious trio, because the women thought themselves better than everyone else. They'd moved into houses formerly occupied by Helen's friends.

It was too late to turn around. They'd already seen her. She didn't need them now, not when her nerves were already frayed to the snapping point. Blanking her expression, she quickened her pace, nodding hello and hoping to pass without speaking. The women were twenty years younger than Helen and career focused like Madison. The few times she'd interacted with them at neighborhood functions they'd acted as if Helen was a housewife because she wasn't smart enough to be anything else.

And maybe she wasn't. She was certainly failing Danny. No. She had her priorities right. Her family had always come first. But if something happened to Danny, how would she support herself? It didn't help that Madison had said the same thing years ago when she'd tried to coerce Helen into going back to school.

But no, she wouldn't think that way. Danny would be fine.

Her neighbors wore perfectly coordinated exercise clothing and each looked as if she'd just stepped out of the salon. Helen hadn't even checked herself in a mirror before racing out. She'd been up since five this morning and hadn't checked her makeup since putting it on.

"How are the renovations coming?" one asked as they drew alongside. They all stopped, forcing her to do the same.

"The remodel's on hold for now." They didn't know about Danny and she wasn't going to tell them.

"We were wondering how long the motor home would be parked in your driveway," the second added.

"Until we no longer need it." She laced the phrase with a saccharine smile.

"What's the holdup? Did you run out of money to pay the contractor?"

The insult snapped her spine as tight as a kite

string. "Danny prefers to do the work himself. He's very skilled with his power tools and loves creating things when his busy practice allows him a few moments of free time."

Since none of these women's husbands even owned a lawn mower, Helen doubted they could identify a power tool at the hardware store. It saddened her to see professional companies mowing their yards and trimming their shrubs. Her sons had learned responsibility by doing those chores, and Adam had made money mowing yards while neighbors were on vacation.

"Isn't having that thing parked in the yard against neighborhood covenants or something?" the third chimed in.

"Danny and I were the first homeowners to buy and build in this development. There were no covenants then and aren't now."

Dear heaven, she was being a bi—witch. Her grandmother would be ashamed. "Now, if you'll excuse me, my husband and son are waiting for their home-cooked dinner."

She hustled back toward her house. Even listening to Danny singing Madison's praises was better than hearing these waspy women buzz.

"THANKS FOR COMING early," Adam said as Madison met him beside the airplane Sunday afternoon. "I hope it wasn't an inconvenience."

As it had every other time, seeing Adam did crazy

things to Madison's equilibrium. "Meeting at three instead of six forced me to juggle a few things, but I managed. What's the rush?"

Adam took her cooler and bag. The accidental touch of their fingers made her heart trip. If it affected him at all he covered it well. Then she noticed the splash of red on his neck and the extra firmness of his mouth. Knowing he wasn't unaffected was not a good thing.

"Dad wants to have a Sunday dinner like the good ol' days. He's afraid he won't be fit company on Tuesday after his next infusion, and he's determined to squeeze in two visits with you each week."

Madison's heart ached in sympathy, confirming she'd totally failed at keeping herself detached from the Drake family.

"How did he handle Friday's?"

"Not great. He'll be weaker each time he goes in. But he was well enough this morning to make demands."

They boarded the plane and Adam fell into his usual takeoff procedures, but the atmosphere wasn't filled with resentment this time. She preferred the tension. It kept her hormones in check.

Flying to get her was both expensive and time-consuming, but if he resented either she had yet to see him show evidence of it to his parents. Andrew never would have been so generous. He'd have made sure everyone knew how much he was putting himself out.

Determined to keep her thoughts from wandering into the danger zone of comparing brothers, she pulled out the stack of veterinary magazines Danny had loaned her and immersed herself in reading each from cover to cover. Adam didn't interrupt and she preferred it that way. Really, she did.

Other than an occasional glance out the window to check the scenery and their progress, she kept her nose in the pages until they'd landed. Not that she hadn't been distracted occasionally by the competent way Adam handled the controls or his deep voice talking to someone on the other end of the radio.

In the same situation Andrew would have demanded her attention and even done foolish things to get it. He used to swerve the car or slam on brakes when she had her face buried in a textbook just so she'd look up. One thing was for sure, she'd have never trusted Andrew at the controls of an airplane. With hindsight she realized he'd often been like a child squealing, "Look at me!" Adam didn't need his ego stroked with attention.

When the wheels rolled to a stop, she marked her place for the transfer from the plane to the car, then read some more. Rude? Maybe. Smart? Definitely.

"Are the articles that engrossing?"

"Yes, but more important, I borrowed the magazines from Danny. I want to return them." She didn't lift her head again until he turned off the car engine and she discovered he'd parked by the Drakes' motor home.

Gathering the magazines she'd finished, she pushed open her door. "Could you unlock the trunk?"

"Why?"

"I need to get some things out of the cooler."

Adam did as she requested. Madison stacked three containers on top of the magazines. Her tower slipped precariously.

"Let me have those." He took the resealable plastic bowls, and again their hands collided. She had the same breath-catching, heart-hiccupping reaction as before. Their gazes met and held, and the awareness of that blasted kiss arced between them. She ducked her head on the pretext of checking to see if she'd left anything behind, breaking the connection.

Four more weeks and she'd never have to see him again. Her life would return to normal.

Helen met them at the door. Everything about her, from her drawn face, flat hair and wrinkled clothing, screamed exhaustion. Madison ached to wrap her arms around her former mother-in-law and reassure her, but the gesture wouldn't be welcome.

"Hello, Helen."

Helen nodded. Her neutral expression brightened when she spotted the containers in Adam's hands. "What did you bring us, dear?"

"Madison brought a surprise."

Helen's lips curled downward. "What kind of surprise?"

Madison climbed the stairs and entered the living area, trying not to be put off by the woman's cool reception and suspicious tone. Danny looked worse than Helen. "Hi, Danny. I brought a few things to try to tempt your taste buds."

He held out his hand. She set the magazines on a small table and crossed to give him the hug he demanded. He wasn't wearing the cologne he usually doused on liberally—another sign that he wasn't himself. Was that because chemo made his sense of smell more sensitive or was he just too sick or tired to care?

"What do you have there, Maddie?" he asked after she straightened.

"I brought batches of my grandma's banana-pudding and chicken-salad recipes, and my tenant's famous double-chocolate brownies."

"You've learned to bake?" Helen asked and Madison grimaced.

"No. I'm afraid that's a lost cause. June made the brownies for us." June had made them for Madison, but she would share.

"Banana pudding is my favorite," Danny said. "And Helen always loved your chicken salad. You're a good girl, Maddie."

"It's the least I could do."

"I'll try some of that pudding," Danny said.

Helen frown deepened. "You haven't had dinner."

"Life's short. Dessert first," he protested.

Helen shot Madison a now-look-what-you've-done look, then retrieved a stack of plates. She gave

Danny small helpings of everything, including the pot roast from the cast-iron Dutch oven on the stove.

Danny went straight for the dessert. He put a forkful in his mouth and rolled it around as if testing it. "Mmm. You never gave Helen this recipe, did you?"

Helen hadn't asked for it or the chicken-salad recipe. "No."

"Serve yourselves." Helen gestured to the plates on the counter.

Adam indicated Madison go first. She fixed a plate, keeping an eye on Helen's drawn face as she did so. Danny's treatment was hard on her. Madison carried the filled plate to her former mother-in-law. Helen looked surprised. "I can fix my own."

"I know you can, but please, sit down. Get off your feet."

She hesitated. "I— Thank you."

Madison returned to the kitchen, fixed herself a plate then sat across from Helen at the table, aware of Adam's eyes on her every step of the way.

Helen watched Danny. "Danny Drake, you're not eating my pork roast."

"My jaw aches too much to chew."

"Why didn't you say something?" Helen protested. "I could have fixed something else."

"Because I whine enough already," he snapped.

"It's not whining, Dad. Your nutrition is important. If you need softer foods you need to say so. Mom can't read your mind."

The three seemed locked in a standoff. Madison

decided to defuse the situation. "Helen, why don't you take a few hours for yourself tomorrow evening? Adam and I will take care of dinner and stay with Danny until you get home."

"Why would I do that?" Suspicion once again filled her tone. Dealing with Helen reminded Madison of trying to befriend a dog that had been beaten.

"Tuesday's chemo is going to be hard on both of you. You should rest up while you have the chance. Go see a movie, grab dinner with a friend, have your hair done or get a massage. Do something for yourself."

"I'm fine. I don't need your food or your help."

"Helen!" Danny protested.

Helen glared at Adam. "Did you put her up to this?"

"No, Mom, and frankly giving you some time to yourself never occurred to me, although it should have. Madison's trying to help."

Madison ignored her hurt feelings. "Helen, you need to take care of *you* so that you have the strength and endurance to take care of Danny."

Helen's anger faded and her eyes filled with tears. Blinking furiously, she turned away. When she faced Madison again she'd regained control. "I don't want to put anyone out."

"You're not. We'll be here anyway. Right, Adam?" Madison turned to the man seated beside her for backup and found him once again studying her as if she were a new species.

"Right. I'll bring Dad an order of breadsticks and some minestrone soup from his favorite Italian restaurant."

"He'd like that." Helen hesitated. "And…so would I. Thank you for suggesting it, Madison. And thank you for the chicken salad. Danny's right. I always loved your grandmother's recipe and if you'll share it I'd like to get it from you."

"Of course." And that, Madison decided, was a step in the right direction toward repaying the Drakes for the kindness they'd shown her before they'd turned on her. Before long she'd have a clean slate, and she'd be able to walk away without a backward glance.

CHAPTER ELEVEN

ADAM COULDN'T TAKE his eyes off the woman seated on the leather sofa. Madison's eyes were bright, her smile wide and the tension that had emanated from her since her reentry into their lives was absent. This was the Madison he hadn't seen in years, only she was an older version—one with more substance than the girl his brother had married. The tough times she'd been through had added character.

She'd taken control from the minute they'd entered the motor home this evening, shooing his mother out the door and insisting she take her time. When his mother had waffled, Madison had promised they had everything under control here, but yes, they would call if they needed her. His mother had left, her reluctance *and* eagerness equally apparent.

For most of the past two hours Madison had entertained his father with stories of her rural practice, often poking fun at the mistakes she'd made or lessons she'd learned the hard way, which had in turn led his father to share embarrassing tales that Adam had never heard before. He couldn't remember the last time he'd heard his father laugh that hard or so much. For that matter, Adam couldn't remember the last time *he'd* laughed as much. How had he never known his father had a sense of humor?

"And then I took a very long shower." Madison concluded her tale of doing a face-plant in a pig sty with a comical grimace.

Holding his ribs, Adam's father chuckled and winced. "Stop making me laugh."

A woman who didn't take herself too seriously was damned attractive, and the fact that she'd been good to his parents made her doubly so.

Adam rejected the idea immediately. He wouldn't become his brother's replacement. He wanted no part of his brother's wife.

Repeating the mantra didn't seem to be working, he acknowledged. He'd have to try harder.

"Good lord, son, I'm parched. Where's that drink?"

Adam realized he'd been so caught up in listening to Madison that he'd forgotten what he'd gone to the kitchen to do. "Coming up."

He finished refilling the glasses and carried them to the den, setting Madison's on the table beside her rather than risking contact. She looked up at him, her face still glowing with amusement. Her beauty took his breath and he couldn't look away.

Seconds ticked past—seconds laden with the memory of what shouldn't have happened—then she blinked and dipped her chin. "Thank you."

Her breathier-than-usual voice hit him low in the gut.

"You're welcome." But as he took his seat at the far end of the couch he had to admit once again that the idea of giving his mother a night out would never have occurred to him. Ditto preparing her favorite foods. Madison had done both. Why?

Neither were the traits of a selfish bitch. And that she'd done so even after his mother had treated her badly six years ago, and repeatedly since her return, refuted a long list of negative thoughts that Adam had held of Madison Monroe.

Who was this woman, if she wasn't the one his brother had complained increasingly about during the last few months of his life?

"You never told me these stories before, Dad."

"You never gave me the chance, son. You always had somewhere else to be when Andrew and I talked shop."

Guilt and regret hit Adam hard and fast. How many other stories had he missed? Would he ever get to hear them?

His father yawned. Adam checked his watch. Almost ten o'clock. His mother had been gone four hours. Unbelievable. "Are you ready for bed yet, Dad?"

"I wanted to wait until your mother returned, but I'm not sure I'll make it."

Adam heard a car door slam outside. "Sounds like her now."

The door opened and his mother breezed in. She'd had her hair done and looked much more relaxed than she had earlier. Adam jumped to his feet to help with the shopping bags draped over her arm.

She quickly pulled them out of reach. "I have them. Sorry I took so long. Time got away from me."

Madison stood. "Not a problem, Helen. Your hair looks great."

The comment seemed genuine.

"Oh, I… Thank you, Madison. My usual stylist wasn't available, so I tried a new one at the mall. I think I like this color better."

"It's more flattering to your complexion. Need help putting anything away before we go?" Madison asked.

She shook her head. "Danny, I can't believe you're still awake."

"Good company."

"Dad, I'll be taking Madison straight to the airport from work tomorrow so you can rest."

His father opened his mouth to protest, then nodded. "That's probably for the best. Gonna miss you, Maddie. Until next week. Sunday dinner again?"

"I can do that." Madison helped Danny to his feet and then hugged him. The expression on Adam's father's face and the way he held on longer than normal said it all. He didn't want to let Madison go—not now *or* at the end of the two months.

His father was in for a big disappointment.

Adam followed Madison out to the car and waited

until they were on the road before asking the question burning inside him. "Why are you being nice to my mother after the way she's treated you?"

He caught a glimpse of Madison's tense, pale face in an oncoming car's headlights. "Because she's going through hell and scared to death. She has no idea what her future holds or if she can handle it." She scratched a spot on her scrub pants. "I've been there, and I wouldn't wish it on my worst enemy."

That was the last thing he'd expected from her. Maybe, just maybe, Madison wouldn't let them down after all.

MADISON CLOSED THE last chart of the day and put it in the box for Danny to review. In a matter of hours she'd be home and she could mark one more week's obligation off her list. Four down. Four to go.

"Madison," Adam's voice echoed down the empty hall. The staff had cleared out twenty minutes ago. Dread, combined with the same old reaction she was now coming to expect, rolled through her. Quickening heartbeat. Shortness of breath. Dampening palms.

"Back here." She rose from Danny's desk as Adam reached the office. The worry on his face did not bode well. "What's wrong? Is Danny okay?"

"He's as well as could be expected after this morning's chemo but, according to Mom, definitely not up for company. It's good that he wasn't counting on us tonight. We have a bigger problem. There's a storm front heading this way. We might have to postpone our flight until morning."

An evening alone with Adam? No way. She couldn't risk it. Not after last night. They'd spent their time working together to convince Danny to eat, then kept him entertained with the worst jokes she'd ever heard. Watching Adam with his father, hearing the respect in his voice and the intelligence in his answers, she'd found more reasons to like him. Reasons that had nothing to do with him looking like her dead husband and everything to do with her actually liking the man, his character, his devotion to his parents and his quick wit.

"No, I need to go back tonight. I have my spay-and-neuter clinic tomorrow."

"What's that?"

"On the first Wednesday of even-numbered months I neuter pets at my costs. I have surgeries booked solid all day. People have already taken off work to bring their animals in. I can't reschedule."

"Someone needs to teach you about running a business. You're losing by giving your services at cost. You should charge more and make a profit. That's capitalism."

"The lower price gets more customers in the door. I'd rather *not* make a profit neutering than *make* a profit euthanizing strays. That's compassion."

He shook his head. "Making a profit would allow you to be more compassionate more often." She opened her mouth to protest, but he stopped the words by holding up a hand. "Save it. Flying into this storm tonight will be rough—far rougher than our last turbulent flight."

Given how she'd worried about him last time, maybe she'd better find another way to get home. "If you get me a rental car I'll get myself home."

"You'd be safer flying above it than driving through it. I'll take you."

"Are you sure?"

"The plane was built to withstand it."

"Can you, as a pilot, handle the turbulence?"

His blue-green gaze held hers. "I have my instrument rating, and I've flown in worse. I don't like it, but I can do it."

His confidence was mildly comforting. "Then I can I handle it, too. Let's go."

She hoped she didn't live to regret her decision.

ADAM SHUT DOWN the engine, peeled off his headset and sagged back in his seat, letting his muscles unkink one by one. Those last fifteen minutes had been the biggest test of his skills to date. They'd completed half the flight before hitting the storm. The wind shear had been unpredictable, and visibility had been near zero. And yes, he wasn't ashamed to admit he'd been scared a couple times.

He glanced at his passenger. Madison's color had improved since they'd touched down. During the flight, lightning flashes illuminating the cockpit had revealed a ghostly pallor and her white-knuckled grip on the armrests. But she hadn't complained.

"You okay?"

She swept back her hair and blew out a slow breath through pursed lips. "Yes. But I'm glad to be on the ground."

He gave her kudos for courage and honesty. A gust rocked the craft on the tarmac. He needed to tie this baby down. "Me, too."

"Will you text me when you land this time?"

He shook his head. He'd had all the adrenaline he could handle for the night. "I'm not flying back in this."

Her mouth opened, closed, opened again, her indecision clear in her eyes even in the dim airport lighting. "I have a guest room. You— You're welcome to it."

He hesitated. She didn't want his company. "If you'll drop me at the closest hotel, I'll get a taxi back in the morning."

Her quiet laugh caressed his ears. "You're in farm country, Adam. The motels here are few and far between and not to your standards. And taxis… Let's just say you can't depend on those out here."

"Then I'll sleep in the terminal."

"There's not a sofa in the place. Only chairs. It may not even be unlocked. I'll bring you back in the morning."

A tough decision. He still hadn't rationalized or forgiven himself for that kiss. But he'd learned his lesson. They were both adults with enough sense not to act on the chemistry between them again. "Then I guess I'll take that guest room."

Even though the rain beat down on them, Madison helped him secure the plane, garnering even more respect from him. When they finished he gathered her things. The building was indeed locked. They hustled around it to the truck waiting on the opposite side.

Andrew's truck. He'd ridden in it before, but not with Madison. He climbed into the passenger seat and immediately her scent surrounded him. For some reason he'd expected remnants of Andrew's overpriced cologne. But his brother had been gone six years. Sometimes it felt like six days, other times six decades.

It took Madison a couple tries to get the motor to catch. When it did, she patted the dash as if she were praising a good dog.

"You need to get that fixed."

"I will."

He closed his mouth and let her focus on navigating through the blinding rain. It was only nine, but thick clouds had obscured any trace of moonlight, and the countryside lacked streetlights. To say it was dark was an understatement. Inching along well below the posted speed, she didn't drive like a woman who was careless of the weather or road conditions. The twenty minutes that passed before she turned off the winding two-lane road and into her driveway felt more like an hour.

The last time he'd come to her house he'd been too angry to be interested in the scenery. The small white farmhouse was set back from the street. The distance seemed farther in the dark. The wet oak trees hung heavily over the gravel path, almost forming a tunnel. Branches occasionally twanged on the antennae and brushed the roof, then a ping hit the roof and he startled.

"It's okay. Probably an acorn or a pecan."

She passed the house. The headlights picked out a two-story barn with sheds attached to either side. The right side had no doors. She drove into that opening. Her high beams revealed pet crates lining the back wall. He climbed from the vehicle and watched as she checked the cages, then nodded. "That's a relief. No guests."

"Guests?"

"I offer a safe-surrender program here. People can drop off unwanted pets or strays they've picked up here or at my office. No questions asked. It's the same program your father has."

"Does that happen often?"

"More often than I like and yet not often enough. Most folks just dump their animals along a country road." She shouldered her overnight bag. "We can leave the cooler here till morning." She stopped at the edge of the shelter, scanning the backyard as if searching for something. Rain streamed down just inches from her toes. Jagged lightning split the sky in the distance.

"Ready to make a run for it?" And then she was gone, sprinting and splashing her way across the grass, zigzagging around puddles and finally onto her screened-in porch.

He dashed into the downpour after her. She held open the door. The porch light revealed her hair clinging to her scalp and her clothing to her torso, delineating curves he'd rather not think about. His heart pounded harder—not from the short run. Rain beat down on the metal roof, almost drowning out the sound.

She opened her back door without a key. "You don't lock your doors?"

"No need to."

Worry for her safety seized him. "You've established a pattern of being out of town Sunday to Tuesday. You should lock your house, Madison."

She flipped on the overhead light. "There's nothing here worth stealing, and if there was, the tenant who lives in that house—" she pointed into the nothingness of the yard "—is a deputy. Anybody who dares to look for trouble will have to deal with her. June may look like a bubbly blonde, but she kicks butt. And Piper, my veterinary assistant, is married to the chief of police. People aren't going to mess with me."

"Locals won't."

"City boy." The affection and humor in her voice

almost made him smile. "Out-of-towners are spotted and tracked the moment they come into town. But thanks for your concern."

Her kitchen was small, cozy, clean. The maple dinette set was probably older than him, but it gleamed from a recent polish, as did the wide-planked hardwood floor. The table had only one place mat. She ate alone.

The floorboards creaked as he followed her toward the front of the house and through an equally lived-in den and a small foyer that turned into a center hall. The place reminded him of his grandparents' house. Both had died when he was young. He hadn't thought of their old farm in decades. He used to love visiting them, and he and Andrew had spent hours exploring the attic and outbuildings.

"Here's the guest room. It's not much compared to yours, but the linens are clean. There's only one bathroom. It's off the center hall. I keep spare toothbrushes, toothpaste, soap and stuff in the cabinet with the towels. Help yourself to whatever you need. You can use the washer and dryer if you want."

The whitewashed double bed looked as old as the kitchen table but in good repair. Ditto the dresser and side table. The quilt, a combination of perpendicular lines that made up blue-and-white squares around a red center, looked hand stitched.

"This is nothing like the home you and Andrew had." He liked it better. It was comfortable, the kind of place you could relax.

"I've told you before, Andrew chose that house and all the furnishings."

"Without your input?"

"Yes. He wanted a showplace. He got one. Good night, Adam."

"You didn't like the house?"

She hesitated, then huffed out a breath. "It was like living in a model home or a museum. I was afraid to touch anything or that I might spill something on the white carpets. I never felt at home there." She pivoted and snatched a raincoat off a hook by the front door.

"Where are you going?"

"To check on my critters."

"In this?" Thunder cracked and rumbled.

"I've been gone three days."

"Didn't you have someone looking after them?"

"Yes. But—I just need to check on them, okay?"

"Have an extra one of those?" He nodded toward her slicker.

Another pause. And then without a word she traveled down a narrow hall to the back of the house. He followed. They passed the bathroom, then he spotted her bedroom through the open door on his left. A brass bed covered in a quilt patterned in giant flowers with petals of different fabrics took up most of the floor space. The decor was feminine without being fussy.

She opened a closet and offered him a yellow

slicker. "The farm used to belong to June's grand-father. This was probably Dr. Jones's."

"He left his clothes behind?"

"He passed away. June sold the farm. I bought it *and* his practice as is with contents. It was easier than trying to find furniture I could afford."

"You could have afforded whatever you wanted if you'd kept your share of Andrew's estate."

"I didn't want… I needed a fresh start."

If she'd wanted to forget her marriage, then why had she kept Andrew's truck? It had to be more than not wanting payments, because six years ago she could have sold Andrew's vehicle for enough money to buy something else.

"You sure want to go out in this, Adam? It's really not necessary for you to get wet again. I can handle it."

He shrugged into the raincoat. Somebody needed to keep an eye on her. "Dad will want a full report on your 'critters.'"

They raced back to the barn, getting drenched before Madison could shove back the heavy door to the center section. He helped her slide it closed. She flipped on a dim overhead light. He turned and spotted the identifying black-and-white stripes of a skunk and froze. He knew enough about skunks from camping to want to avoid upsetting the animal.

She went straight for the skunk, opening a cage he hadn't registered in his shock over seeing the animal. The habitat was massive with multiple levels, tunnels and climbing things. "Hey, Buster."

She scratched under his chin and stroked his back, then scooped up the creature and nuzzled him. She glanced over her shoulder. "It's okay. He's been de-scented."

"Madison, why do you have a skunk?"

"Because once his owners got over the novelty of having him they decided he was too much trouble. They were going to set him free, but he's too do-mesticated to survive in the wild. He would've been coyote food in no time. I haven't been able to find him a new family yet. Skunks are too mischievous for most people. They steal things and sometimes tear up stuff while searching for entertainment. Kind of like ferrets."

He had no experience with ferrets, either, but be-fore he could ask her to elaborate a shrill whistle pierced his ears, startling him and drawing his at-tention to a smaller cage and a shaggy-haired guinea pig. "That's Wilbur. His treats are in the bin behind you."

Adam hesitated, not because he was afraid, but because he also had no experience with guinea pigs.

"Andrew and I never had pets. Dad wouldn't allow it. I got around his edict by volunteering to take care of classroom pets during school vacations. Ham-sters, gerbils, turtles. A rabbit once. My teachers liked the idea of sending the animals home with a veterinarian's kid."

He hadn't thought about that in years. "But Andrew was never one to be outdone. He convinced Dad to let him work at the office during our days off. I guess he was smarter than me. He got paid."

Her sad smile reached across the top of the cage. "Making money doesn't make you smarter. Loving what you do is its own reward."

Wilbur squealed.

"He won't stop whistling until he gets some attention. He doesn't bite, and if you scratch his back he'll be your friend for life."

Adam dug out a treat, opened the door and offered it to the black-and-white hairball. It nuzzled his hand. Adam scratched as directed and was awarded with a chortle of approval. The moment Adam stopped the critter scuttled to the other side of his cage to try to get Madison's attention.

"In a second, buddy," she responded. "You're spoiled rotten." She returned the skunk to its enclosure.

"I can't remember not having pets. On a farm they're everywhere. Learning to care for them was part of growing up and learning responsibility."

A trio of mangled, scarred cats wound around Madison's ankles, demanding her attention. One was missing an eye. Another had partially chewed-off ears. Madison picked up the first cat, nuzzled it and talked nonsense to it, then she put it down and went onto the next.

When Madison finished with the felines she spent

a few minutes with the guinea pig, then crossed to a stall door on the left side of the building. He wasn't sure what he expected on the other side of the wooden gate, but the knee-high goat was a surprise. She petted him, and he rewarded her with a series of comical jumps and twists in the air. A goat doing tricks. Now he'd seen everything.

"Why a goat?"

She checked the trough and water bucket. "Ned peed on his previous owner's vehicles. They hit him with a baseball bat to knock him off the car and broke his front leg. They were ready to give him to the migrant workers for grilling. But he has so much personality I couldn't let that happen. Plus, he's pretty good at keeping my fence lines weeded."

She was more relaxed, showering affection on her "critters" than he'd seen her to date. On her turf she was a country girl in her element. But if this was the girl his brother had fallen in love with, why had Andrew tried to turn her into something else?

She left the goat to check on the horse he'd noticed on his first visit. The horse received the same TLC the others had. "Is he somebody's reject, too?"

"Yes. Right after I moved here one of Dr. Jones's clients asked me to euthanize him. The husband and wife had lost their jobs and couldn't afford to keep Bojangles. They'd tried to sell him, but he was undernourished, needed some medical care and wasn't very attractive. I couldn't destroy him without giving him a chance. Then I realized how much I missed riding and adopted him."

"Dad mentioned transference. What was he talking about?"

She bit her lip and hesitated, then shuffled, fussed and fidgeted. "In my case, the animals I rescue are substitutes for the loved ones I couldn't save. Each of my pets is a castoff or an orphan."

The ones she couldn't save? Andrew? Her baby? Her family?

And then it hit him. This mismatched group of castoff pets was her family, and she'd genuinely missed them when she'd been in Georgia, and like a parent, she needed to hug each "child." Clearly each animal had missed her, too, and greedily lapped up the affection.

What would it be like to have that kind of welcome when he came home? He might never know. With his long hours it wouldn't be fair to have a pet. Eventually, he'd like to have a wife and children who'd race to meet him at the door the way he and Andrew once had their father. But he'd yet to meet anyone who interested him more than his work.

One thing was certain. A woman who nurtured this barn full of misfits was not capable of turning her back on her own child. His brother hadn't exaggerated about Madison's emotional detachment.

Andrew had flat-out lied.

CHAPTER TWELVE

MADISON LATCHED BOJANGLES'S stall door and took another look around, soaking up the scents and the comfort of coming home.

She would never admit it to Adam, but during the last ten minutes of tonight's flight she'd doubted she'd ever see this old barn or her critters again. She hadn't been that scared since the night of the car accident, when she'd been waiting for the ambulance and praying their injuries weren't as bad as she'd suspected.

Fear had taken over her brain in those last turbulent eons of the flight, and she'd wondered if she'd die alone and if anyone would miss an old maid with only a farm full of strays for family. Piper and June would be upset for a little while. But in the long run, would the world be any different because she'd been here?

No. Sad fact.

Given her gloomy mood, she dreaded being alone in the house with Adam. He was smart, ambitious and cared about his parents—everything she'd found appealing in Andrew, without his negative qualities.

Watching Adam's face when Wilbur had purred his approval over being petted had been like watching a boy open birthday presents. Endearing. Adorable.

But just because Adam was handsome and had a knee-weakening boyish smile didn't make him an eligible partner. It didn't matter that he was calm in a crisis and had strong, steady hands on the yoke of the bucking plane. He was not Mr. Right or even Mr. Right-This-Minute.

If only his touch didn't electrify her… If only he didn't have adorable crinkles around his eyes when he smiled… If only her pulse didn't skip when their eyes met… If only she didn't ache to be held tonight, to have someone make her not feel so alone and insignificant.

She couldn't—wouldn't—go there. The temporary fix wouldn't be worth the long-term hassle.

She'd come out to the barn to escape and count her blessings, never expecting Adam to insist on accompanying her. So much for peace, quiet and regrouping. But they couldn't stay here all night. They both had to get up early tomorrow.

"Time to get wet again." She dashed out of the shelter without waiting for a response. She sensed more than heard him behind her in the heavy downpour.

He stopped beside her on the porch. His hood had fallen off during the sprint and water beaded in the dark strands. He sluiced the rain from his face, then shoved a hand through his damp hair. It spiked in every direction. He looked deliciously disheveled and attractive, like a man fresh from the shower. She shut down that wayward, rabble-rousing thought.

He reached for her and she froze, heart stalling, lungs seizing. Anticipation burst through her veins. Only, instead of grabbing her, he reached past her and snagged a piece of paper that had been stuck to the freezer behind her. She hadn't noticed the sticky note on their first trip inside.

She wasn't disappointed. She *wasn't*.

"'Madison,'" he read. "'Thanks for helping with Red. We made peach ice cream this week, and I know it's your favorite. I left some in your freezer. Bill and Sue.'" He looked at her, one eyebrow hiked.

"Sweet." She pulled open the door and spotted the newest of several dishes that didn't belong to her. The fast-food dinner they'd eaten en route to the airport was long gone. Maybe a scoop or two of ice cream would soothe her unsettled stomach. On second thought, if she ate it now she'd have to offer some to Adam, and that meant more of his company. Not a good idea. She shut the door.

"People come onto your back porch while you're not at home and leave food in your freezer?"

"Yes. I realize that might sound strange by Nor-cross standards, but it's the country way. I often get paid in food, services or IOUs."

"You make it sound like you're not in this profession for the money."

The idea surprised a laugh out loud from her.

If only he knew how fine a line she walked every month with her budget. When she had both rental houses occupied she had a little more wiggle room. "Hardly. I'm fortunate that I had grants and scholarships, and then my parents' life insurance policy to pay for college. I don't have student loans hanging over me. Otherwise, I'd be in trouble."

"You have a pattern of living off life insurance payouts."

She stiffened at the implication. "I used both my parents' and Andrew's to invest in my future. I didn't go on cruises or party it all away. Andrew's life insurance paid for my farm and my practice."

He studied her through narrowed eyes, then the assessment morphed into approval that warmed her to her core. Seconds later the kinetic connection she'd felt in the office before the kiss returned. Goose bumps lifted her skin. If she was smart she'd hurry to her room and put the barrier of a solid wood door between them.

She pivoted abruptly, hung her dripping rain slicker on a peg outside the back door and reentered the house. "You can have the bathroom first."

"Thanks." He'd hung up his coat, as well.

She stepped into her bedroom. He walked past and she pushed the panel shut and walked to the window overlooking the side yard. The area light in the barn gable cast enough of a dim glow for her to see there were no new branches down and no wiggling baby squirrels on the ground. She had nothing to keep her from lying in that bed and thinking about the emptiness threatening to engulf her.

But if she felt alone and disconnected she had no one but herself to blame. She kept people at a distance and had chosen not to open herself up to even the possibility of another romantic relationship. The decision to guard her heart had not come without consequences.

She flopped onto her bed and stared at the ceiling. She knew every noise this old house made, which meant it was all too easy for her to pick up the sound of Adam moving around the guest room, and then as he made his way to the bathroom between their rooms. He opened and closed the cabinet. Water sang through the pipes. The shower curtain scraped along the metal rod then back again. She hadn't had a man in her shower since she'd moved in. A mental image of Adam naked bloomed in her mind. She closed her eyes and groaned.

Down hormones. Down.

Danny. Think about Danny. He had a struggle ahead, and Helen faced a tough road as his caregiver.

But instead of her former in-laws, she saw Adam's laughing face and the surprise lighting his eyes when his father had shared his story of slipping in a poodle puddle and splitting his head open on an exam table. Danny had confessed he'd been so embarrassed he'd begged his vet tech to stitch him up rather than take him to the E.R. And he'd forbidden anyone to tell Helen, because he hadn't wanted to worry her.

Helen and Danny had always had the kind of relationship Madison envied. They'd been friends as well as husband and wife, with never a harsh word spoken. But something had changed in the past six years. Had Danny's diagnosis caused the gulf between them? Or had it been going on longer than that? Since Andrew's death? If so, Madison had another log of guilt to pile on her fire.

The water shut off with a clank. She pictured Adam, wet and naked, stepping from behind the shower curtain. Her stomach dropped faster than it had when they'd hit air pocket after air pocket during the turbulent flight. What was wrong with her?

The problem was she liked and respected Adam more than she ever had Andrew. With Andrew she'd been blindly, stupidly in love. She'd seen his flash and charm and totally missed his lack of substance. She'd admired his ambition, not realizing that he undermined others to achieve his goals.

She'd awakened slowly to Andrew's personality quirks, but by then she was married to him and that meant she'd do her best to make the relationship work. She'd vowed she would never emulate her mother and seek affection elsewhere.

Not a memory train she wanted to ride.

The bathroom hinges creaked and the shifting floorboards marked Adam's return to his room. She rubbed her burning, churning belly. The discomfort had to be a cry for food. Didn't it? She'd never be able to sleep with all that irritation. She needed a snack. Shower first or ice cream?

She couldn't handle the idea of stepping into a stall still warm from Adam's steam. Ice cream won. But for insurance's sake she'd give Adam five more minutes to get to bed before venturing out. She rose and moved around the room by rote, putting her damp clothes in the hamper, changing into her shorty pajamas and going through her usual night-time routine. Silence descended, broken only by the rain on the roof and the wind whipping along the eaves, making the old house pop and settle.

Then time was up. She pulled on her robe. Praying the wet weather wouldn't make the door swell and stick, she wrapped her fingers around the crystal knob, twisted gently and opened the panel. *Whew. No scrape.* She stepped into the hall and came face-to-face with Adam exiting the bathroom.

Every cell in her body snapped to attention. He wasn't wearing a shirt, and the urge to trace the curve of his pectorals, to tease the tiny buttons of his nipples, hit her viscerally. She yanked her attention from that taboo territory to his blue eyes.

His gaze held hers for the briefest of moments, then burned a path from her head to her feet, making her wish she'd kept on her damp scrubs. She curled her bare toes into the floor, pushed back her hair and scrambled to find a way to escape before she made a mistake she couldn't undo. "I thought you'd gone to bed."

"I left my watch and cell phone in the bathroom. I need an alarm." He lifted a hand, displaying both. The action made his thick biceps contract. Her abdominal muscles did the same.

"I don't have a clock in the guest room, do I?" she blabbered, and could have kicked herself for being an idiot.

"No."

"Sorry." Her mouth was dry. Her pulse pounded against her eardrums.

"No problem."

Neither of them moved. "The um…storm's getting worse," she blurted into the awkward silence.

"Sounds like it. Madison, I owe you an apology."

"Why?"

"The first time I came here I resented the hell out of my father bringing you back into our lives. But you're not the woman I thought you were. You're… more compassionate and generous than I'd been led to believe."

The compliment sandbagged her and undermined her defenses even more. "I… Apology accepted. G-good night, Adam."

He remained where he was, squarely blocking the hall. She debated taking her heartburn back to bed.

"You think that ice cream's any good?"

The question, accompanied by that boyish grin, knocked her mentally off-balance. "Sue makes the best peach ice cream I've ever tasted. She and Bill grow the peaches on their farm, and Sue's father owns the dairy that supplies the cream. The ingredients don't come any fresher."

"Any chance there's enough for two and that you're willing to share?"

How could she refuse that glimmer of anticipation in his eyes? Wise or not, she couldn't. "That's actually where I was headed. If you'll grab the ice cream, I'll get the bowls."

"Deal."

Given the emptiness welling inside her that she knew ice cream couldn't fill, this would probably be another decision she'd regret. But then, her life had been liberally littered with those.

THUNDER BOOMED CLOSE by, rattling the house. Adam put the last spoonful of ice cream into his mouth and let the rich dessert slide down his throat. Madison was only a scoop behind. She lowered the utensil to the bowl and licked her lips. He caught himself following the movement and averted his gaze.

"Didn't I tell you it was the best?" she asked.

"You didn't exaggerate. I'll take care of the dishes." He collected the bowls, rose and looked around. "No dishwasher?"

"No. June's grandfather was old school and never installed one. I didn't see the point in going to the trouble or expense just for me. I don't use that many dishes."

Something they had in common. "I hear that."

She extracted a bottle of dish liquid and a sponge from the cabinet beneath the sink. "You can rescind your offer to wash up if you want since it's hard manual labor."

The teasing tone of her voice made him smile. "I think I can handle it. It's the least I can do since sharing means you won't get seconds. Not even my great-grandmother's peach ice cream was that good."

She got a faraway sad look in her eyes. "My mother used to make homemade vanilla with my grandmother's ice cream freezer. My sister and I would fight for turns at cranking the handle."

He knew very little about her life before Andrew other than that she'd grown up somewhere in tornado alley. "Andrew and I did the same. I remember being disappointed after my grandparents passed away and Mom bought an electric machine. Wow. I haven't thought about that in twenty years."

Lightning struck nearby, making the fine hair on his arms lift. "That was close."

Then the lights flickered and went out. The instant total darkness of the countryside was a surprise. He couldn't see his hand at the end of his arm, and he couldn't see her beside him. But he could feel her and hear her breathing. The awareness of Madison was unsettling.

"You're off the hook for washing up. I'm on a

well. No power means no well pump. We can't turn on the water. Stay put. I'll get a light."

The sound of her bare feet padded toward the front of the house. He heard the scrape of a match—the old-fashioned wooden kind—then the tinkle of glass. A glow lit the den. Madison returned carrying an old brass hurricane lantern.

"Know how to use one of these?" she asked.

"I camp."

"Then you can take the lamp. I don't need it—I know this house as well as I know my own face."

"You're used to taking care of yourself."

"I'm pretty self-sufficient. Good night, Adam."

Another of Andrew's tales bit the dust. His brother had claimed Madison expected everything to be done for her when she was at home.

"At least let me walk you to your room."

She looked ready to argue, then shrugged and headed down the hall. A louder clap of thunder shook the walls, followed by a crack then a heavy thump outside. She darted ahead into her bedroom and to the window overlooking the side yard.

"A branch came down."

He joined her, but couldn't see anything except the glare of the flame on the glass. He set the lamp on a dresser, then stood beside her at the window until another flash of lightning lit the lawn. "It's a big one, but it doesn't look like it landed on anything."

"No. But we're lucky it wasn't an entire tree. The

ground is saturated from all the recent rain and oaks have shallow root systems. With winds like this it's not unusual for them to topple over." She opened the window and waited. He didn't know for what.

"What are you doing?"

"Listening for the cry of a critter that needs rescuing. I'm glad we landed before the worst of the storm hit." She closed the window, then wrapped her arms around her middle. Their shoulders brushed.

Awareness jolted him like an electric charge. "The storm rattled you."

"Didn't it you?"

"Yeah."

"I wasn't sure we'd make it," she confessed with obvious reluctance.

His brother would have blustered about being in control the whole time, never admitting weakness, fear or being wrong. Well, he wasn't Andrew. "There were moments I had my doubts."

"You never let on."

"I didn't want to worry you unnecessarily. And I was too busy praying." He added the last as an attempt at humor.

A smile tweaked a corner of her mouth. "Me, too."

In that moment he realized he actually liked Madison. Given other circumstances and other histories, he'd have wanted to know her better.

Something changed as they stood staring at each other. Then her lips parted and her pupils expanded, telling him something he didn't want to know. Ever since that kiss he'd wondered if he was the only one hijacked by an attraction he shouldn't feel.

Negative. The electrical charge sparked between them now.

The small circle of lamplight intensified the intimacy of their situation and sharpened his senses. Here in her room, with her bed only feet away, her scent was stronger, more potent, but still subtle. Her warmth trespassed into his space and sweat beaded on his back and streaked downward, making him glad he'd put on his shirt before eating ice cream.

He wanted to blame his overheated status on the power outage that had shut down the air-conditioning. But what tugged at him was the same unexplainable magnetic pull that had grabbed him in the workroom at his father's office. He hadn't understood it then and couldn't explain it now. All he knew was that he wanted her. Madison. A woman who was off-limits.

A smart man would retreat before he did something stupid like stroke the worry from her brow or rescue her bottom lip from the pinch of her teeth. His feet ignored his order to leave.

Who was this woman who fiercely protected the ones no one else wanted? She appeared tough on the outside, but was loving and loyal to her collection of rejects. And while she had every reason to keep giving his family the cold shoulder, she'd been far nicer to his mother than she deserved.

He was undeniably drawn to Madison. She was

a walking contradiction, an enigma he wanted to figure out.

The hollows of her cheeks appeared deeper in the dim light, as did the dip between her mouth and chin. He traced the former, then the latter. Her breath hitched. The pulse at the base of her neck fluttered wildly beneath his fingertip.

"Adam." Her voice was more plea than protest.

She tilted her head in invitation. Even as he told himself he shouldn't, his fingers slipped into her silky hair and he lowered his head. Her lids drifted closed a split second before his lips brushed her brow, her cheek, the bridge of her nose.

Then he discovered the flavors of sweet cream and peach lingering on her mouth, but her flesh was anything but cold like the ice cream. The heat of her tongue touched his and hunger engulfed him.

She wound her arms around his waist and fisted her hands in his shirt, pulling him closer. Close enough that her breasts pressed into his chest, burning him through the thin layers of their clothing. Close enough that her hips nudged his.

Close enough and yet not nearly close enough.

Arousal rushed through his veins with every accelerating beat of his heart. He bunched his fists in her hair, kissing her harder, deeper. She mirrored his actions, fueling the fire in his gut as she met him stroke for stroke. He skimmed his palms down her back. She shifted against him until the softness of her mound cradled his thickening flesh. A mew of approval slipped from her mouth into his. She shivered, then kneaded him like a cat with her short nails. Now he knew why cats purred.

Her touch, her kisses, shouldn't feel this good. They shouldn't make him this hot or make him *want* this badly. This wasn't right. He knew it. Damn it, he *knew.* But he couldn't push her away. He unknotted her belt, then shoved the robe aside and found the hot sliver of skin between her pajama top and bottom. Her muscles rippled beneath his fingertips.

She reciprocated by plowing her hands under his T-shirt. Her delicate touch along his ribs sent a shudder racking through him. She caught his hands, stilling them and flattening them over her hip bones. He battled resignation, regret, unsatisfied desire and disappointment. Stopping was the right thing to do. Even if it would likely cripple him.

She slowly guided him upward, inch by tantalizing inch, along her waist, over her rib cage, until he cupped her breasts. She broke the kiss with a gasp. Her desire-filled eyes found his, and the hunger in their depths knocked the breath from him. He simply savored her shape, then he circled his palms, allowing her taut tips to tease him. Each go-round coiled his body into a tighter spiral of need and took him closer to the point of no return. All the while he held her gaze, watching her eyelids grow heavier.

Then she blinked and her fingertips skimmed a trail across his back, his sides, his abdomen, searing him. She outlined his navel and his muscles jumped, flicked his nipples and his insides fisted. She shrugged out of her robe and pushed at his shirt, urging it over his head. He stripped his away, then hers, and drank in the sight of her.

She had curves where a woman should. Her breasts were small but perfectly formed, the tips puckering and begging for attention. Her waist dipped in, then eased back out to hips that held up her low-riding pajama pants. The drawstring tied below her navel riveted his attention. He wanted to unwrap the rest of her, to taste all of her.

"Adam, I need…" Her eyes closed, opened, and the want in them rocked him to the core. She gulped air. "I need you to hold me."

He didn't have to be asked twice. She stepped into his arms, fusing her body to his. The intense heat of her skin melding to his hit him like nothing he'd ever experienced. The fusion of their lips was just as potent. His head spun. His lungs tightened. He'd had no idea the groove below his pectorals was an erogenous zone until her nipples brushed him there and sucked the air from the room. Everywhere he touched was as smooth as satin, only warmer.

Soft lips found his collarbone, teasing him with a series of butterfly kisses, then her tongue traveled the same path. He gripped her bottom. Her muscles tensed and she swayed against him, back and forth like a pendulum, multiplying his need exponentially until all he could think of was satisfying this overwhelming craving for her. He struggled for balance and restraint, but he was on a slippery slope.

He stroked the length of her thighs left bare by her short pajama bottoms, up and down until he became entangled in the fabric. Frustrated by the barrier, he stabbed his hands beneath the waistband. Her butt was smooth, warm, firm. Her shuddery gasps rewarded him when he traced the skin beneath her hip bone, then found curls.

He palmed the texture, finding the way it tickled his hand incredibly arousing and erotic. He hadn't been with a woman who didn't shave her intimate area in a long time. And then he discovered the slick crease. She jerked in his arms then widened her stance, giving him better access. Her tongue found his nipple and mimicked the circles he drew on her tender flesh, shocking him with a current of desire. Her breaths quickened. Her body stiffened. Her teeth grazed gently, and he almost lost it. Clamping his jaw, he battled his way back from the edge.

A moment later she buried her face in his chest and clung to his shoulders. Spasms of release shook her and a whimper escaped her hot mouth. Then her knees buckled. He caught her, swept her into his arms and placed her on the bed. A split second later his jeans were on the floor.

She lay there, long and lean and beautiful, her dark hair spilling across the quilt. He wanted to be against every inch of her. He yanked her drawstring, then stripped her bottoms. She sat up, reaching for him and encircling his erection. She stroked him with one hand and hooked the other around his hip, urging him closer. He teetered on the verge of control. He wanted to bury his face in those dark curls and taste her, but he couldn't wait another second. He joined her on the bed, parted her thighs and drove into her.

Slick heat welcomed him and overwhelmed him. He tried to slow his movements, tried to tamp down his rapid response by focusing on her pleasure. But he couldn't douse the flames. She had her eyes closed, her head thrown back and her spine arched as he sank into her again and again. He bent to capture a nipple, to suckle and nip one tip then the other. Her moan and the embrace of her inner muscles rewarded him.

In the near darkness he could see the flush of her approaching release on her chest, rising to her face. Then it hit her and she cried out. Her orgasm was a beautiful thing. Contraction after contraction squeezed him, then she relaxed and her eyes fluttered open.

With pupils expanded and lips parted, she caressed his biceps, his pectorals. Her nails flicked his nipples and an electric sensation shot straight to his groin. Her smooth legs twined around him, pulling him even deeper. She grasped his butt with her strong hands, digging in her short nails as another orgasm rocked her. Release exploded from him, gushing like a broken dam until he was spent, empty, drained.

He collapsed to his elbows and tried to right his world. Tried to figure out what in the hell had happened. Sex had never been that powerful for him.

Sex. With his brother's wife.

CHAPTER THIRTEEN

SHAME, REGRET AND panic set in before Madison's skin dried. She had turned to the one man she never should have for solace.

"I'm sorry. I don't know what—" Mortification stole her words. She let her legs fall back to the mattress. "That shouldn't have happened."

Adam went rigid above her. "No."

He rolled to his side, his neutral tone giving nothing away. Unable to look at him, she closed her eyes and scooted to the edge of the bed. She grabbed the corner of the quilt in an attempt to cover herself, but it wouldn't budge. He was lying on it. She yearned to escape, but her robe was on the floor on his side of the bed. Retreating meant brazenly circling the room naked. She didn't have the guts.

"I'm not…usually like that. The flight… The storm… I thought we were going to die."

"Were you pretending I was Andrew?" His clipped words cut straight to her heart.

Shocked that the idea had even occurred to him, Madison gaped at him for a full ten racing heartbeats. The easy way out of her embarrassment would be to say yes. But even if it was true—and it wasn't—she couldn't do that to Adam. Nothing about Adam felt like Andrew. Smelled like Andrew. Tasted like Andrew. Adam was stronger, more passionate, more...everything. How could two men with identical DNA be so dissimilar and affect her so differently?

She raked back her hair. Her fingers caught in the tangles they'd made. Wishing she could selfishly lie to save face, she reluctantly looked into those familiar and yet unfamiliar blue-green eyes in the flickering light. But with the lamp behind him, she couldn't even begin to decipher the emotions behind that shadowed, probing stare.

"Adam, your brother never crossed my mind."

He held her gaze for several tense seconds as if weighing her veracity, then nodded. She wished she could turn on the lights to see if he believed her, though conversely she was thankful for the darkness to help hide her shame. He rose, his firm buttocks and thighs flexing as he bent to reach for his pants and then stepped into them. Her mouth watered and not even regret could dampen the warmth rekindling low in her belly. The urge to reach out and trace each firm curve, each corded muscle, the veins on his arms, was almost too strong to ignore. Almost.

Then he turned and the glow from the lamp illuminated his back. Red trails ran parallel to his spine. Horrified at her lack of control, she stared at her clenched hands—hands responsible for those marks. She hadn't responded that passionately, that uninhibitedly, ever before. Not even with Andrew. At least she hadn't broken his skin. She wouldn't have the additional embarrassment of having to render first aid.

Why had Adam felt so good in her arms, inside her body—even better than the satisfying sex she'd shared with Andrew? There had to be a logical reason. Maybe her biological clock was going haywire. Or maybe the chemical cocktail released when she'd feared death had heightened her senses? Yes, that had to explain it.

But then an old saying she'd heard echoed in her head, sending a chill across her skin. The first time you did something wrong it was a mistake. The second time it was a choice. This was the second time in five years Madison had turned to someone in desperation—trying to fill a void by filling her body with someone who had no business being there.

Last time had been a horrible experience. In the heat of the moment she'd called her date Andrew. This time the man in her arms had been the only one in her thoughts.

The need to escape intensified. Gathering every grain of confidence she could dredge up, she circled the bed, conscious of those hard eyes tracking her every step of the way, snatched up her robe and wrapped it around her, belting it tightly.

"Adam, I don't do affairs. Even if I did, one between us would be too complicated. Helen still hates me. Danny refuses to accept I won't take over his practice. And in four weeks I'm walking out of your lives forever. This thing between us can't continue."

"I agree. Tonight was a mistake."

She winced even though he was only echoing her sentiment. "We're both mature adults. Let's just forget this happened. Okay?"

He zipped and buttoned his jeans, then faced her. Something worrisome in his eyes held her captive. "I didn't use protection."

Her stomach did a crazy loop-the-loop. Panic raced through her heart, chased by an unmistakable sense of…yearning? Her hands automatically covered her stomach. A baby… Every maternal instinct she thought she'd suppressed caught wind like a sail billowing to life.

Then reality rained down like a hailstorm. Cold and stinging. A baby would tie her to the Drakes for the rest of her life. It was one thing for her to be cast aside, but she would never allow anyone to hurt her child that way.

Please, please, don't let me fall pregnant. Not now.

That would be too cruel. She was a smart woman. There were alternatives…if only she could think of them. The morning-after pill made the most sense. But where could she get one without the Quincey gossip grapevine knowing what she'd done? And could she take it?

She tried to think rationally, calmly. "The chance

of me getting pregnant is slim. There's only twenty percent in any given cycle if a woman is trying to conceive—and we weren't trying."

But doubt sprouted its ugly head. Andrew had bragged about how fertile he must have been to knock her up on the first attempt. And Adam had the same DNA.

Adam's mouth flattened and his nostrils flared. "You do this often enough to research that?"

She grimaced. "No. One of my clients was having trouble getting pregnant. I did some research for her. Do you? Do this often, I mean? Do I need to worry about sexually transmitted diseases?"

"I had a complete physical right after Dad's diagnosis. I'm fine. You?"

"I'm healthy."

He nodded. "Then you're right. Our best bet is to forget this happened."

"Right. Okay. I will if you will." But could she do it? she asked herself as he pivoted sharply and left her room.

Could she forget she'd had the best orgasms of her life with a man who was the spitting image of her husband? A man who wanted her out of his life almost as badly as she wanted to be gone.

"G'MORNING, DOC."

Madison jumped at the sound of June's voice calling across the yard. She'd been so busy dreading facing Adam this morning and trying not to think about how she'd tossed and turned, unable to sleep on sheets that smelled like sex, like *him,* that she hadn't heard her tenant approach. "Hi, June."

June, in her deputy uniform, offered a mug of coffee. "You're up early. Checking the damage?"

More like hiding from it. But she nodded.

"The storm took out power to most of Quincey. Any casualties?"

Not of the animal variety.

Madison sipped the brew, stalling while she searched for an acceptable answer. "No orphans as far as I can see."

"You're jumpy. Have trouble sleeping?"

Another sip allowed her to avoid eye contact. "After the first branch fell, I kept waiting for trees to follow."

"It has been an exceptionally wet summer. I'm surprised you made it back last night. I thought your flight would be grounded."

If they'd stayed in Norcross, would last night have happened? "The final leg was rough and scary."

June's eyes narrowed. "Are you okay?"

"Yes. Just thinking ahead to how busy today's going to be."

"Oh. Right. The clinic."

Maybe she'd give Adam the spare keys and let him drive himself to the airport. She'd be in surgery all day and wouldn't need a vehicle. That way she wouldn't have to spend time alone with him. After the office closed she'd hitch a ride to the airport to pick up Ol' Blue. Yeah, that would work.

But she needed to get rid of Adam without June seeing him. "Are you heading into the office, June?"

"In a few. First, I'm going to drive around and check for storm damage. I'm sure I'll be busy later handling the crowds your spay-and-neuter clinic brings to town."

June added the last bit tongue in cheek. Madison forced the expected smile. "Well…I don't want to keep you. Thanks for the coffee. I'll return the mug later."

"Madison, are you sure you're okay? You seem agitated."

The back door opened before Madison could answer and Adam stepped out onto the porch. He spotted the two of them and stopped. Madison silently groaned.

So much for the incident passing undetected.

June's quiet chuckle carried across the humid morning air. "Good for you," she whispered.

Madison's cheeks caught fire. "It's not… We…" She took a deep breath and tried to gather her thoughts. "Let me give him the keys to the truck so he can get to the airport."

"You want to get rid of him?"

Gulp. "He needs to get back to Norcross. The storm grounded him overnight, and you know as well as I do that even bedbugs refuse to check into our highway hotels."

"I'll take that as a yes. I'll give him a ride. You might need the truck, and I have nothing better to do."

No. No. No. Horrified, Madison scrambled for an excuse. "June, that's not necessary. I—"

"I have to drive out that way anyway. I promise not to grill him. Much." With that, June pivoted on her heel and strode briskly toward Madison's back porch. She yanked open the screen. "Hi there! I'm Deputy Jones—you must be Adam. I'm going to give you a ride to the airport so Madison can get to the office, if that's okay? Her day's packed. Ever ridden in a patrol car before?"

"Sounds good and no, I haven't. But, Deputy Jones, would you mind if I have a moment with Madison first?"

Madison cringed. Morning afters… She'd never had one and didn't think this was going to make her want another one.

June's posture turned intimidatingly official. "Is that necess—"

"It's okay, June. Can you give us five? Or do you need to go?" Wishful thinking.

"I'll wait. Right out here."

Madison hustled into the house without another word and shut the door behind Adam before June changed her mind and took it upon herself to follow. She hoped June would forgive her the rudeness, but this wasn't a conversation for three.

Adam's hard gaze met Madison's. "You called the cops?"

"No. She's my tenant and my friend. I told you about her." She couldn't remember ever being more uncomfortable. At the same time her mouth dried and her pulse quickened as she soaked up the impact of his stubbly chinned masculine appeal. If the circumstances had been different, she could imagine waking up to that face and staying in bed another hour…or three.

No. Don't imagine that.

Too late. Her body flushed and her skin dampened. She curled her toes in her boots, then cleared her throat. "Have a safe flight home."

"What happened last night does not change your promise to my father."

"I know that."

"Let me know if your period starts or if you're late."

The intimacy of the topic made her cheeks burn, but if she had conceived—and she prayed she hadn't—this was only the first of many more uncomfortable discussions.

"I will. But I'm, um…not expecting it this week."

"Let me know either way," he repeated. "I'll see you Sunday."

And then he strode out the back door, taking all the oxygen in the room with him. Madison sank onto a kitchen chair and put her head on the table. At the moment, being pregnant seemed like the worst thing in the world that could happen.

And yet—

No. There was no "and yet." Being pregnant would be bad. She couldn't afford it emotionally or financially. And she definitely couldn't stand to come face-to-face with her forbidden attraction to her brother-in-law on a regular basis.

GIVEN WHAT HAD happened the last time Helen had interrupted Danny in the bathroom, she hated to knock. But he'd been in there a very long time. Dinner was getting cold and she didn't want to eat alone. Adam wasn't joining them tonight. The storm had forced him to stay overnight in North Carolina and as a result he'd gotten to work late and wanted to stay to make up the time.

What was Danny doing? Was he okay? She hadn't heard the shower or toilet. Bracing herself for a confrontation that she didn't have the energy for, she tapped on the door. No answer. Her worry multiplied.

"Danny?" She turned the knob, and found him standing at the sink, a brush in his hand. A brush filled with hair. More strands littered the white marble countertop.

Poor Danny. She saw fear and worry on his face. First the debilitating sickness from the chemo, and now this. His cancer was becoming very real—to both of them—and not something Danny could breeze through like a virus.

She entered the bathroom, wrapped her arms around his waist from behind and rested her chin on his shoulder—something she hadn't done in ages. Their gazes met in the mirror. "It's just hair, Danny. It'll grow back."

"I was hoping I'd be one of the few who didn't lose mine."

"I know." She massaged his shoulders, and again realized she hadn't done this in a long time. It used to be a regular occurrence when he'd had a stressful day. After dinner she'd knead and he'd talk. She missed the feel of his muscles, but she missed their discussions even more. He was in great shape for a man of sixty-one. Other than the cancer.

They would get through this, and maybe one day they'd share those postdinner moments again. She gathered her resolve. "I bought hair clippers when I was out the other night."

He frowned. "Why?"

"Because we were warned that this might happen, and it's better to be proactive rather than reactive. You know what the pamphlet said. 'Take control. You decide when to go bald.'" Just saying the word *bald* made her tongue feel thick and foreign in her mouth. "Do you want me to get them?"

He swallowed, closed his eyes then opened them again and stared at the strands in the brush. His chest rose and fell. "Yes. It's time."

She went into the bedroom and dug the bag out from where she'd hidden it in the back of her closet. Hoping it would have never come to this and that she could return the clippers unused, she'd kept the receipt. She'd been a step behind on getting the right foods in the house—she wouldn't be caught unprepared again. For Danny's sake she'd be positive and strong and ready to stand by him no matter what came next.

She took a much-needed moment to mask her anxiety, then returned to his side. Her hands shook as she opened the box and removed the parts, lining them up in a precise row. She plugged in the set and oiled the blades the way she'd seen Danny do a hundred times on the set they used for their boys when they were young. A familiar popping sound emitted when she turned on the clippers.

She tried to focus on happy memories instead of what was about to happen. "Do you remember when you used to give the boys their summer buzz cuts?"

"Yes." His expression was stoic, but his voice revealed his strain. But at least he hadn't fussed at her about living in the past this time. "Andrew always complained, but Adam took it like a trooper."

True. She'd forgotten that. She offered him the clippers. He hesitated—this man who never hesitated about anything. "Danny, don't you want to…?"

"You do it."

"But… Are you sure? I've never—"

"It won't matter if you mess it up, Helen. It's all

coming out anyway." He snatched a towel from the rack and draped it around his shoulders, then put down the toilet lid and sat on it.

Her heart raced like a hummingbird's. Her hands trembled even more. She loved his thick salt-and-pepper locks, loved to tangle her fingers in the strands, loved to brush them back from his brow. But it had been a long time since she'd done either.

When had she stopped? Would she ever get to do so again?

A sob rose in her throat. She choked it down. With the clippers in her right hand, she tilted his head forward with her left, stroking the cool strands one last time. Tears stung her eyes, but she fought them back. He was upset enough without her blubbering all over him. Besides, she needed to see clearly if she didn't want to take off his ears.

"Ready?"

"As I'll ever be."

She wasn't. But she placed the clippers at his nape, took a deep breath, then pushed them upward anyway. Dark strands rained down on her hands, Danny's shoulders, the floor, leaving a stark white scalp behind. And regret. Oh, Lord. What had she started? It was too late to turn coward now. She lifted the clippers and repeated the process again and again until all but the top of his head was bare.

She glanced up at the mirror and saw tears on her husband's cheeks and the dam on her control broke. For a few moments they stared at each other, twin rivers running down each of their faces, then she pulled herself together, snatched a tissue from the box for him and another for herself. Crying never fixed anything, her grandma had always said.

"It's going to be okay. We are going to be fine." She tried to infuse as much confidence into her voice as possible. Blinking furiously, she tucked her chin and finished the job, then eased away the hair-covered towel.

He looked up at her. Shock rooted her to the floor, then it ebbed. She ran her hands over his stubbly head, then cupped his jaw in her palms. "You are actually quite handsome without hair. I never realized what wonderful bone structure you have."

"Don't lie to make me feel better."

"I'm not. Look."

He turned toward the mirror and when he did, she spotted an inch-long scar she'd known nothing about. "Danny Drake, what happened here?"

The blush on his cheeks was as unexpected as it was charming. She hadn't seen him blush since before their wedding. "It's a long, boring story."

"Lucky for you, I have nothing but time. Let's get out of these itchy clothes. You can tell me about it in the shower."

"In the shower?"

"Yes. We haven't showered together in a long time."

He rose. "No. We haven't."

He might not be interested in making love, but

she would show him to the best of her ability that she still loved him and desired him.

In case she never had the chance again.

MADISON WRAPPED A towel around her hair, put on her robe and padded to the kitchen to scrounge up dinner.

Her hot shower had done little to alleviate the tension and dull ache in her muscles from her marathon workday. Spotting the two women seated at her kitchen table stopped her in her tracks. Unexpected company was not unusual in Quincey. For these two to drop in was even less so. But Piper and June's avid expressions warned this was not going to be a relaxing evening of girl talk. At least not for her.

She wrapped her arms around her middle. "This is a surprise."

"We brought dinner," Piper said.

"You didn't have to do that."

"Gus barbecued a pig for the men's church supper tonight. I confiscated some for us," June added.

Only then did Madison notice the three takeout boxes on the counter. "I'll get us some tea."

She retrieved the pitcher from the fridge and fixed three glasses, wondering how she could keep what she'd done a secret. She stalled by collecting utensils, the salt and pepper shakers, hot sauce and napkins. Then there was nothing left to do but take her medicine.

"You haven't had a man spend the night for as

long as I've known you," Piper said before Madison's bottom settled in the chair.

"He slept in the guest room." Not a lie.

The containers squeaked simultaneously as the girls opened them and the delicious aroma of hickory smoked pork filled the air. She might find her appetite if they'd change the topic.

"Really? Then how do you explain that big hickey on your neck?" Piper asked.

Horrified, Madison slapped a hand to the right side, where Adam's love bite had sent her into the stratosphere of pleasure. She hadn't noticed a mark in the mirror, but it had been steamed from her shower.

"You slept with him," June added, wide-eyed.

Confused, Madison looked from her tenant to her assistant. Piper shrugged and grinned shamelessly. "I was bluffing."

Madison's hand fell to her lap. Busted. "It was a mistake."

"Why?" Piper asked.

"Because he's Andrew's brother."

"Andrew has been gone a long time. There's nothing wrong with two single adults finding pleasure together if it's consensual. It was, wasn't it?" June tacked on the last in her official deputy voice.

"Of course, Justice."

"Hey, no need to get ugly and call me that."

"It is your name."

"Hello!" Piper chimed in. "We were talking about

Madison's one-night stand." Madison winced. "What June means, Madison, is that your night of passion is okay as long as you used protection."

Madison did her best not to react.

"You didn't use protection?" June demanded.

"I didn't say that!"

"You didn't have to. You swallowed and your lashes twitched. That's your tell when you're upset."

"I have a tell?"

"Everybody does. I study body language, remember? Basic Interrogation Techniques 101. But back to your wild night with Studly Did-He-Do-You-Right?"

She wanted to hide. "I'd really rather not discuss it."

"Tough. You didn't pretend Adam was his brother, did you?"

"No!" Madison sagged back in her chair, pretty certain if she ate anything it would come back up. Piper and June weren't going to let this go. She might as well surrender.

"We flew straight into the storm. I didn't think we would survive the flight. And I...I didn't react well. The sex wasn't planned. It just...happened. And he really did sleep in the guest room...afterward. I didn't lie about that."

"It's okay," Piper said. "Don't beat yourself up."

"It's not okay! And it was wrong. He and I both know that. It can't happen again."

June tsked. "If it had been me, what would you have said?" She held up a hand, halting Madison's answer before she could find it. "I'll tell you what you'd have said. 'Go for it, June. Have fun, but be careful.'"

"You had sex, Madison. You didn't steal another woman's husband," Piper said. "Was it good?"

Madison's face flushed even hotter. "Piper!"

"All I'm saying is you're overdue, and if it was good, why not continue the relationship?"

"I'm walking out of the Drakes' lives in four weeks. Forever."

"Unless you're pregnant," Piper pointed out.

Horrified, she slapped her hands over her ears. "Don't say that. I won't be. The likelihood of that happening is low."

Please, please, please, let that be true.

Piper reached across the table and caught her hand. "It happened to me, and I handled it badly. I kept Roth away from his son for eleven years. That was a mistake. If you've conceived you have options, and you need to consider them all and find the one you can live with. But I don't recommend hiding your pregnancy from Adam as one of them. June and I will help you no matter what. Got that?"

Madison searched Piper's sincere blue eyes, then June's bright green ones, seeing confident assurance in both. A lump rose in her throat, choking off words. She'd never had this kind of support before and didn't know how to handle it. Unable to speak, she nodded.

It was only then that she realized that by monopolizing her time, Andrew had taken yet one more thing from her during their marriage. He'd kept her from making friends in college and during vet school, isolating her so that she'd be more dependent on him. Typical narcissistic behavior.

The bastard.

And yet one more reason *not* to get involved with the Drakes again.

ADAM KNEW HE was in trouble when found himself looking forward to seeing Madison. He tried to blame his eagerness on his curiosity about the woman who had so many hidden facets. But curiosity didn't fill his nights with erotic reenactment dreams that made his heart pound and his sheets sweaty.

He'd made a mistake—one he wouldn't repeat. But the desire he'd felt for Madison had overwhelmed his common sense twice now. The best way to guarantee that wouldn't happen again was to take preemptive action.

Madison might not be the terrible person his brother had accused her of being. She might be the savior of every stray animal in North Carolina and even his father's practice—and possibly Danny Drake's sanity—but she'd been behind the wheel in the accident that had resulted in Andrew's death, and there was something haunting in her eyes that hinted that she wasn't telling the whole truth.

She'd proved repeatedly that she was generous

with her time. Not only had she looked out for his mother, but she knew how to take care of his father and little old ladies who'd lost their pets. She hadn't learned those skills by practicing textbook veterinary medicine. She was obviously as compassionate with her patients' owners as she was with their pets. People didn't leave surprises in the freezer of someone who did their job and nothing more.

Was there even a hint of truth to Andrew's stories about his marriage or his mother's suspicions? He suspected not, but he needed to know for sure, now more than ever. His preoccupation with Madison bordered on obsession. Last night while he'd tossed and turned he had come up with a way to get his answers.

If anybody could point him in the right direction, it was the retired cop who worked part-time security for the hospital. Adam caught up with him in the parking lot Friday evening. "Roger, how can I investigate a car accident?"

"Recent?"

"Six years ago."

Roger tossed his uniform hat into his car and rubbed a hand over his high-and-tight haircut. "That complicates things. You can't go to the site to measure preaccident skid marks or check the postcollision impact and debris field. And I'm guessing you don't have access to the car."

"It was totaled and hauled to the junkyard."

"And it's likely been stripped, crushed and sold

for scrap since. You'll be limited to the original accident reports and insurance claim forms. There are companies that specialize in auto accident investigations. Why didn't you hire one at the time? Or has our wonderful legal system dragged the case out this long?" Bitterness snarled in his tone.

"The case never went to court, but information has recently come to my attention that makes me question whether the crash was accidental or deliberate."

"Reliable information?"

"My mother." The men shared a grimace.

"Kind of have to follow up on that one, don't you? Was the driver charged?"

"Only for driving too fast for the conditions. She paid the fine without contesting." He'd always considered that an admission of guilt. Now he wasn't sure.

Roger frowned. "That charge is a judgment call on the officer's part. It could mean anything or nothing."

"My brother and his unborn son died as a result of the wreck."

"That would have been a homicide or manslaughter charge."

Homicide or manslaughter? Charging Madison with such a severe crime seemed…abhorrent. If he hired a private accident investigator he could probably keep the findings to himself. But he had to have the facts. For his sake. For his mother's sake.

"I need to know what happened."

"Tell you what, Adam. Email me the details. I know a guy who went into accident investigation after he left the force. I'll forward everything to him and see if he's interested in digging up an old case. If he is, I'll have him call you. But I have to warn you, he's not cheap."

"The truth will be worth the price."

CHAPTER FOURTEEN

MADISON HAD SPENT most of the week working herself into a tangle of nerves and trying to build the courage to face Adam again. She'd planned how she'd act and rehearsed what she'd say in an attempt to convince him that Tuesday night had meant nothing to her and that she could forget the passion she'd found in his arms and move on.

It wasn't lying if she intended to make it so.

Then she'd arrived at the airport and discovered Adam had sent one of the coowners of the plane to pick her up. Her adrenaline level had crashed, but thankfully her cardiothoracic surgeon pilot hadn't noticed. He'd been too busy yammering about the conference he'd attended over the weekend and about how his revolutionary procedure had been the hit of the event. He'd been flying over her area on his return trip and had volunteered to pick her up for Adam.

He'd been a narcissist to the bone, and she'd had enough of those to last a lifetime. Too bad she hadn't been smart enough to know the difference between confidence and conceit when she'd met Andrew.

She'd ignored her pilot as best she could and had begun to prepare herself all over again for confronting Adam upon landing. But in the terminal she found Helen, not Adam, waiting. Her stomach did another roller-coaster swoop. Of disappointment? No. Definitely not. She simply wanted—no, needed—to get the encounter with Adam behind her.

She never would have expected him to be a coward. Ducking and diving or flat-out denial had been Andrew's M.O. when he'd done something wrong. She'd expected better of Adam, the one who claimed he faced his fears and who'd accused *her* of running from hers.

"Where's Adam?" she asked Helen, noting her mother-in-law looked better, more rested and less like she was teetering on the edge of a breakdown than in previous weeks.

"He couldn't get away from the hospital. Didn't his coworker explain?"

"No. He was too busy bragging about his brilliance."

Madison headed toward the parking lot, but Helen lagged behind, looking as if she had something to get off her chest. "You told Danny's staff about his cancer."

Madison stopped inside the double doors and braced herself for an ugly argument. "Kay asked a direct question—I told you I wouldn't lie. Danny hadn't informed them of his situation—he promised me he would."

"Danny has never had more than a sniffle or a twenty-four-hour virus in his life, and none of those kept him from the office. He wanted to believe he'd sail through this, too, that he was somehow stronger than most people." She tucked her hair behind her ear. "I guess we both did. We didn't expect the treatment to be as difficult as it has been."

Compassion lowered Madison's defenses. "That's why you need a support team, Helen."

"Lisa, Jim, Susie and Kay have each visited this week, bringing food, entertaining Danny and shooing me out of the house. Danny really needed that this week, Madison." Looking uncomfortable, she shifted on her feet and tangled her fingers. "And I...I did, too. Thank you."

Taken aback by the tears of gratitude brimming in Helen's eyes and the emotional wobble in her voice, Madison nodded. "You're welcome. Danny's staff thinks the world of him, and they have a vested interest in his return. They need to contribute, as much as *you* need their help. They want the best for him, and they'll be there for him long after I'm gone."

"I can see that now. So does Danny."

They continued to Helen's car. "I should warn you before you see him tonight that we had to shave his head."

If Danny had been half as enamored of his hair as Andrew, Madison knew that was a biggie. "That must've been tough on both of you. How are you holding up?"

Helen blinked. "Me? I'm fine. He's the one..." She sighed. "I'm managing. His hair was one of the first things that drew me to him. And with it gone it's just such a visible reminder that...I m-might lose him. It's hard for me seeing him suffer and not being able to fix it. I always took good care of my boys."

"Yes, you did. To the exclusion of looking out for yourself most of the time."

Helen held up a hand to halt the words. "You don't need to say, 'I told you so.' You warned me that I was unprepared for life without Danny. And you were right. Once I get him through this, I'll think about going back to school or getting certified for something."

"Good idea."

"I admit, in the past when you pushed me to find a career I thought you were comparing me to your mother. I know she and your father were unhappy, because she was trapped, but—"

"You're not my mother." She didn't mean to snap the words, but she didn't want to talk about the horrible discovery that had driven her from home.

Helen stiffened, looking affronted. "I know that."

Madison shook her head. "I meant you would never do what she did."

"No. I wouldn't do that to Danny. Ever." She checked her watch. "Speaking of Danny... He'll be waiting. We should go."

"Helen, cancer treatment is a marathon, not a sprint. Let anyone who offers to help *help*. You can't do this alone."

"You learned all this from your patients?"

"In a small town all we have is each other, rather than a surplus of psychologists. Sometimes an ear is all people need. You absorb a lot if you're willing to listen."

Again, Helen shuffled her feet. "Madison, I—I'm sorry I've been so difficult. Standing by my baby's bedside and watching him slip away was the hardest thing I've ever done. I kept clinging to the hope that Andrew would wake up, and…I couldn't do anything. I couldn't help him. I needed to blame someone. You were the easiest target. I'm sorry."

Madison had waited six years for that apology, but it still surprised her. "You were hurting. You'd just lost your son."

Helen's gaze bounced around the empty terminal before returning to Madison. Pain, confusion and regret mingled in her eyes. "For a long time I wondered… No, I convinced myself that the wreck wasn't an accident."

Madison flinched. It wasn't any easier to hear a second time what Adam had already told her. "Helen, I would never have intentionally hurt Andrew or my baby."

"I see that now. But Andrew had told me you two were having problems and that you didn't want little Daniel. I believed you were rejecting my son and my grandchild. I became defensive because I couldn't imagine my life without my children—no matter how they came into being."

No matter how they came into being?

The odd phrasing alerted Madison. Had Helen known about Andrew's trick?

"You thought I didn't want Daniel even after I asked you about watching him while I worked?"

Helen lifted one shoulder. "I didn't know what to believe. You were telling me one thing and Andrew was saying another. And you wanted to go back to work six weeks after giving birth. I just couldn't imagine not wanting more time.

"Despite how hateful I was then, you still came back for Danny. You interrupted your life and your practice for us. I know coming here every week hasn't been easy, but I don't know what we'd have done if you'd refused." Her voice wavered. She blinked furiously, then dug in her purse for her keys.

Madison circled to the trunk of the car, giving Helen a moment to get herself together. "You'd have hired the service and managed fine."

"You don't understand. Madison, having you here is a reminder of when life was still perfect, when we w-were still a fa-family."

A family who had no idea how devious and manipulative their son had become. Or did they?

Madison watched her mother-in-law struggle until it became impossible to resist the need to comfort. She dropped her gear and wrapped her arms around

Helen. She was more than a little surprised when Helen hugged her back so tightly it almost crushed the breath from Madison's lungs. Helen held on for a very long time.

The embrace felt familiar, like coming home. Warning bells rang in her subconscious, but she didn't pull away. Helen trembled as if fighting for control, then she stepped back and swiped her damp cheeks. Her expression turned all business.

"Let's get you to the house. I left dinner in the slow cooker. Danny's going to want to hear about your week. He's been following the weather on television. It sounds like you've had some stormy days."

Acceptance from the Drakes felt good. Too good. But it was treacherous ground. She had to keep her emotional footing, because if she allowed herself to travel that path, it was only a matter of time before she'd slide back out into the cold again. And if Helen ever found out what had happened with Adam, then it would be sooner than later.

And God forbid if there was a baby.

IT WAS ALMOST two o'clock Monday morning when Adam dragged himself into his house. Madison's floral fragrance lingered in the air. She was here. Adrenaline flooded his veins.

He'd received no response to his text telling her he was sending someone else to pick her up, and after last Tuesday's mistake he hadn't known what to expect. Could he have blamed her if she hadn't returned? No. He'd crossed a line and had sex with his brother's wife.

Yes, Andrew was gone, but she would always be Andrew's girl, and Adam had never taken anything that belonged to his brother. Not his toys, his clothes or his women. Too bad Andrew hadn't felt the same.

Pushing aside the negative memories, he headed toward the kitchen. Tonight he could feel Madison's presence rather than just hear the echo of his own footsteps, and for some reason it was comforting to know the place wasn't empty.

He dismissed the crazy thought. All he felt was relief that he wouldn't have to track her down or find a last-minute substitute veterinarian for tomorrow. He'd been fine without Madison before and he would be again.

He passed through the foyer. The earring his housekeeper had found wasn't on the credenza where it had been since Wednesday. The small gold hoop had been the first thing he'd seen each night when he arrived home and the last thing every morning when heading out—to remind him of Madison and what had happened during the storm. Madison must have picked it up.

The sight of her cooler sitting in its usual spot by the back door halted him short of the refrigerator. He'd been waiting for a call from her all week. Was she pregnant? Would there be long-term repercussions from his loss of control?

"I never would've taken you for a coward."

Her quiet voice behind him yanked every muscle in his body taut like a puppet master pulling slack from the stings. He pivoted. Every inch of Madison's skin was covered save her bare feet and head. Loose pajamas concealed her legs and her short robe was belted tightly at her waist—the same robe she'd shrugged out of that night. Her long, tangled hair draped her shoulders.

"What are you talking about?"

"After your nasty comment about me running from my problems, *you* are avoiding *me*."

"I texted to let you know I'd been held up and sent a picture of Saul so you'd know who to look for."

"I didn't get a text. All I know is your conceited friend was at the right place at the correct time with the same plane. He told me he was my ride. I tried to call to verify. You didn't answer. I almost didn't get on that plane."

"I had my phone turned off." He pulled it out of his pocket, turned the gadget back on and saw the Message Undeliverable icon by the text he'd tried to send her. He flipped it around so she could see it. "I'm sorry. The text didn't go through. Sometimes that happens when I'm deep in the hospital building.

"Speaking of pawning off on friends, you pawned me off on yours. Deputy Jones interrogated me all the way to the airport. She probably dusted the cruiser and ran my prints after dropping me off."

Madison grimaced. "June's protective. If you weren't hiding from me, then what kept you at work?"

"I was trying to avert the nursing strike. The deadline was midnight tonight."

Caramel-colored eyes, narrowed with distrust, searched his face as if trying to weigh the truth of his statement. Had Andrew lied to her the way he had to his family? Probably. Another reminder that Andrew had been far from perfect. Having Madison back forced Adam to face that harsh reality on a regular basis. He'd be glad when the accident report came through. Pete Lang, the investigator, had promised to get on it as soon as he could.

Then Madison's gaze met and held his. "Fine. But if you have to send someone else for me again please don't send *him*. He's convinced he's the greatest surgeon ever born."

"His ego is matched only by his surgical skills. He's one of the best, but he's a little hard to take in big doses."

They shared a smile, then awareness of what they'd done invaded the room, seeping into the cracks and crevices until they were surrounded by it. Memories rushed forward. The warmth of her skin. The taste of her mouth. The wet heat of her body gripping his. His temperature rose and his pulse jackhammered against his eardrums.

Sex. That was all it had been.

But damn, it had been good.

He needed to get her out of here before he did something stupid like give in to the temptation. "I'm sorry I woke you."

"I wasn't asleep. Have you eaten?"

"Not since breakfast."

"Yesterday?" She barely waited for his nod, then crossed to the refrigerator and pulled out a pot. "Your mother sent some chicken and dumplin's and told me to make sure you ate."

"Madison, I can feed myself."

She gave him a look that should have made his thickening anatomy duck for cover. "I know that."

"Are you pregnant?"

She gasped at his blunt question. "I don't know yet."

"When will you know?"

"Soon, I hope. I've never been the regular type. Stress tends to throw off my cycle."

"If you are—"

"I won't be." Her quick denial made it clear she didn't want to discuss the possibility.

"If you are, what will you do?"

She bit her lip, ducked her head and busied herself by reaching into the cabinet for a bowl. Her hands shook as she ladled out the stew, very precisely covered it with plastic wrap then put it into the microwave and turned on the machine.

"Madison."

"I don't know, Adam."

"Ignoring a problem won't make it go away."

"I'm not ignoring anything. I just refuse to panic unless there's a need."

"Will you panic if you are?"

Her throat moved visibly, and the pulse at the base—the one he'd laved with his tongue—fluttered wildly. "A baby would…complicate things."

His gaze dropped to her flat stomach. Andrew's words echoed in his head. "You don't want children?"

"I never said that. I'm trying to be practical. The timing is wrong. Child care is expensive. Money is tight. I barter animal care for what I can't afford, but I wouldn't be willing to let just anyone look after a child in trade for services rendered."

"You wouldn't be so tight for money if you joined a larger city practice and put your training to better use."

"We've been through that. Quincey needs me."

He wasn't going to change her mind about that tonight. "If you are pregnant you could move back here."

"No!"

"I'll help financially wherever you end up."

"If I am, it's not your problem."

"I'm equally responsible." He paused. "Would you have it?"

She closed her eyes tightly. Seconds ticked past. Her hands shifted toward her navel, then she yanked them back to her sides. Her lids lifted. "I don't know."

"If it turns out that you're pregnant, I want to know and I want to be part of the decision making."

"I—I'll let you know."

What would he do if she was and decided to keep the baby? They lived too far apart for him to be a decent father. Would he have to leave the hospital he'd worked so hard to improve in order to spend time with their child? To do that he'd have to leave his parents.

When he'd first started at Mercy he'd considered it a temporary stop, a rung on the ladder to a larger, more prestigious hospital. He'd planned to get his mother past her emotional meltdown, then move on. But he'd become invested in the hospital's people, in Mercy's growth and continued improvement. Instead of limitations, he now saw potential, and he no longer wanted to move up and out.

He wiped a hand across his face. A child with his brother's wife. How could he have been so careless? He'd never been a slave to his desires before. Why now? Why Madison? What about her turned him irresponsible?

How would his mother handle Madison having his child? He shook his head. For once he wanted to borrow Madison's philosophy and not anticipate trouble. If it happened, he'd deal with his mother.

The microwave beeped, making them both jump. She fetched the bowl and a spoon and put both on the bar in front of him. "Did the nurses strike?"

He let her change the subject. He'd said his piece and he was too drained to press the point. "No."

Residual anger from the past week's events made

his jaw so rigid it was hard to eat. He shoved a bite into his mouth anyway.

"And…? That's all you're going to give me?"

He chewed, gulped, washed down the food with the glass of iced tea she'd provided. If she insisted on talking, then the nursing issue was a safer topic than the awareness of her he couldn't shake.

"We're an excellent hospital. Voted one of the best in the state for the past two years. But one malicious person with a chip on her shoulder created an atmosphere of discontent that contaminated others around her. It took time to make the rest of the staff see past her poison. But we did it and averted the strike."

The positive outcome was the only reason he wasn't pounding out his frustration with the weights in his gym now the way he had every other night for the past few weeks.

"Did *you,* personally, stop the strike?"

"Why do you ask?"

"I hear pride in your tone."

Perceptive, wasn't she? He lowered his spoon. "I was part of a team."

Her head tilted as she assessed him and her dark hair glided across her shoulder, making him recall the feel of the silky strands slipping across his skin.

"Andrew never would've shared the credit."

Another unpalatable truth. "No. He wouldn't have."

He shoveled in another mouthful and chewed

while reviewing the facts as he knew them. "You seemed happy with Andrew. Did I misread the situation on my visits home?"

"I was happy."

The slight emphasis on *was* combined with the flatness of her voice indicated otherwise. "Was...?"

"He's gone. I'm not. I'll see you in the morning."

"Stop running, Madison."

She paused but didn't turn. Her fists clenched by her side. "I. Am. Not. Running. Stop accusing me of that."

"Then why are you so eager to escape this conversation?" And why was he trying to detain her? Letting her go would be better for both of them. He was in a weird mood tonight, tense, his nerves and thoughts tangled, similar to the way he'd been after the flight. Probably due to lack of sleep. But he wanted company. Madison's company. He needed to understand what had happened six years ago, and the only way to get answers was to dig.

She slowly faced him. "I'm not versed in awkward 'after' encounters."

That couldn't mean what he thought it did, could it? But the flush on her cheeks said more than words. Andrew had bragged that Madison had been a virgin when they'd met and how he'd been the one to teach her everything. As much as Adam wished he could forget that long-ago conversation, it played in his brain like annoying elevator music.

"You haven't been with anyone since Andrew?"

The pink deepened into red. "I didn't say that."

"You're an attractive woman. You could have any man you wanted. Why wouldn't you satisfy a basic human need like desire?"

She looked flustered by his compliment. "Because I didn't want to feel cheap."

That stung. "Do you feel cheap now?"

She bit her lip and flipped back her hair, feigning a nonchalance her troubled eyes refuted. "No. I—I..."

"You what, Madison?"

"I don't feel cheap, Adam, but I do...regret what happened."

The blend of vulnerability and latent hunger in her eyes tugged at him. "You didn't answer my previous question. Have you had a relationship since Andrew?"

She stiffened to rigid attention. "That is none of your business."

No. It wasn't. But the need to know was as compelling as the need to take his next breath. "There's nothing wrong with moving on after a decent amount of time, Madison."

"That's what I hear."

But not what she believed.

He searched her face, noting the shadows in her eyes. His father had been right. She'd been grieving when she left them six years ago. Was she still mourning her loss?

"Do you still think of him when you close your eyes?"

"Sometimes."

Revulsion rose in his throat. Despite her denial, had he been a substitute for his twin?

"Not in the way you mean," she added hastily.

"Then how?"

"I'm a goal-oriented person. I had my future mapped out. Then it all changed. I was so naive. I never saw it coming."

He could understand that. Andrew's death had shocked them all. But her plans weren't the only ones that had been derailed. If she'd stayed he wouldn't have had to move back to keep an eye on his parents. And if he hadn't, where would he be now? Would he have continued his climb to larger hospitals and more responsibility in an effort to impress his father? Would he have become as ambitious as his father? Would he have ever found a facility that provided the satisfaction Mercy did?

"Did you ever consider sticking with your plan to join Dad's practice?"

"I lay in that hospital bed alone mourning the death of my child and then my husband. Not once did any of you come to check on me or to update me on Andrew's condition. That proved to me that the only tie I had with your family was Andrew. With him gone I didn't belong, and after the confrontation with your mother, coming back was not an option."

It shamed him to admit he'd never once thought of visiting her. He'd been too wrapped up in watching his brother slip away.

"You didn't visit Andrew, either."

"I was hemorrhaging and they wouldn't let me move. No one offered to wheel my bed down to ICU. I didn't know that was an option, so I didn't ask. By the time the doctors gave the okay for me to get in a wheelchair, Andrew was gone."

"I'm sorry. You should've been allowed to say your goodbyes."

She glanced away, her fingers picking at the hem of her robe. "Yeah. Adam, your mother and I have worked out a truce. If she ever finds out what we did… It won't matter to me because I'll be gone. But you—"

"She won't find out. Stop beating yourself up. If not for the fact that you're my brother's wife, there'd be nothing wrong with what we did."

"I haven't been Andrew's for a long time."

No. She hadn't. Technically.

The need to make her understand that her desires were normal and moving on was okay swelled within him. He rose and moved toward her even though a smart man would have kept the counter between them.

She backed quickly. "Stop right there. This chemistry between us is…strong but wrong. We both know that complicating an already bad situation isn't a good idea."

He stopped close enough to touch her. Only sheer willpower prevented him from reaching out to test the warmth of her soft cheek. "What happened to your marriage?"

Panic flashed across her face. "The past is over and rehashing it won't change anything. Let it go. It's late. We have to be up in four hours. I'll see you in the morning." She bolted from the kitchen.

Running. She might deny it, but she did it.

He locked his knees, determined to be wise enough not to follow her. Everything she'd said, everything she'd done to this point, raised questions for which he *needed* answers. The more time he spent with Madison the more he wondered if he'd known his twin at all.

He would find out the truth about Madison and Andrew's marriage. But not tonight.

ADAM'S TELEPHONE RANG Friday afternoon, shattering his concentration. He realized he'd been staring blindly at the budget report, lost in thoughts of Madison. Again. Trying to figure her out had occupied too much of his mind lately. He snatched up the phone on his desk. "Adam Drake."

"Hey, Adam. Pete Lang."

Adrenaline kicked through Adam's veins when the accident investigator identified himself. *Finally. Answers.*

"I wanted to let you know the accident looks pretty straightforward to me. Dark, deserted road. Black ice. According to the officer's report your sister-in-law admitted she and your brother were arguing at the time, so throw distraction into the mix. For what it's worth, your brother's blood alcohol level was double the legal limit, but your sis-in-law had none on board."

"She was pregnant."

"Trust me, buddy, that's no deterrent to some people. Looks like a tragic accident to me."

Disappointed and simultaneously relieved, Adam sank back into his seat. "How much do I owe you?"

"Nothing yet. I have to admit something about this case is nagging me. Can't put my finger on it, but it doesn't feel right, and I learned a long time ago to trust my gut. In my opinion, given her slow speed, the wreck should've been survivable with property damage only. Let me think on it and get back to you."

"Thanks, Pete. I look forward to your full report."

So he'd learned nothing to derail his desire for Madison. But he was known on the job for his persistence. He wasn't giving up.

SATURDAY MORNING MADISON stared at her office wall, thumped her pen on the file in front of her and tried not to think of Adam or the way they'd tap-danced around each other Monday and Tuesday. The sexual tension between them had been so strong she'd nearly choked on it. But they'd managed to act wisely and keep their physical distance by staying at his parents' Monday evening until they were too exhausted to keep their eyes open and then heading to the airport directly from Danny's office Tuesday.

She pressed a hand to her crampy stomach. She wasn't pregnant. Her period had started Wednesday morning. And even though she should have called or texted Adam to let him know, she hadn't. How did you break that kind of news?

"Congratulations. You're not going to be a father!"

"Whew, we escaped that one!"

"I'm not knocked up."

Nothing she'd come up with had sounded right. But it wasn't only the awkward wording that had kept her from contacting him—it was the hollow ache of disappointment that had blindsided her. The list of reasons why having a child now was a bad idea was extensive. Logically, she knew that. But emotionally, the emptiness was very real. And very scary. Surely she hadn't wanted the complication of a baby?

She scanned her immaculate office and her bare, save the file in her hand, desk. Even with her abbreviated hours, every appointment slot wasn't filled. She spent a lot of time cleaning or reading research articles and waiting for her next patient to arrive, because she couldn't sit still without thoughts of Adam taking over her brain. Her every-other-Saturday hours were no exception.

She'd left Piper up front with her nose buried in parenting magazines thirty minutes ago. Madison suspected it wouldn't be long before her assistant decided to have another baby—if she wasn't already pregnant. Madison was happy for her. Piper had reunited with the love of her life, and together she and Roth were finally forming the family they should have eleven years ago. Why not add to their happiness? Madison could expend her unexpected maternal instincts on Piper's baby.

She made the last notation in the chart and pushed it aside. On Mondays and Tuesdays she barely had time to dictate chart contents to Lisa, then skim and sign off on her entries. Danny's practice kept her on her feet both mentally and physically. She missed that bustle and even the total exhaustion at the end of the day. She even missed having her feet and back ache and her thoughts whirling with everything she'd seen and done.

The front door opened. She checked her watch. She only had one more patient scheduled before she closed at noon, and Mr. Rouse had never been early in all the years she'd been treating his bloodhound.

More than likely her visitor was an emergency case. Others' misfortune put money in her pocket. She hated that, but it paid the bills. She shot to her feet and hustled toward the front of the office.

Danny and Helen stood by the reception desk, shocking her to a standstill. Danny's face was ashen, but curiosity lit his eyes as he craned his head, examining every nook of the waiting and reception areas. Helen looked uncomfortable, then she spotted Madison and her gaze turned apologetic.

"I tried to convince him not to come, but he insisted."

"I can't sit around and stare at the same walls every day. I'll go crazy."

"I think you already have," Helen quipped. "The drive was too much for you, Danny. I told you it would be."

"I slept most of the way. And if I'm going to sleep all day in that bed, does it really matter whether it's parked or rolling?"

Madison had never heard them bicker like this. Then his words registered. That bed? Panicked, she crossed to the window. The Drakes' motor home filled her small parking lot. So much for keeping her past and her in-laws a secret from the rest of Quincey. A motor home that cost more than most of the locals' houses would definitely garner unwanted attention.

Quincey didn't get many visitors unless they were lost or searching for antiques. Tongues had probably started wagging as soon as they drove through downtown without stopping.

"Didn't you have chemo yesterday, Danny?" Madison asked.

"Yes. We left right afterward. Helen drove most of the way yesterday and the remainder this morning."

The clearing of a throat reminded Madison they

weren't alone. "Helen, Danny, this is Piper Sterling, my assistant. Piper, Helen and Danny Drake."

Piper's eyes widened. "Nice to meet you. You've had a long drive. I have some of my mother's cookies and a jug of sweet tea in the back, if you're interested in refreshments."

"Thank you, young lady—maybe after I've seen Maddie's office."

Madison's heart sank. How could she refuse the grand tour when he'd come this far? "There's not a lot to see."

Helen stepped toward the counter. "Piper, I'd love some of that tea while these two talk shop."

"Great. Come with me." She shot Madison an "I tried" look, then led Helen toward the back room, leaving Madison with a man who looked as if he'd rather lie down for a long nap than explore.

"Are you sure you don't want to rest for a minute? The ride had to have been difficult."

"All I do is rest, and I can sleep or vomit in a moving vehicle. Show me your lab."

"I'm expecting one more patient. I can show you around until he arrives."

She led Danny down the hall to the back of the building. He moved more slowly than usual, taking a moment to glance into each treatment room, then he paused in the doorway to her lab and scanned the long narrow space.

"You keep the place spotless."

"My teacher had high standards."

A smile twitched on his lips. He'd been an exacting taskmaster. Danny nodded. "He was a bit of a perfectionist."

"The equipment is old and not state-of-the-art like yours, but it still works," Madison defended.

He headed straight for her old microscope and stroked a hand along the arm. "This is the same model I had when I started out. Bought mine used. It was all I could afford. The original owner of your practice probably purchased this equipment new when he opened his doors. It's all about the same age." He said it with fondness in his voice rather than condemnation.

"He did. I found the receipts. I'm not much on buying fancy gadgets when the old ones still work."

He moved onto her centrifuge. "This is the way we did things in the good ol' days before time and money became the gods everyone worshipped. There are times I miss those days."

"Your practice has grown so much that I doubt you could manage without the time-savers."

"I have to delegate everything. No time to do any of this myself." His sweeping arm indicated the other equipment. "The lab used to be my refuge. Now I own a million-dollar building and there's nowhere in the place I can go to get my thoughts together."

"You could cut back."

"Success is measured by the number of digits on the books each day."

She debated arguing, but the sound of the front door opening derailed her. "Danny, it sounds like my patient's here. Why don't you join Helen for a snack? I'll be right with you after I get through."

Disappointment filled his face. "Would you mind if I sit in, the way you used to with me? I miss being in the office."

Advertising her relationship with Danny and Helen was the last thing she wanted, but how could she refuse? "You should consider popping into your office a few hours a week if you feel that way."

"We'll discuss that when we get back. So what do you say?"

"Sure." With dread-laden footsteps she headed into the hall to meet the newcomer. Mr. Rouse carried a huge wooden box. Charlie trotted along at his feet, tail wagging. No leash, of course, despite the sign in her waiting room saying all pets should be restrained, but Charlie was always well behaved.

"Morning, Doc. I brought you a little something." He set the crate loaded with corn, tomatoes, cucumbers, squash and blueberries on the counter. "I know you love my Cajun-spiced smoked hens, so I roasted an extra one. And you haven't been around to tend your garden, so I wasn't sure if you had produce."

She deliberately ignored the hint of a question in his statement. "Thank you, Mr. Rouse. Your chicken is delicious, and your corn is the sweetest in Quincey. I appreciate you bringing it in."

Piper and Madison would divide the goodies later.

Rouse's hound headed for Danny instead of going straight to Madison's treat pocket the way he usually did. He stood on his back legs, planted his paws on Danny's shoulders and nudged his chest. Danny winced slightly.

Rouse's face turned as red as his neck. He reached for Charlie's collar. "Sorry about that, sir."

Danny waved him back. "Not a problem. What's his name?"

Danny scratched the dog beneath his floppy ears, then snapped his fingers and pointed at the floor. Charlie immediately went to all four, then sat.

"Charlie."

Danny stretched out a hand. He'd been the one to teach Madison to carry treats in her pocket. She dropped a couple into his palm. He fed them to the dog. "You're a smart boy, aren't you, Charlie? I had lung cancer surgery last month, and I'm currently undergoing chemo. Charlie smells it."

Rouse's eyebrows disappeared under the brim of his hat. "Dogs can do that?"

"Yes. Dogs can sniff out cancer, seizures, diabetes and a number of other human ailments. They're far more sensitive than us humans, even though we think we're smarter."

That was her cue. "Mr. Rouse, this is Dr. Drake. He'd like to sit in on our visit today, if that's okay?"

"Sure. Sure. Nice rig out front. Yours?"

Danny stood slowly, as if his joints were hurting. "My home on wheels."

"The missus and I talked about getting one if we ever sell the farm. She has grand ideas about visiting all the grandkids in one. They're spread all over the country. Kids don't stick around and farm anymore."

"No, they don't. A motor home's not a bad idea if you think retirement won't make you crazy. I'm Maddie's father-in-law. My wife and I drove up to spend the weekend with our girl, then tomorrow we'll take her back down to Norcross with us. Maddie's been helping out in my practice while I recuperate. That's why she's been scarce here."

Rouse's eyes lit with curiosity as he shook Danny's hand, and Madison's stomach sank. The privacy she'd fought so hard to maintain had ended with Danny's words. Before the sun set today Quincey's residents would know all of her business and be hot on the trail for more.

CHAPTER FIFTEEN

"MIND IF I use your shower?" Danny asked as he descended from the motor home ahead of Helen into Madison's driveway. "I would love to have some good water pressure."

"You're welcome to use my bathroom…and even my guest room, if you like, Danny." Madison's hesitation was slight, but it was there nonetheless.

"That would be wonderful. I'm sick of that bed and that motor home," he answered before Helen could politely decline.

Embarrassment scorched Helen's face. If Danny weren't injured, she'd dig an elbow into his side. Men could be so obtuse. You didn't invite yourself to stay in someone else's home—especially when their body language contradicted the reluctant invitation.

"We could get out of the monster home and back into our house much sooner if you'd agree to hire someone to finish the renovations instead of insisting on doing it all yourself."

"I like tinkering, and I know how you want it done."

"You can't do it right now or in the foreseeable

future, and I can easily explain what I want to a contractor. I explained it to you, didn't I?"

Madison looked uncomfortable, making Helen realize she should've kept her mouth shut. Arguments between a husband and wife should be kept private.

"I'm sorry, Madison. Use her shower if you must, Danny, but we'll sleep in your *home on wheels*." Helen threw his earlier words back at him. "You claimed it's the most comfortable mattress you'd ever slept on right after we bought it."

"I'd rather stay with Madison." Danny had a stubborn streak a mile wide, and he'd dug his heels in. His petulant tone told her she'd never win this argument.

She didn't know about sleeping under Madison's roof, but Helen wasn't ashamed to admit she wouldn't mind taking a look inside her home. The old country cottage looked more like something from an Americana calendar than the architectural masterpiece Andrew had bought.

Madison's gaze followed a car slowly passing on the street. The occupants tooted the horn. Juggling the box her last patient had given her—in lieu of payment—she lifted her hand.

"Let's get out of this hot sunshine." Madison turned toward the house and Danny tottered along beside her.

"I'll get our bags," Helen grumbled to herself. She ducked back inside the vehicle, retrieved their suitcases and followed.

The wooden screen door slapped shut behind Danny as she descended the metal steps, and the familiar sound brought back memories of happier, simpler times. It reminded her of hot afternoons sipping lemonade and eating watermelon outside, of sticky fingers and smiling boys rinsing off in the water sprinkler. Back then Danny had had time for her and his sons. He hadn't worked every possible hour.

But those days were gone. Her grandparents had passed away when the boys hit their early teens. Her grandmother had gone first, then her grandfather just a few weeks later—some claimed from a broken heart. The house had been sold. Nana and Pops had been her surrogate parents since her teens when her mother had grown tired of being a single parent and dumped Helen before taking off for parts unknown.

Maybe that was why Helen had bonded so strongly with Madison. Madison and her mother had butted heads just as much as Helen and hers. The difference was Madison had left by choice. Helen had been dumped like smelly garbage. But neither of them had seen their mothers again. As for Madison's father... Well, at least she'd known who he was. Helen hadn't.

She shook off the ugly memories and approached the porch. Two weathered white rockers swayed in the breeze. They, like the house, could use a fresh coat of paint. A few potted geraniums by the steps would be a nice touch, too...and maybe some Stargazer lilies and gardenias to scent the hot summer air and add color to the yard.

Not her problem.

She climbed the stairs, pausing at the top to take a good look at the countryside, including an old red barn and an attentive horse that looked as if he wanted to come out and play.

Madison opened the front door. "Come in."

"Thank you for inviting us, but I don't want to impose. We'll stay in the motor home tonight if you'd prefer."

"You're welcome here, Helen."

"I apologize for my little snit fit out there."

"It's okay. You've been under a lot of stress. Did Adam ask you to come for me?"

Dear heaven. How had she forgotten to call her only living son? "No. In fact, he doesn't even know where we are. I need to tell him that he doesn't need to make the flight. We left in such a rush I didn't have a chance. If you'll show me where we're staying, I'll set all this down and then give him a call."

"This way."

The front bedroom was small but homey. The hodgepodge collection of mismatched pieces was charming and fit together perfectly. It was worn, but dusted. She could tell from the knots and stitching that the log-cabin quilt covering the bed was homemade, not one bought at a box store or made overseas. The wooden floorboards creaked as she crossed them—another memory-evoking sound.

"This is very pretty, Madison."

"Thank you. Some of the furniture came with the house. The rest I found in yard sales, then refinished."

Madison's home had warmth and heart—something Andrew's designer showplace house had lacked. "Why didn't you tell Andrew you preferred this simple decor?"

Madison briefly lowered her gaze. "I did. He wasn't fond of vintage furniture. He called it 'other people's junk.'"

That sounded like him. Andrew had always preferred shiny and new things.

"If this is your style I can see why you were less than thrilled when Andrew surprised you with the house. At the time I thought you were ungrateful."

"It was more than that, Helen. We couldn't afford that big house or the furniture he bought. We had a budget and he wasn't sticking to it."

Helen had suspected as much, but Andrew had assured her he'd bring in extra business to his father's practice to cover the large monthly payments.

"I'll leave you to get settled. Danny wants to explore, but I'm trying to get him to rest first. I've parked him on the screened porch beneath the ceiling fan with a glass of lemonade. Join us after you've talked to Adam or stay inside out of the heat, if you prefer. The bathroom's down the hall. Help yourself to anything you need."

Madison pivoted and left Helen staring after her. Helen had forgotten how helpful and considerate her daughter-in-law had always been. Madison had been like the daughter she'd never had. She'd missed that closeness. She hadn't realized how much until now.

Had the house being out of their budget caused the argument and put fury in Madison's eyes at the graduation party? Or had it been the unplanned pregnancy? If Andrew had twisted Helen's suggestion and forced Madison's hand, what would happen if Madison ever found out Helen had unintentionally planted the idea? Would Madison forgive her? Or would she leave them in the lurch before Danny was ready to return to work?

No matter what, Madison could not find out about that long-ago conversation between Helen and Andrew—because Helen no longer wanted Madison to leave. She was good for Danny, and if she joined the practice, then maybe Danny would have time for something besides work. Helen missed Sunday dinners, lazy days with her husband, the drives in the country, the weekends by the lake or on the beach. She wanted them back. And Madison was the ticket to making that happen.

THE SOUND OF the motor home's engine faded as the Drakes pulled away, leaving Madison stranded on Adam's sidewalk.

She climbed the steps, trying to prepare herself for the encounter ahead. She liked to keep her emotions in a tidy box, but nothing about how she felt around Adam was logical or controlled. Around him she was an emotionally disorganized mess.

She lifted her hand to ring the bell, but the door opened before she could press the button. Her heart and lungs stalled then sprang back into action at double their regular rate—a result of Adam startling her. That was all—nothing to do with her being eager to see him.

The tingle in her fingertips and below her navel, combined with the anxious bumblebees-buzzing-through-her-veins sensation that had only gotten stronger as the motor home approached Norcross, called her a liar.

"I'm not pregnant," she blurted to derail the feeling, then wished she'd shown more finesse. She tried to read his face. Was he relieved or torn the way she'd been? She couldn't tell.

"When did you find out?"

Guilt needled her between the shoulder blades. "Wednesday."

"Five days ago? Madison, why didn't you let me know?"

His terse tone made her hackles rise. She should have. She knew that, but...but... Well, she hadn't. "I was busy, and then your parents showed up unexpectedly. I've been entertaining them."

"Since yesterday. A text would've sufficed."

"Yes, I suppose. I'm sorry. I didn't know what to say."

"The same thing you just said." He stepped back,

opening the door to let her into the house, then he took her bags from her. "No cooler?"

"No time to pack one."

He headed down the hall. She followed him into the guest room, resigning herself to two more nights of dancing around this crazy connection they had.

"When did your marriage turn sour?" Adam demanded.

This wasn't a conversation she wanted to have, but judging from his determined expression and by the way he'd conveniently blocked the bedroom doorway, she wasn't going to wiggle out of it easily. That didn't mean she wouldn't try. For his sake.

"Adam, it's late and I'm tired. I thought we'd never get out of Quincey for all the neighbors dropping by on the pretext of bringing me things when they only wanted to check out your parents. Can we save this discussion for another time?"

Her life in Quincey would never be the same. But that was a worry she'd fret over later.

"I need to know how many lies Andrew told."

Even she didn't know that answer. "Please let it go. He was your brother. Your memories of him are all you have left."

"What happened to your marriage, Madison?"

"You have no idea what you're digging up."

He leaned against the jam. "I'm not leaving until you talk. You had a plan, then it changed. How?"

The fight drained from her. She was tired. Tired of carrying the secrets that weighted her down like the old burlap feed sacks she used to help her father unload. Tired of running from the truth. Tired of Adam thinking the worst of her. Tired of covering for a man who'd betrayed her.

What was the worst that could happen? The Drakes would tell her to leave and never come back? Not finish out the time she'd promised Danny? That was what she'd wanted all along anyway, wasn't it?

Wasn't it?

She wasn't sure anymore.

Adam's opinion of her mattered—too much. She'd hoped—*prayed*—the crazy, wound-up sensation she experienced around him was only misplaced sexual attraction, but it was far more. Her reactions whenever he was near, her disappointment each time he hadn't come to pick her up and the way he monopolized her thoughts when they weren't together proved that. A woman didn't experience highs and lows like that or a single-minded preoccupation for someone who didn't matter.

But she'd get over it. Wouldn't she?

She shoved back her hair and took a deep breath. "I had a plan to finish college and then vet school, setting myself up for a financially secure career. Then I met and fell in love with your brother.

"I tried to stick to my goals and begged Andrew to wait until I'd graduated to get married. But he was insistent and persuasive. I finally agreed to marry him, but only after he promised we'd wait until I was established in your father's practice before we started our family. Five years. That was the plan."

"Accidents happen."

"Yes. They do. And I believed that's what happened to me. I was going to make the best of it. But from the moment Andrew learned I was expecting he changed. He became controlling and demanding. His charming side vanished. He resented the time I spent at school instead of in Norcross, claiming we had limited time to be just us—a couple—before we were a family. But I was too close to graduation to quit. I apologized to him repeatedly because I thought I'd screwed up my birth control and that our problems were my fault. And no matter what I did, he wouldn't let up about how I'd messed up 'the plan.' I felt like I couldn't do anything right.

"Then I found out that my getting pregnant wasn't an accident. Andrew had planned it."

"What?"

"He'd had too much to drink at my graduation party and started bragging that he'd found a placebo that looked like my birth control pills and switched them out." She waited for Adam to call her a liar.

"That's why you were arguing."

She nodded.

"Go on," he said through clenched teeth.

"I was upset. I couldn't believe he'd pull such a stunt when he *knew* why having a career was so important to me. On the way home he told me when and where he thought I'd conceived. He said there had to be something wrong with me for not wanting to stay home and raise our children—not just the one I was carrying but our future children, too. He wanted me to throw away seven years of education and my dreams and be a stay-at-home mom like Helen."

"Why is a career so important to you?"

Yet another secret she'd carried. She'd only told Helen and Andrew. "My mother barely finished high school, and she'd never had a job. She wasn't happy with my father, but she couldn't leave him because she had no skills to support herself. She got her kicks with other men instead." Bile burned her throat. "I had no clue until early my junior year in high school when I got sick at school and went home early. I caught my mother and a stranger in our guest room. I was horrified. I raced out to the fields and told my dad. He just shrugged and said not to worry about it, as long as she was at home with us every night.

"I hated them both for lying and letting my sister and I believe everything was all right—that we were a normal happy family." She wrapped her arms around her middle and stared blindly out the window. "That day I swore I'd never be dependent on anyone or let myself get so miserable that I convinced myself cheating was an acceptable option."

"What did you do?"

"I worked my butt off to get every scholarship and grant I possibly could. Once I left Lafayette I never went back. I'd lost all respect for my parents and I couldn't stand to be under their roof."

"That's why you always came to our house for vacations instead of going home."

"Yes."

"It's also why you pushed my mother to go back to school or get a job."

She nodded.

"Andrew claimed you were trying to cause problems between our parents."

Shocked, she faced him. "I would never do that. Danny and Helen had—*have*—a marriage I envy, the kind I wanted for Andrew and I. Sometimes I wonder if their strong relationship isn't part of the attraction I felt for Andrew."

Silence filled the room. Adam's brow furrowed, but he wasn't defending Andrew over the failure of her marriage the way she'd expected. Nor was he condemning her.

"Madison, do you know why I didn't go into veterinary medicine?"

She shook her head.

"Andrew was excessively competitive. He couldn't stand to be second best at anything, and his methods for getting ahead weren't always…fair. From the stories I heard, you were outshining him at the office. My guess is that he sabotaged you to stop you."

Shocked, Madison stared. "But I did my best because I wanted him to be proud of me. Why sabotage someone he claimed to love?"

"He loved himself first. The rest of us fell somewhere in line behind him. Luckily I had an epiphany in high school and decided not to compete with him. I chose a different career path and moved away from Norcross as soon as I could."

"But you came back."

"I came back for Mom. Dad doesn't ever ask for favors. When he called and said Mom was in a depression and he couldn't get her out of it or get her to talk to anyone, I dropped everything."

Andrew had looked out for number one. Adam had put his family first. The last thing she needed if she was to resist the attraction she felt for him was yet another reason to admire him.

"Madison, I hired an accident investigator to look into the wreck."

She was already on shaky ground. He couldn't have knocked her more off-balance if he'd pushed her down. "What? Why?"

"Andrew's and Daniel's deaths weren't your fault, and you need to know that."

"But I was driving. We were arguing. I took my eyes off the road—" To tell him she wished she'd never married him and never conceived his child. But she couldn't tell Adam that.

"The police report stated you were driving below the posted speed limit when you hit black ice and skidded off the pavement. My investigator said the wreck would've been survivable if the guardrail had functioned properly. But it failed. There are lawsuits pending against the company for similar accidents. You should probably file one, too, to get yourself a cushion to live on if you keep seeing patients for perishables. Andrew's and Daniel's deaths were a tragic accident—not negligence on your part."

Chaos erupted in her brain. Six years' worth of questions, doubts and recriminations bombarded her. "Are you sure?"

"I'm sure."

Not her fault.

A lump rose in her throat, choking her. Her eyes burned. She would not cry. She'd cried gallons of tears already. She wrapped her arms around her middle and tried to hold on to her fraying composure.

"Madison?" Adam's voice seemed to come from a great distance away.

Not her fault. Dizzy, she gulped in huge breaths. She hadn't killed her baby and husband.

MADISON'S PALLOR ALARMED Adam. "Madison, are you all right?"

She didn't answer. In fact, she looked as if she wasn't aware of him. Then she started shaking.

"Madison." He gripped her shoulders and turned her. She looked at him blankly, then blinked.

"You're sure their deaths weren't my fault?" she whispered again with hope in her voice and eyes.

"Positive. The investigator said it should've been a property-damage-only incident. You did nothing wrong."

"I thought—" She hiccupped in a breath. "And then your mother said— I believed she was right. I killed them both, and I couldn't blame her for being sick at the sight of me, so I left.

"You're right, Adam—I ran and I hid and I didn't tell anyone about my past. Not even Piper and June, my closest friends, knew everything until you came and I had to explain, but now after your parents' visit everyone knows." The words fell over each other so quickly he struggled to decipher them.

She looked shattered without a vestige of color. Fearing she'd faint, he led her to the bed and sat, forcing her beside him. She perched on the edge, every muscle and sinew in her body as taut as an elevator cable.

This woman who cried over having to euthanize a stranger's old, dying dog had been blaming herself for her own child's death? He couldn't imagine the hell someone that sensitive had gone through. Though he knew he shouldn't, he took her into his arms. She resisted for a moment, then leaned into him. A sob, seemingly dredged up from deep in her soul, escaped, then she lost it, burying her face against his chest.

Minutes passed. Ten. Twenty. He cradled her, letting the storm of her tears wash over him. The quivers rocking her shook him to his core. He stroked her back, his fingers gliding over her hair in an attempt to soothe her. Madison had been there for every stray that crossed her path, but no one had been there for her—especially not his family, who'd called her one of their own.

A tornado of feelings tore through him. He felt protective and territorial—neither of which he'd experienced for a woman. But overshadowing both of those was anger. Andrew hadn't deserved Madison, and his brother's lies and cruel, manipulative games during the last year of his life had not only torn their family apart—he'd nearly destroyed the woman he was supposed to love above anyone else.

Adam gritted his teeth on the fury welling inside. If his brother was here tonight, Adam would do something he had never let Andrew provoke him into doing no matter how badly it had been deserved. He'd kick Andrew's sorry ass for the way he'd treated Madison.

But that option wasn't open. The only thing he could do was help Madison pick up the pieces of her life.

CHAPTER SIXTEEN

AN OBNOXIOUSLY CHEERFUL mockingbird's song dragged Madison from a heavy sleep. She opened her eyes to darkness. But for the bird to be singing it had to be near dawn. She turned her head to check the time. Her clock was missing. Disoriented, she rolled over and found the glowing digits on the wrong side of the bed.

And then she remembered where she was—Adam's—and what she'd done last night. She'd lost control and bawled all over him like an orphaned calf. She'd cried until her head throbbed and her throat felt raw. She remembered being numb with relief, then…nothing.

Embarrassment burned over her, making her wish she could pull the covers over her head and refuse to come out of the room. But she couldn't. It was Monday. She had to fill in at Danny's office. How would she face Adam after making such a fool of herself?

She swung her legs over the side of the bed. Her waistband dug into her skin. She reached to adjust the fabric. Denim. Not pajamas. Her jeans. She'd fallen asleep with her clothes on. The remainder of the evening snapped into place like puzzle pieces. The last thing she remembered was Adam holding her. What had happened after that? Her pulse tripped faster. She must've fallen asleep in his arms. How long had he stayed? She turned on the lamp but the pillow beside her was empty and smooth. No indention from his head.

The discovery that Daniel's and Andrew's deaths hadn't been her fault had rocked her. She'd lived with the guilt, pain and fear that someone would find out for so long. A fresh wave of relief flowed through her, leaving her feeling lighter than she had in years. Adam couldn't possibly know what he'd done for her.

An appetite like she hadn't experienced in ages gnawed her stomach. She made a quick trip to the bathroom, splashed her face and brushed her teeth and hair. Her shower would have to wait until after she'd eaten. She padded barefoot into the kitchen without turning on any lights and the smell of coffee teased her nose. The room was empty, but the red light on the coffeepot glowed.

Adam was up. Adrenaline tricked into her system. The flicker of citronella torches outside the windows caught her attention. Adam stood facing the pond, flanked by flames on each corner of the patio.

Bypassing caffeine and food she made her way across the kitchen. The sound of the door opening brought his head around. With a wary expression he searched her face as she descended the steps, and who could blame him? She'd had a meltdown last night. He probably wondered if he was in for a replay.

"Good morning," he said cautiously. "You're up early."

"So are you, and yes, it is a good morning." She'd slept more soundly than she had in a decade. No nightmares.

Even in the dim, dancing light she could see he'd already showered and shaved. His damp hair and jaw gleamed in the torchlight. Shadows danced on the white dress shirt encasing his broad shoulders and black pants covered his long legs. His feet were bare, and for some reason that boyish habit made her smile.

Not only was he handsome enough to make her toes curl, he was kind. Neither were traits she would have attributed to him before the past couple weeks.

"Adam, thank you for last night. I'm sorry I bawled all over you."

"No problem. You were overdue."

"Why did you hire the investigator?"

He sipped coffee and stared at the dark lake for so long she thought he might not answer. "Because the generous, caring woman I've come to respect and admire is nothing like the selfish one my brother described. I had to know the truth."

The compliment poured over her like champagne, making her skin tingle. "I'm sorry to taint your memories of Andrew. But thank you. You might've done it because you needed answers, but you've given me the one thing I haven't been able to find for myself in six years. You've given me peace."

"I'm glad. I'm sorry for what he did to you, Madison. To all of us. Now I have to figure out how to tell my mother."

Horrified, she gasped. "You can't."

"Madison, she needs to know you were wronged."

"Please, Adam, Andrew was her son. She still calls him her baby. Don't ruin that for her."

"Why do you insist on protecting everyone but yourself?"

She shifted, uncomfortable with the question. "I'll be gone soon, but her memories of Andrew will remain with her for the rest of her life."

He set his coffee mug on the table and closed the distance between them. "You're too generous, and you're the one who pays the price. Put yourself first for once. Go after what you want."

He said it with admiration in his eyes rather than recrimination. What she wanted was him. With Adam she felt alive and attractive and hopeful for the first time in ages. She was attracted to his intelligence, his kindness to his parents and the generous way he'd pursued the truth at the cost of his own precious memories. He called her generous, but he was the unselfish one.

June and Piper were right. Why couldn't she enjoy a relationship with someone she liked and respected? And then in two weeks they'd go on with their lives.

She cradled his jaw in her palm, savoring his smooth, warm skin. He stiffened, but he didn't push her away. Their eyes locked and held. Desire swelled between them. "Madison?"

The huskiness of his voice sent a thrill through her. "What if I want you, Adam?"

His pupils expanded, then he covered her hand with his. "I don't want you to regret this later."

"I won't."

He moved closer, erasing the gap until his chest brushed hers, and the contact was electric. Then he lowered his head. His first kiss was as tender as moth wings fluttering against a lamp. One stroke, two, three—each time he lingered a few racing heartbeats longer. He eased back, his palms skimming up her arms to cup her shoulders. He searched her eyes in the rising sun, then cocked an eyebrow, as if asking one more time if she wanted to pursue this.

Instead of answering with words she rose on tiptoe, laced her fingers through his thick hair and took his mouth with hers. This was not a mindless need to fill a void or reaching out to someone because she couldn't stand to be alone. Not this time. She wanted, needed, ached for Adam.

He gripped her waist and pulled her forward, pressing her body so close to his that even a breath of breeze couldn't have squeezed between them. His heart thumped against her chest and her head spun from the dizzying passion in his embrace. She clung to him, returning each devouring kiss with her own ardor. Then he eased back again, grasped her hand and led her inside.

He didn't stop until they stood by his bed. Grasping the hem of her shirt, he slowly dragged it over her head. Cool air danced on her hot skin, and then his burning gaze slid downward from her eyes to linger on her breasts. Her nipples tightened beneath her bra. He took a moment to thumb each one through the fabric, tightening the knot of desire in her belly so much a moan slipped from her mouth.

He bent to kiss her cleavage, tracing the line of cotton with his tongue. The moan morphed into a gasp. His knuckles brushed her belly as he loosened the button of her jeans, then slid the zipper down. Her knees nearly buckled. Hot palms cupped her hips and skimmed the fabric away. She kicked her clothing aside.

He gobbled her up with hunger-darkened eyes, eradicating even the slightest bit of self-consciousness as she stood naked before him. "Your first night here I thought you were too skinny. But I was wrong."

Worry hit hard and fast. Andrew had often criticized her size. "I'm not always this thin. My weight fluctuates."

"It's not the size of these—" he palmed her breasts "—or this that matters." He caressed her flat stomach. "It's the size of this that interests me." He scraped a circle over her heart with one blunt-cut fingernail. Goose bumps rose on her skin and a shiver rippled over her. "You're a beautiful woman, Madison. Not just on the outside."

Objections bubbled to her lips, but she bit them back. Because of his habit of hardcore honesty, she didn't doubt for one moment he believed what he said, and at the moment that was all that mattered.

"Thank you, Adam."

She made quick work of his shirt buttons, brushing the breadth of his chest to get to his firm, supple skin. Hard, tiny nipples abraded her flesh, arousing her even more. She hooked her fingers behind his buckle. All the while he caressed her back, her waist, the undersides of her breasts, distracting her from her task of removing his pants. Heaven help her, she'd never get them off if she couldn't focus.

And then finally he was as naked as she. His body was a work of art, a perfect example of how a man in his prime should look—long limbs, corded muscle, a thick erection. Her mouth watered and her heart pounded with the anticipation of touching and tasting as much of him as she could. Last time had been too hurried.

He pressed his lips to the sensitive skin between her shoulder and neck while his hands burnished over her, building a passion in her belly that threatened to consume her. Then his teeth grazed her, sending a shudder racking through her.

He caressed her bottom, then following the line the elastic band of her panties usually occupied, he dragged his fingertips bilaterally around to her front, one slow, torturous inch at a time, and urged her legs apart. Her nerve endings danced with excitement. He combed his fingers through her curls, then found the slick crevasse of her desire, locating her center with his first breath-stealing stroke.

Her plan to map his muscles, to savor each inch of him, evaporated. She had to cling to his shoulders to stay upright. The slow up-down slide of that finger absorbed 100 percent of her attention. Tension gathered. Her legs stiffened and quivered. She dug her nails into his shoulder and held on when her legs weakened. And then it happened. Orgasm pulsated through her in wave after wave, spreading tingling heat throughout her body.

Her knees wobbled as the sensation receded, and he caught her, lifting her into his arms, then laying her in the center of his big bed. He opened a nightstand drawer, then retrieved and applied protection before following her down. His limbs and torso aligned with hers, and he felt so good against her it was almost more than she could bear. Impatient, she wound her legs around his, opening herself to him.

"Open your eyes, Madison. Look at me."

Understanding instantly, she did as he bid, forcing her heavy lids up to the doubt in his eyes. She cupped his face. "Make love to me, Adam. I need you inside me."

And then he filled her in one long, deep stroke, forcing the breath from her lungs. Each subsequent thrust pushed her still-aroused body back up to that plateau, and each swivel of his hips urged her closer to the edge. She strung kisses along his collarbone, tasting the fragrant side of his neck, his clenched jaw, then he captured her mouth with his in a kiss so carnal, so unrestrained, that when her next release imploded her cry filled his mouth.

She threw her head back to gasp for breath and opened her eyes just in time to see his face contort, jaw muscles straining as he erupted inside her.

And then the room went still. In the aftermath their gasping breaths mingled. The sensual haze slowly cleared. He shook his head. "I haven't tasted you yet."

And just like that her ebbing desire returned full force. "Maybe next time?"

A grin lifted one corner of his mouth and his blue-green eyes sparkled with mischief. "I like the way you think, Doc."

Her heart swooped like a seabird diving for fish. In that instant she realized she was falling for her husband's identical twin. Another Drake. The thought terrified her. Her fight-or-flight instincts kicked in. But if life had taught her anything, it was to seize each moment while she had it, because it could be gone in the blink of an eye.

Before she could gather her thoughts Adam glanced at the digital clock. His expression turned to one of frustration. "I guess I'll have to wait. We need to get you to work. We'll have to hurry if we don't want to be late."

And that, Madison remembered, was why she was here. To do a job. And when that ended...so would this.

THE EMPLOYEES' CARS were already in the parking lot when Adam turned into Drake Veterinary. Madison checked her watch. They were running a few minutes later than usual, but still well ahead of the first scheduled patient.

Adam sat up straighter. "What in the—?"

"What?"

"That's Dad's Corvette."

She spotted the convertible at the far end of the lot by the building's entrance and her heart went straight to her throat. "Danny's here?"

"Has to be him. He won't let Mom drive the 'Vette. What's he up to?" Adam speculated.

How could she face Danny after what she and Adam had done this morning? She gulped down her panic and tried to think. Danny couldn't possibly know what had happened an hour ago, and as long as she kept calm he never would.

"I've been pushing him to come in for a few hours when he feels up to it. I guess today he feels like it."

Adam pulled up to the front door, parked and shoved open his door. She grabbed his arm. "What are you doing?"

"I'm coming in with you."

That would only make facing his father worse.

"No need to make yourself late. I've got this. I'll call you if it's anything other than routine."

He turned his palm over and held hers on the console, lacing their fingers. Her pulse skipped and the tingly, satisfied feeling she'd ridden to work with became an achy I-want-more-of-that weight in the pit of her stomach.

"Madison, Dad has taken a big step by coming in. It would be rude to leave without saying good morning."

Thoughtful and considerate. And right, unfortunately. Her heart melted a little more. Why couldn't she have met Adam first? He was a genuinely nice guy. No. Cancel that crazy, irrelevant thought. She didn't want to be part of the Drake family again. She couldn't trust her heart to any of them—especially one who had identical DNA to the man who'd betrayed her. She'd always wonder if or when they'd turn on her again.

Too late, a little voice in her head whispered.

"It is a big step for him to not only come in but to drive himself in." It was embarrassing that simply holding his hand could arouse her. Her gaze dropped to his mouth. She wanted him to lean across the space and kiss her. But not here where they might be seen. Then before she did something she'd regret, like initiate the embrace, she shoved open the door and bolted for the building.

Adam beat her to the entrance and opened the door for her. Danny sat in the waiting room with everyone gathered around him like a king holding court. Madison stopped abruptly. Adam grasped her waist to keep from barreling over her.

"You have to stop doing that," he whispered into her ear.

His breath stirred stray tendrils, and desire shimmied over her. She glanced over her shoulder at him and their gazes locked. For a second all she could think of was this morning. To cover, she pasted on a huge smile and turned back to the room's other occupants.

Danny was looking straight at them. "Danny, this is a big surprise. I'm glad you're here," she said.

"Had to see what these disreputable characters were up to." He grinned and his staff smiled back. "Morning, son."

"Dad, it's good to see you getting the 'Vette out of the garage."

Danny smoothed a hand across his bald head. "Letting the wind blow through my hair."

Everyone laughed, as he'd no doubt intended. "Madison, my girl, you used to be an early bird and the first one in the office."

Her cheeks caught fire. "I'm sorry. I overslept."

Adam stepped forward and hugged his father, then straightened. "Give me a call if you need anything. I'll see you tonight, Dad. Madison, walk me out?"

Another rush of heat hit her. "Sure."

Conscious of all eyes on them, she followed him back outside. "Keep an eye on him," Adam said.

"I'll try to make sure he doesn't tire himself out so much that he needs a ride home. On the other hand, if he does, maybe he'll let me drive the 'Vette."

He chuckled and the rich, deep sound danced along her nerve endings. "Not going to happen."

He caught her hand and squeezed, holding her captive for a dozen heartbeats. "Have a good day. I'll see you this evening."

The words were nothing special, but the hunger in his eyes promised something rather extraordinary after the dinner with his parents. Her mouth dried and her heart raced. "I'm looking forward to it."

"Not half as much as I am." He climbed back into his car and left. She realized she was staring after him like a lovesick teenager, then snapped into action and went back inside. The staff had scattered to their positions throughout the building.

Danny rose from the chair. "Looks like a full day ahead. Working as a team again is going to be good."

"Yes, it is. But take a break whenever you need to."

"Step into my office."

Filled with anticipation, Madison followed him down the hall. When he'd been her mentor, every morning had started with *Step into my office,* then Danny would go over the highlights of the day, the patients they were expecting, the interesting things she could expect and how they would handle each incident. He'd often given her topics to research before tricky patients arrived. Those mornings had been some of her most valuable learning experiences.

He sat behind his desk, and she took her usual spot, perched on the seat across from him. There were no files waiting on the surface as there had been years ago.

"Andrew was always the most charming twin, the most outgoing, the one with a ready smile. People gravitated to him. Like they did me," he added with a sardonic shrug.

Her expectations crash-landed, but she kept her mouth shut. It was only natural for him to feel nostalgic for the days when the three of them had worked together and Andrew had occupied the chair beside her.

"But the downside to that was that everything always came too easily to him. He never had to fight for anything, so he never learned how. That made him lazy. Adam, on the other hand, always set a goal just beyond his reach, then he plotted to get what he wanted. Sometimes he failed, but he tried again and learned from the experience. He always saw the big picture and not just the flashing lights and bright colors immediately in front of him.

"When the boys went to separate colleges I think Andrew missed Adam's stabilizing influence. Then he found you and you became that for him."

Yet another conversation she didn't want to have. "Danny—"

He held up a hand the way he always had when he wanted her to hold her questions until the end. She bit her tongue, but every cell in her body wanted to run.

"You and Adam have more in common than you know. You're both fighters. You both look out for the underdog. You both play fair and have a strong sense of right and wrong. You make long-term plans instead of only seeing the present. Adam is a much better match for you than Andrew ever was."

Horrified by where she suspected this was headed, she shook her head in denial. "He's just giving me a ride and a place to stay, Danny."

A smile, so like Adam's, lifted one corner of his mouth, and mischief sparkled in his eyes. "Adam always had a good head on his shoulders, even if he didn't go into veterinary medicine. He'll be a better partner for you than Andrew was."

No. No. No. "Danny—"

"I'm telling you that you have my blessing, Madison. Helen's is going to be a bit harder to get. Though she'd deny it to her last breath, Andrew was always her favorite, because he made her feel important. He ran to her with every little thing. But we'll work on her. Between the three of us we'll win her over." He winked.

"Doctors, your first patient is here," Kay's voice said through the speaker on Danny's phone.

Dismayed, Madison rose on shaky legs. Having Danny's approval should've been a good thing, but considering she intended leaving them all in two weeks, it was the last thing she wanted. It would be just one more way she'd disappoint her mentor.

HELEN DRIED THE last supper dish and put it into the cabinet. Her vegetable lasagna had been a big hit. Danny had eaten more than she'd seen him consume since his treatment had started. Even Madison had eaten well, something she hadn't done since returning.

Exhaustion from Danny's half day at the office weighted his eyes, face and shoulders, but he was happy, and Helen would take that over Danny being bored and cranky any day.

But something was off with them and she couldn't put her finger on what it was. She'd refused help with washing up because she wanted to watch the trio. Adam had checked his watch four times since she and Madison had cleared the table. That wasn't like him. Though he was always punctual, Adam was her patient son.

Madison had spent the evening with her attention focused on Danny and Helen, ignoring Adam almost to the point of rudeness, and that was out of character for her. Had Adam and Madison argued? But neither seemed angry.

Adam caught Helen staring and rose. "Mom, is there anything we can do for you before we leave?"

Tell me what's going on, she wanted to say, but didn't. "Do you have to go so soon?"

"Dad's had a big day. He needs to rest before chemo tomorrow and so do you."

True, but... "When will you be back?"

Heavens, that sounded needy. But it was as if he couldn't wait to get out the door. And she'd enjoyed tonight—it had been almost like old times.

"I'll stop by Wednesday after work to give you a chance to get out and go to the store or whatever you want to do."

She instinctively wanted to refuse, but she had unfortunately learned she couldn't handle everything by herself. She could thank Madison for that. She searched Adam's face, trying to read him, but couldn't. Andrew's moods had always been easier to gauge than Adam's. Danny rose and hugged Madison. As he drew back he winked. What was that about?

All afternoon she'd heard "Madison this" and "Madison that." He couldn't stop talking about his morning in the office, but she wasn't jealous anymore, because today she had her old Danny back— the one she'd had before Andrew's death—and again, she had Madison to thank for it.

Madison approached, and her wariness was hard to see. She briefly embraced Helen. "Consider your new recipe a success. It was delicious."

"Thank you, dear. I guess we'll see you Sunday night?"

"Definitely."

Helen looked from one face to another. It was as if

the three of them knew something she didn't. What? And then it hit her. Her birthday was next month. Were they planning a surprise party? Surprise parties weren't Danny's or Adam's cup of tea. But they were Madison's. That had to be it. She wouldn't let on that she'd guessed and spoil their surprise.

The door closed behind Adam and Madison. She folded the dish towel and caught Danny looking at her.

"She's a good girl, our Madison," he said.

"Yes, she is."

"It's good having her back."

"Yes. I've…I've missed her."

"You know I'm still hoping to convince her to move home and join my practice."

"She'd never leave her clients in the lurch, and you have to admit her farm is quite adorable. She's put a lot of work into it. And her animals… She'd never abandon that ragtag bunch. Could you find someone to take over for her?"

"Who would want a practice that doesn't pay the bills?"

"It would have to be someone who wants to semi-retire and maybe only work three or four days a week and who already has a healthy retirement account."

"I don't know of anyone off the top of my head, but I'll think about it and I can put out discreet feelers."

"Please do. In fact, I think I'll whip up some food

for her to take back this week and surprise her at the airport tomorrow before she leaves. You heard her friends. Madison doesn't bother to cook for herself. She lives off yogurt, fruit and sandwiches. But she loves my cooking."

Danny smiled. "You're mothering her, Helen. That tells me you want her back, too."

Helen hesitated, hating to admit she'd been wrong. But Danny was one of those men who would move heaven and earth to give her what she wanted. He spoiled her with everything except his time these days. If she said it out loud he'd become even more determined.

"Yes, Danny, I want Madison to come home to Norcross. I miss having her as part of our family."

And that was that. Danny would make it happen.

CHAPTER SEVENTEEN

MADISON FOUGHT THE urge to squirm in her seat. Each mile closer to Adam's house was a mile closer to being in his arms. The looks he'd given her during the ride from the office to the Drakes' had nearly made her self-combust. She'd had to quit glancing his way lest Helen or Danny see her hunger reflected on her face.

Adam turned the car down a road they hadn't traveled before. She sat up straighter. "Where are we going?"

"We're taking a short detour."

She tried to hide her disappointment. "Why?"

He cut her a smile sexy enough to make her toes tingle. "If I told you, then it wouldn't be a surprise."

Loving the twinkle in his eyes, she swallowed her protests. Andrew's surprises had rarely been pleasant. But, she realized, she trusted Adam in a way she'd never trusted her husband. Curiosity replaced frustration.

Ten minutes later he turned into the gravel lot of an old white cinderblock building. The hand-painted sign read Denton's Dairy Bar, Home of the Freshest Homemade Ice Cream, and the parking lot and picnic tables were packed with patrons.

"You're craving ice cream? Now?"

His chuckle rippled over her like a caress. He parked and twisted in his seat. "Madison, I'm as eager to get home as you are. I have a taste for something they don't serve here—you."

Her breath hitched. She flushed all over.

"But we have never been on a date, and I know how much you like ice cream."

"This is a date?" The silly, romantic gesture melted her. She was a sure thing. He didn't have to win her over, but in delaying his gratification for some one-on-one time, he'd made her feel young and giddy, as if her heart hadn't been ripped from her body six years ago, smashed to bits then returned in broken fragments.

"I was afraid Mom would keep us so late Denton's would close before we got here. Do you want to taste my version of the best homemade ice cream or go home?"

"Ice cream first. Then you." Fire lit Adam's eyes and, subsequently, her belly. "And Adam, it's a perfect date."

"I still owe you a candlelight dinner."

Her pulse fluttered faster. "I'm more of a roadside-ice-cream-stand girl."

He rewarded her with a quick peck on the lips, then returned for a second and a third. She wanted to wrap her arms around him and hold on, but the console prevented her. They were both gasping by the time he lifted his head and whistled under his breath.

"G-rated parking lot. No more of that. What flavor ice cream do you want?"

She'd never considered eating ice cream as foreplay, but he'd turned it into exactly that. Anticipation simmered in her veins and happiness swelled inside her. A smile she couldn't contain stretched her lips.

She scanned the menu board. "The specialty of the day. A waffle cone of blueberry cheesecake, please."

He winked. "Coming right up. Find us seats if you can."

She made her way to the only vacant table. Minutes later Adam wound his way through the noisy families and sticky-fingered children without flinching.

He passed her a cone. "Live dangerously. It's a double scoop."

"Thank you." Then the hospital executive dived into his treat with boyish excitement. She couldn't look away. Like her, Adam found his thrills in simple pleasures. This was the life she'd always wanted.

A cold drip ran across her fingers, snagging her attention.

She dutifully ate her dessert, lapping up the time spent with Adam along with the smooth, creamy sweet. This was what a relationship was supposed to be.

Neither spoke while they raced to consume the melting ice cream. Once the cleanup was done he captured her hand. "I want you to consider helping Dad beyond the time you stipulated. I know it's an imposition, but, Madison, I've just found you. I'm not ready to let you go."

Her pulse skipped, and if her heart could sigh, it would. Those were the perfect words to end a perfect night. How could she walk away in two weeks?

And that was when she realized she'd done the worst thing she could possibly do. She'd fallen totally, irrevocably in love with Adam Drake.

MADISON DIDN'T WANT to go home, she realized with a sinking stomach as they pulled into the crowded airport parking lot Tuesday night. That was a first. She loved the sanctuary of her farm and practice.

Last night had been wonderful. After their date Adam had taken her home, then straight to his bedroom, where they'd made love the first time with explosive passion, then again so tenderly she'd had to hide tears in her pillow afterward. She'd lain in his arms all night, too tangled up in emotions to sleep.

She'd fallen in love, a state of vulnerability she'd sworn to never enter again. But being in love with Adam was a no-win situation. Even if he wasn't a Drake, a relationship between them would never work. He loved his job at Mercy Hospital. And she wouldn't leave Quincey.

Her marriage had taught her that long-distance

relationships were a struggle. How long would it be before the cost and inconvenience of getting together would outweigh the pleasure? How long before he resented the time she spent on her practice instead of with him? Or could they make it work? The odds were against them, but could they beat them?

Adam reached across the console and squeezed her hand. "It's going to be a long five days."

They'd made love again this morning and his gentleness had soldered him so deep into her heart she might never recover. Then over breakfast Adam had revisited the request she'd strategically dodged last night. He'd managed to persuade her to continue coming to Norcross for as long as Danny needed her.

Determined to soak up every moment of his company, she covered her doubts with a forced smile. "I can't wait until Sunday."

He leaned over to kiss her. She met him halfway. His lips were firm, his tongue slick and hot. The carnality of his mouth contrasted with the chasteness of the distance the console and the public location forced between them. She was limited to combing her fingers through his thick hair and cupping his strong jaw.

Kissing in the car was something most teenagers did, but she never had. His thumb stroked erotically over the pulse drumming at the base of her neck. She wanted it lower. She needed his hands, his mouth on her breasts, on her body, the way they'd been this morning before work. She craved—

A hard pounding on Madison's window startled them apart. Helen stood on the opposite side of the glass, glaring in. The shock on her face echoed through Madison. She'd seen that expression on Helen before, and it filled her with trepidation.

Adam cursed under his breath. "Stay in the car. I'll handle this."

He exited the vehicle and circled to Madison's side, planting himself between Helen and Madison. "Mom, calm down."

"I will not calm down." Helen leaned around him to point at Madison through the glass. "You already stole one of my sons from me. You can't have the only one I have left!"

"Madison didn't steal anyone, Mom. Andrew's death was not her fault. It was an accident. Nothing more. You need to move on."

"She was driving and he's dead. That's all that matters. Now she's trying to make you move away."

Madison had never had anyone defend her before, and the fact that Adam did so now surprised her, but she had to fight her own battles rather than let him ruin his relationship with his mother.

Dreading what was to come she opened her door. "I'm not trying to take Adam from you, Helen. I know he loves his job too much to leave Mercy."

He shot her a quick, questioning glance. "Tell her what Andrew did to you, Madison."

He didn't know what he was asking. Madison shook her head. "Adam, don't."

"Tell her or I will."

"Please don't," she begged him.

"Don't tell me what?" Antagonism dripped from the words.

"Andrew sabotaged her birth control and got her pregnant intentionally to keep her from joining Dad's practice. The reason they were arguing the night of her graduation party was because he got drunk and bragged about what he'd done."

Helen paled and staggered back a step. "No. You're lying."

Her hoarse, whispered words were almost inaudible with the surrounding airport noises.

Madison had to stop Adam before he did irreversible damage. She grabbed his arm. "Adam, the past is over. Let it go."

His hard face didn't soften. "Andrew is the one who lied. Repeatedly. He had to be the center of attention and Madison had outshone him at the office. The only way he could stop her was by eliminating her as competition."

Trembling and pale, Helen shook her head. "You've concocted this...this tale to turn him against his own brother. I'm sorry you ever came back."

Helen stormed back to her car, which was parked a half dozen spots away behind a minivan.

Madison had a feeling she was going to be sorry, too—for a very long time. The last thing she'd intended was cause Helen more pain or drive a wedge between mother and son, but it was too late. Returning to Norcross would only exacerbate the situation. She'd have to say a final goodbye to Adam tonight. The realization opened a deep well of pain inside her. She wanted to run, to hide, to escape and lick her wounds in private.

She faced him. "You should follow your mother. She's very upset. But if you would, please, rent me a car before you go. I don't have a credit card."

He stared after Helen's departing taillights. "She's irrational now and won't listen to reason. She needs time to calm down. I'll talk to her tomorrow night."

"You shouldn't have told her."

His troubled gaze held hers. "If we're going to try to make our relationship work, she's going to find out eventually anyway."

She wanted so badly for a life with Adam to be possible. But it wasn't. They had too much against them. "Adam, there is no us beyond this brief interlude. Long distance relationships don't work."

He stared at her for a long time. "If distance wasn't an issue, would you even be interested in trying?"

She wrapped her arms around her middle, but it did nothing to alleviate the sense of loss engulfing her. She searched for the words to lessen the blow and couldn't find them. "It doesn't matter what I want. I can't come back to Norcross."

"You're going to run because of my mother's outburst?"

"It's not running. It's reality. I'm not welcome here."

"What about your promise to Dad? Does your word mean nothing?" The harsh words lacerated her.

Her head snapped back as if he'd slapped her. "Forcing your mother to play hostess to me when she hates my guts isn't the right thing to do. It's an imposition."

"Call it whatever you want, Madison, and make any excuses you want. I call it cowardice. Let's go. We're running out of daylight."

He stalked toward the general aviation terminal, leaving her to follow. And that was that. She'd finally found a man she could love, trust and respect. And she had to let him go.

She'd gone into the affair with no expectations of forever, so why did the ending hurt so bad?

HELEN DROVE HOME by rote. She wanted to deny Adam's claim that Andrew had tricked Madison. But how could she when the heinous thought had already crossed her mind?

Why, oh, why, had Andrew always needed to brag about every little success? By boasting to Madison he'd started an argument that had very likely led to Madison's distraction that night, making the wreck that had killed Andrew and Daniel partially Helen's fault.

If Danny and Adam ever discovered her part in the tragedy, they'd never forgive her. Danny would probably even leave her. Her heart palpitated with panic.

Danny's doctors had told them the last CAT scan

had shown no sign of cancer. Danny's prognosis was very good. But she could lose him anyway, all because she'd offered motherly advice.

The horrible secret coming to light was all Madison's fault. If she hadn't come back—

No, Helen admitted with the weight of the disaster settling on her shoulders. Madison had refused to come back. Helen had browbeaten her into agreeing. If the secret came out and Helen ended up alone, she had no one but herself to blame.

And if Madison and Adam ended up together, she'd lose Adam, too, even if Danny found someone to buy Madison's practice, because twice now Helen had struck out in anger and said horrible things. Madison had forgiven her once. But her doing so again was unlikely.

Those two times with Madison were the only times in her life that Helen had allowed her mother's nasty personality to come out of her mouth, and it shamed her. But seeing Madison kissing Adam had been so shocking, so *wrong*. Madison was Andrew's wife. She had no business kissing his brother.

No, it was more than that. Madison was the only woman to ever threaten what Helen loved most. All the Drake men loved Madison, and Helen was very, very afraid her husband and sons might love Madison more than they did her.

The motor home came into view. She desperately wanted to keep driving. But she couldn't. Danny needed her. She'd left him in bed to carry the food to the airport. *The food.* She smacked a hand against her forehead. She'd forgotten all about the turkey-and-spinach enchiladas she'd made for Madison. The container was still in her trunk.

Her sweat-slickened hands slipped on the steering wheel. Nerves. She was almost sick with them. She parked and decided to leave the food in the car. It would spoil, but she'd rather throw it out than explain to Danny why she hadn't delivered the food.

Did he know about Madison and Adam's... involvement? Was that what everyone but her had known about during dinner last night? That had to be the reason behind all those secretive smiles. And the little speech Danny had given her about trying to get Madison to move back to Norcross meant he condoned the relationship.

If she didn't want to lose her husband and her son, then she had to make sure no one ever learned about the conversation she'd had with Andrew before Madison became pregnant.

And she had to find a way to make Madison forgive her. Again.

MADISON WASN'T COMING back.

Adam sat on the back patio listening to and empathizing with the bullfrogs' sad calls. In all the years he'd lived beside the pond he'd never heard them until Madison had mentioned them. She'd opened his eyes to a lot of things.

Like doing the job because you loved it rather than

for financial reward or someone else's approval. Like keeping secrets that tore you up because letting them out would hurt others. Like always taking the high road when striking back would be so much easier.

Despite his mother's continued bad behavior, Madison had never retaliated. He couldn't imagine the personal cost of maintaining that smile in the face of so much hostility. And she'd never told any of them what Andrew had done to her—not until Adam had forced it out of her.

He needed sleep, but he didn't dare close his eyes. Every time he did he saw Madison, pale and shaky at the airport when she'd informed him it was over. He'd asked her if distance weren't an issue would she be interested in a future with him, and her hesitation had eviscerated him.

He swatted another mosquito. He'd been sitting out here feeding the bloodthirsty insects ever since returning from the airport because she'd slept on the screened porch, and his whole house smelled like her. His sheets bore the scent of the love they'd made. *Love.* The word hit him like a fifty-pound medicine ball to the belly, knocking the wind from him. He'd fallen in love with Madison Monroe. His brother's widow. The shock wave of the discovery rocked him.

If what they'd had was just sex, he'd have politely accepted the end, the way he had with Ann. No hard feelings. No pain. But that wasn't the case. Because of Madison, he'd learned the difference between making love and having sex.

Long-distance relationships don't work. Her words echoed in his head.

Logically, he agreed. He couldn't keep flying back to North Carolina every weekend. Not only was the fuel cost high, but the other owners of the plane were beginning to complain about Adam commandeering it so often. They had cut him some slack because of his father's condition, but that wouldn't last.

Life without Madison seemed unpalatable. But so did this pain, this emptiness, the sense of being off course and not knowing how to get back on track.

She wouldn't leave Quincey. He didn't want to leave Mercy. If he wanted a future with her, then one of them had to make the sacrifice. Madison's pets, her clients, her friends had been there for her when his family had not. He wouldn't take her support system away from her. That meant he'd have to put Mercy and all the work he'd invested in the hospital behind him.

He could do that. He would put Madison ahead of his career any day—even if it meant taking a backward step to a smaller facility. That might not garner his father's approval, but impressing his dad wouldn't give Adam a fraction of the satisfaction that holding Madison in his arms at night or seeing her smile first thing in the morning did. He was not his father or his brother. He would not be blinded by ambition, and he wouldn't sacrifice her happiness for his own.

Filled with a sense of purpose, he rose and headed

inside. Sleep now, then first thing in the morning he'd put his plan together. And once he did, he was going after the woman he loved.

BEFORE HE COULD pursue his future, Adam had to clear up the misconceptions of the past.

He tossed the papers on the table of the motor home. "I hired an accident investigator to look into the wreck six years ago. The fatalities weren't Madison's fault."

"I never thought they were," his father protested.

Adam eyed his mother. She fidgeted under his hard stare—as she should. "She did. Mother, before you lose your temper and unjustly accuse someone again, you need facts, not misinformation. Because of your attack last night, Madison's not coming back."

Danny bolted upright. He shot a scowl at Helen, then refocused on Adam. "Maddie promised me eight weeks."

His mother paled, then tossed her hair. Had he seen relief in her eyes? "She's left us before. It's not like this is the first time. We'll get by. I'll call the veterinary service."

Fury burned in Adam's chest. "Tell him the truth, Mom."

Panic filled her eyes. "I don't know what you mean."

"Madison left six years ago because you told her to go."

"What?" his father asked.

"After Andrew's memorial service, Mom told Madison that the sight of her made her sick."

"Helen!" His father looked dumbfounded. "You're the reason Maddie left?"

"I was hurting, and I—"

"Do you think she wasn't hurting, Mother? She lost far more than you did. She lost her husband *and* her baby *and* her family—us. You lost one son."

"I—I—"

He didn't let her finish. His disgust of the situation and his part in it robbed him of compassion. "Madison lay in that hospital alone, laboring and delivering Daniel stillborn, then mourning him and Andrew. Alone. None of us visited her. She depended on strangers to relay updates on Andrew because none of us bothered."

Danny looked shocked. "I never thought to... I kept waiting for Andrew to prove the doctors wrong and wake up. That boy was too damned ornery and hardheaded to die. I kept hoping for a sign...."

"We all did, Dad. All these years I've faulted Madison for abandoning us and her responsibilities. I had listened to Andrew's lies, and I believed she was cold and selfish. But that couldn't be further from the truth. Madison did the right thing in leaving because we Drakes kept hurting her. We abandoned her long before she left us. And Andrew—"

Anger snapped off his words. It took a moment to regain his composure enough to speak.

"Andrew didn't deserve a generous, caring woman like Madison. Maybe I don't, either. But I love her. And I want to marry her if I can convince her to give me a chance. If either of you can't accept that, then you're going to lose your second son. Because I'll walk out that door, and I won't bring her back for more abuse from you or manipulations by you." He glared at his mother, then his father.

"I'm looking for a position near Madison, and I'm going to beg her to make a place for me in her life. Whether or not she and I ever see you again depends on your actions, Mother—whether you can make peace with her. And if she can forgive the wrongs this family has committed against her. Frankly, I wouldn't blame her if she never spoke to any of us again."

He turned his attention to his father with years of pent-up frustrations. "Dad, I've spent my life competing with Andrew to win your approval. I'm done. The only person I have to impress is me. And Madison, if she'll have me."

"You have my approval, Adam. You always did. Was I disappointed that you didn't join the practice? Of course I was, and I didn't handle your decision well. But while I was hurt that you didn't want to work with me, I respected you for forging your own path. I am proud of you, son. You've done well."

Adam searched his father's face and saw sincerity in his eyes, but the accolades he'd been waiting for most of his life did nothing to alleviate the emptiness Madison's departure had created. "Thanks, Dad."

Then he left. He had a lot of work ahead of him and a nearly impossible task. But he had never quit just because the odds were against him, and he wasn't going to start now.

CHAPTER EIGHTEEN

MADISON PACED HER back porch Saturday morning, tripping over the trio of cats. Her friends had ambushed her with breakfast and support. They'd sat at her table sipping coffee while she'd poured out the whole story, holding nothing back. And they were still here.

"Are you sure you want to do this?" Piper asked.

"You don't owe the Drakes anything," June added. "Not after the way that hag's behaved."

For two days Madison had been trying to work up the courage to make the phone call she needed to make. Her conscience wouldn't leave her alone until she did. "I keep my promises. It's only two more weeks."

"Two more weeks of hell," June interjected. "I'm sorry now that I encouraged you to sample your brother-in-law's wares. I never intended for you to get your heart broken."

That pretty much summed it up. Her heart hurt. She couldn't sleep. Every moment of every day she missed Adam. Not even her animals filled the void.

"Adam is—" What could she say? That she loved

him and ached without him? "He's a very good person and deserves to be happy. I have no regrets."

That much was true. Even knowing how it would end, she wouldn't forfeit those precious hours of getting to know him and falling in love with him.

All week she'd wrestled with her dilemma. She'd promised Danny eight weeks. But keeping her promise meant risking another painful encounter with Adam. How could she look at him, loving him the way she did, and leave him again? She could play it safe and run from her problems, as he'd accused her of doing, or…she could prove him wrong. If she wanted to be able to live with herself, she had to do the latter.

Her decision had nothing to do with Adam's accusation of cowardice and everything to do with her integrity. Okay, that might not be the whole truth. Adam's opinion counted. Too much. She wanted him to think well of her even if they couldn't be together. She wanted him to remember her as someone who always did the right thing even if the right thing was the hardest thing.

June rose. "If you insist on making the call alone, we'll hang out at my place. Shout if you need us, you hear? We've got your back, Madison. No matter what. Even if I have to carry a can of whoopass down to Georgia."

A surprised laugh burst from Madison, but her eyes stung, too, because they meant it. "Thank you.

Thank you both. For understanding and for being here for me."

"You did the same for me," Piper said and gave her a hug.

Then they headed across the lawn toward June's cottage. Madison waited until they were inside, then took a deep breath and pushed the call button before she found another excuse to delay her.

"Hello."

Her heart stalled. Danny's deep voice sounded so much like his son's. Like Adam's.

"Hello," he repeated.

"Danny, it's Madison."

"Maddie, my girl, I've been thinking about you. How are you?" His concern came through loud and clear. But if she wanted to make it through this call without breaking down, she had to steer clear of emotions and stick to business.

"Have you hired a substitute vet for Monday and Tuesday?"

"No."

"Then I want to come back. I promised you eight weeks and I keep my promises."

"I know you do, Maddie. And you're welcome here anytime."

"But I have conditions."

His chuckle filled her ear. "I suspected you would. You always wanted to clearly understand the procedure before picking up the instruments. What are your requests?"

"I need a place to stay. A hotel this time. Not Adam's or your place."

"Done."

"And I won't come by the house. If you want to talk shop, call me."

"I understand. I don't like it. But I understand."

"And one final thing…" This was the biggie. "Don't tell Adam I'm coming."

"Now, Maddie—"

"That's nonnegotiable. Those are my requirements. Take them or leave them."

"I'll take 'em. And, Maddie, I don't like the idea of you on the highway in that old truck. I'll get you a rental car."

"You don't have to—"

"For my peace of mind, I do. Would it be okay if I come in a couple hours each morning and work with you?"

"Danny, I don't think—"

"I promise I won't try to change your mind and persuade you to stay."

Her stomach churned. He did need to ease back into the office. It made sense. "Okay."

"I'll text you the arrangements once I've made them. And, Maddie, thank you. Thank you for everything you've done. I couldn't have made it through these past six weeks without you. Helen knows that. And so does Adam. We all miss you."

The words rocked her. She hardened her heart. "Don't make me regret coming back."

"I won't. You have my word."

ADAM SETTLED ACROSS the motor home table from his father Tuesday night. The atmosphere wasn't the same without Madison. He'd enjoyed hearing her talk shop with his dad in a way he'd never enjoyed the same with Andrew. Probably because she focused on the patients rather than her prowess, and the intelligence and excitement in her eyes for her job was a turn-on.

"We missed you last night," his mother said as she set a plate in front of him. She was still a little stiff. None of them had forgotten her part in this.

He nodded his thanks. "I was searching job advertisements for a position closer to Madison."

"About that…" His father sounded less than his usual confident self. "Your mother suggested I put out feelers to try to find a buyer for Madison's practice."

"Why?"

"Because I still want Madison taking over my practice, and you've put a lot of effort into turning Mercy into a top-rated facility. I'd hate to see you walk away from all that hard work before you reap the rewards."

More approval. He soaked it in, but in the end, it

didn't matter. "Madison is as possessive of her clientele as you are of yours—for different reasons. They've become her family. If I have to make a lateral or backward move to be with her, it'll be worth it."

Looking resigned, his father nodded. "Just as well. I've had no luck with my search. Her practice doesn't make enough money to tempt anyone I contacted."

"I appreciate the effort, but there are several good hospitals within an hour's drive of Quincey. I'm optimistic. How did the substitute vet service work out?"

His father took a sudden interest in his chicken pot pie. Adam's neck prickled a warning. "Dad."

"I didn't call them."

Adam lowered his fork. His father had never shut down for a full week—not even to spend time with his sons. Usually Adam's mother had taken the boys on vacations and their father joined them on the weekends.

"You kept the office closed?"

"No. Madison came. I went each morning to help."

A bolt of energy shot through Adam. "Then why isn't she here for dinner?"

His father shot a lowered-brow gaze at Adam's mother. "She refuses to come to the house."

No surprise there. "Why didn't you tell me she was in town?"

Danny sighed. "Madison made me promise not to. It was a condition of her returning."

A stab of pain hit Adam square in the heart. Madison had been in town for two days. And she'd chosen not to see or speak to him. It made him wonder if he was wasting his time searching for a job in North Carolina. Could she have forgotten what they shared so easily?

Adam swung his gaze to his mother. "Did you know about this?"

"No." The shock on her face was too genuine to be faked. "I knew your father went into the office, but nothing else."

"Where did she stay if not here?"

"A hotel. And I rented a car for her. I didn't want her on the road in Andrew's old truck. And I sent a mechanic to the rental agency to repair the truck. I'm looking out for our girl until you can take over. I want her back in the family, son—just as much as you do. And I'll do whatever it takes."

But his father wanted her here. He refused to accept that wasn't going to happen. Getting Madison back meant giving instead of taking—something at which his family wasn't adept.

HELEN QUICKENED HER steps, trying to outpace her worries.

It had been an uncomfortable week. Both men were still angry with her. Adam was cranky and kept his visits short. Danny kept his nose buried in a book or his computer rather than talk to her.

He was never going to find anyone to buy Madison's practice. Nobody wanted to work for vegetables and auto maintenance like Madison did. Who wanted a practice that could easily be managed in three days and leave you twiddling thumbs the remainder of the week?

Danny needed to find someone who wanted and could afford to semiretire. Someone who had other hobbies and liked having time on his hands to pursue them. They needed to find someone whose wife wouldn't mind having him underfoot more days than not. She missed a step and caught herself before taking a pratfall on the asphalt.

Her heart pounded and her chest tightened as an idea sprouted. Was the answer right under her nose? Was Danny the veterinarian they needed to find?

No. That would mean moving away from Adam and the house that held all of her happy memories of her boys. She couldn't do that, couldn't leave the notches in the doorjambs marking their growth, the handprints the boys had left in the concrete when they'd poured the patio and countless other precious mementos.

The yammer of female voices broke into her concentration. She looked up and spotted the women she always tried to avoid. How sad was it that she couldn't even go out for a walk without encountering unpleasant people. And then clarity struck.

The world and her neighborhood had changed. But she'd remained frozen in the past. This wasn't the family-oriented place it had been when her boys were small and she'd been friends with their playmates' parents. The area had been overrun by the very types of career-driven, catty women she detested.

Quincey, on the other hand, was like this place had been in its glory days. Neighbors dropped by to say hello. They exchanged food and friendship. Everyone they'd met at Madison's had been so kind. Nosy? Of course they were, but only because they cared about Madison. Not one of her and Danny's neighbors had even stopped by or called to ask if she or he needed anything. Their friends had downsized after becoming empty nesters, and they'd lost touch.

But if she and Danny moved to Quincey, she'd have to sell the house and leave her memories behind. No, they were embedded in her heart and her head. They'd move with her.

Could she do it? Could she leave everything familiar and dear and start fresh somewhere else? Yes, she could. Would Danny agree? Doing so would give him and Adam their heart's desire. Madison. In Norcross. Heading up Drake Veterinary Hospital. But Danny wouldn't be working with her. That might be a sticking point. She'd have to persuade him. And maybe if she had more of Danny's time, she could save their marriage.

Eager to run her idea by him, she kicked her walk

into high gear and passed by the women without wasting her breath on a greeting they wouldn't appreciate anyway. Adam's car was gone when she reached home. Perspiring and out of breath, she barged into the RV. The den was empty as was the bedroom. She found Danny in the shower. She jerked open the glass door, snatched the towel off the rail and threw it at him.

"What in the hell, Helen?"

She wouldn't let his harsh tone put her off. "I figured out a way to give everyone exactly what they need. Madison. Adam. You. Me. I have a plan."

"You're not making sense."

"Are you going to dry off and listen or just stand there?"

"Hold your horses." Scowling, he toweled dry.

Helen could barely contain herself. She had been the one to make a mess of everything, and if this worked it would set her world right again. "Where's Adam?"

"He's flying up to see Madison."

"Perfect. Get dressed. I'll tell you what I've come up with on the way."

"On the way to where?"

"Madison's."

"Tonight?"

"Yes."

"Are you crazy?"

She stopped and took a deep breath. Was she? "No. Danny, for the first time in a very long time

I'm seeing clearly. I've wronged Madison. You have no idea how badly. I owe her an apology—a big one. I'm going to pray the whole way that she accepts it and forgives me."

He studied her for so long she thought he'd refuse, then he padded into the bedroom, picked up the Corvette keys and tossed them to her. "Pack us a bag and load her up. If I'm going to ride all night I'm going to need more legroom than your sedan offers."

She frowned as he pulled on his clothes. "Are you up to driving seven hours?"

"No. But you are."

"You're going to let me drive your Corvette?" He barely let her sit in it.

"It's about time I let you see how well she handles. But don't go getting attached. You won't be taking any joyrides without me."

MADISON PULLED HER truck into the lean-to and automatically scanned the cages in the dark. No guests. Good. She was too exhausted from the long drive to deal with newcomers.

Ol' Blue had started with nary a hiccup when she'd picked it up at the rental car place, and for that she was thankful.

She grabbed her bag from the passenger seat, threw open her door and made her way to the house with her gaze on the ground, watching for unexpected guests in the grass. A squeak on her back porch brought her eyes up. A shadow rose from the chair.

Her heart stalled, and all of Adam's cautions about strangers came rushing forward. She backed toward the truck.

"Madison, it's me."

Adam. Her heart did a crazy leap at the sound of his voice. "What are you doing here?"

"We need to talk."

"It's one in the morning, Adam."

Frustration crossed his face. "Give me five minutes."

They stood awkwardly on the porch. She ought to send him away. But she couldn't. She wanted to brush the worry from his brow and take him to bed. Most of all, she wanted to just hold him. But that would only add new lacerations to her already bleeding heart.

"You could've waited inside."

"I'm not entering your house uninvited even if you did leave the door unlocked again."

She bristled at the chastisement. "Quincey's safe. I told you that."

"For my sake, would you please exercise a little caution?"

For his sake? Did that mean he still cared? And did it matter if he did? The same problems still kept them apart.

She pushed open the door and gestured for him to precede her. "Why are you here, Adam?"

"There's an opening at one of the hospitals in Raleigh. I'm hoping to talk to the hiring supervisor tomorrow and see if I can get an interview for the position."

Confused, she scanned his face. "Why leave Mercy? For more money?"

He crossed the kitchen and stopped in front of her, then he lifted his hand and stroked her cheek. Her insides swooped like a barn swallow. She couldn't stop herself from leaning into his touch and greedily gobbling it up. The look in his eyes stole her breath.

"For you. I tried to let you go. But I can't."

His words weakened her resolve to do the right thing. "One person sacrificing his or her happiness for the other doesn't work, Adam."

"I won't be sacrificing. I loved the challenge of turning Mercy around. I can find that challenge elsewhere. Madison, I'm in love with you. I want to marry you."

Her knees nearly buckled. She was so tempted to say yes, to forget the cost if she did. "You can't. You don't know the whole story."

"Then tell me."

Her mouth dried and her pulse pounded her eardrums. "The night of the wreck, my last words to Andrew were that I wished I'd never married him and never gotten pregnant. If he had survived I would have divorced him."

"As you should have after what he'd done. He

betrayed you, Madison. My family, myself included, seems to have spent a lot of time hurting you.

"Now let me tell you my story. At first I was blinded by deceit. Then I became intrigued with a woman who cried with a stranger over the loss of an old dog. I was fascinated by one who'd risk getting struck by lightning to shower her love on a bunch of rejects nobody else wanted. I learned to respect her when she repeatedly ignored a firestorm of negativity to help a man to whom she owed nothing. But I fell in love with a woman who bottled up all the pain she'd been dealt just to keep from hurting others. You're a very special lady, Madison Monroe, and I don't want to contemplate a life without you."

He was saying all the right words—words that filled her heart so full of hope it almost burst. Then denial kicked in. So she squashed the hope. "You can't turn your back on your family. The day will come when you'll resent me for coming between you."

"This is not about my family. This is about you and me. You never have to see my mother again if you don't want to. I won't expose you to her venom."

He didn't know what he was saying. She shook her head. "The first rule of veterinary medicine is that a cornered or hurt animal often strikes out at anyone close by—even someone trying to help them. Your mother was hurt and striking out. I was the closest target. I don't have to like it, but I do understand her behavior."

"You're being more generous than she deserves."

"She's your family, Adam, and family is important. You'll never know how important until they aren't there to love, to hate, to argue with, to hug. Never willingly cut those ties. They may not be there when you wake up and want to go back."

"Like yours wasn't?"

She nodded.

"Madison, I need to know if you feel anything for me or if I was just scratching an itch for you."

The insecurity in this usually confident man's face was hard to take. And she'd put it there. She had to ease his mind, even if it opened her up to more pain.

"No, Adam, you weren't just scratching an itch. I tried to convince myself that was all it was. Neglected hormones running amok, or something like that. Then I blamed the attraction on your resemblance to Andrew. But it was neither of those. What I feel for you is so much more.

"I admire your integrity and the way you put your family first." She took a deep breath. If she said it, she couldn't *un*say it. But it was a risk she had to take. "And I love you too much to take you away from them."

Air hissed between his teeth. "You love me?"

She stared into those hope-filled blue-green eyes and prayed he could see the truth in hers. "Yes, Adam, I love you. But even if we could work out our family issues, you've invested your heart and soul into Mercy. I would never ask you to walk away from that."

"Where I work doesn't matter as long as I can come home to you each night. We're a team, Madison. We're best when we work together."

She stared at him, soaking up the words and the conviction behind them and the serrated edges of her heart started to seal, giving her a sense of hope. And then the realization that *she* was the problem, not his family, sent her into a mental spin.

The only way she could have what her heart most desired was by leaving Quincey. She tested the idea and it didn't fill her with panic. Instead, it filled her with a sense of freedom. Then she figured out why.

"Quincey is my hidey-hole, my safe spot where I curled up to lick my wounds and heal. Thanks to you, I don't need to hibernate anymore. I think I'm ready to rejoin the world. If I move to a bigger practice I can help more animals…but I can't leave my clients here in a lurch."

"Madison, I'm not asking you to move. I'm telling you I will."

"It's because you're not asking that I'm volunteering. There's bound to be another small-town vet like me who's struggling to make ends meet and won't mind coming in a few days a week to supplement his or her income and care for my patients. As soon as I have Quincey's pets covered I'll join you in Norcross, and you can stay at Mercy."

"But you love it here. What about your friends and your critters?"

"Adam, one thing I've learned is that when you find love you need to hold on tight and never let it slip away. I'll visit Piper and June, and I'll find homes for my critters. And then you and I can be together."

A slow grin spread across his mouth. "You're a very smart lady, Dr. Monroe. I love that about you."

"And you're a very generous man. I love that about you." She stepped into his arms, ready to face tomorrow and determined to find a way to make this work.

"I'll make you a deal. You look for your veterinarian. I'll look for a job closer to Quincey. We'll take the first opportunity we get. Either way it's a win-win situation if we get to be together."

He was willing to make sacrifices and so was she—they'd be equal partners in love and in life. And that was exactly what marriage should be.

"Then, yes, Adam, I'd love to marry you."

POUNDING WOKE MADISON from a deep, satisfying sleep. She stirred and it all came rushing back. Adam on her porch. His proposal. Making love.

The knock sounded again, harder this time, clearing the remaining fog from her brain. *At her front door.* Friends came to the back. She checked the clock. 6:00 a.m. Then she eased out of Adam's arms. Cool air from the ceiling fan teased her bare skin.

"What is it?" he asked in a sexy, sleepy voice that made her warm and tingly all over.

"Probably a client with an emergency patient." She pulled on the first clothes she could find—the scrub suit Adam had removed last night.

He sat up, scrubbing sleep from his eyes like a two-year-old. "This happen often?"

The sheet fell to his waist and her mouth watered. "Often enough. Go back to sleep. I'll be back as quickly as I can."

Finger combing her hair, she shuffled to the front door and interrupted the third set of knocks by yanking it open. Helen—the last person Madison expected to see—stood on her welcome mat with Danny behind her.

Only a disaster could bring them to her doorstep again. "What's wrong?"

"We need to talk to you," Helen said, then her gaze went over Madison's shoulder. "Both of you."

Madison turned to find Adam had followed her. Thankfully he'd put on his wrinkled clothes. She stepped back and opened the door. "I'll start the coffee."

"Why are you here?" Adam asked.

"Because I have the answer to all of our problems." Helen looked quite smug when she said it, but there was also a light of excitement in her eyes and none of the animosity Madison had expected.

No one spoke while Madison bustled through getting the brew started. She was grateful for the busy-work. Helen and Danny sat at the table. Adam leaned against the door frame, arms folded, his face an unwelcoming mask.

"So...what brings you here so early?" Madison prompted.

Danny grimaced. "We would have been earlier if I hadn't insisted Helen pull over at the rest area for a couple hours. She's a little too fond of driving the 'Vette."

Adam straightened. "You let her drive the 'Vette?"

His father nodded. "Might want to sit down, son. She has a lot to get off her chest and a doozy of an idea that's so crazy it might work."

Adam remained standing. The room went silent.

Helen shuffled in her seat and studied her hands, then took a deep breath and looked up. "I owe you a huge apology, Madison. More than one. I need to back up to before you became pregnant."

Madison didn't want to rehash those bad days. "Helen, I don't think—"

"Please, this is important. I can't live with this on my conscience a moment longer." Desperation clouded Helen's eyes.

Madison gulped and nodded for her to continue.

"Andrew always came to me with his problems. And...he thought you'd become one of them."

"He lied," Adam stated starkly.

"Yes, son, I know that. Now. He blamed Madison for making him look bad at work when he really needed to change his own lazy ways. You earned all those accolades because you never took short-cuts. I know this because your fondest mentor—" she nodded toward Danny "—used to tell me stories of what you'd done and how hard you worked. But back then I didn't listen to your boss. All I did was worry about my boy and how he measured up."

The torment in Helen's eyes was hard to take. "Helen, you don't have to—"

"Let me finish, Madison. Then if you want me to never speak of it again, I won't. Andrew claimed all you cared about was your career. You put it ahead of everything, including him. I hated seeing him so upset. And then I made a critical error." She ducked her head and fussed with the seam of her pants. "I told him that would change when the babies came along.

"And then he announced your pregnancy a few months later. From his cocky tone, I suspected even then that the surprise pregnancy might've been a surprise only to you."

Shocked, Madison searched for words. "You knew?"

"I suspected. Andrew didn't like to lose. And I hated myself for planting the seed. Then when Adam confirmed it…"

The pain in the woman's voice was more than Madison could bear. She placed her hand on top of Helen's. "You can't take the blame for Andrew's actions."

"I knew my son and his weaknesses. If I hadn't said what I did then—"

"No. Stop. *If* Andrew twisted your words to suit his purposes, that's not your fault. Your comment to him would have been true *if* he'd waited the five years we'd agreed upon. In fact, that's why I wanted to wait until I was established in the practice—so I could afford to take time off with our child. Andrew's choices were *not* your fault," she repeated when Helen's doubtful expression didn't change.

"How can you be so nice when I've been such a bi—witch?" Tears brimmed in her eyes.

Sympathy wound around Madison like a kudzu vine. "Because I know what it's like to live with guilt. We each have different methods of coping, but we're reacting to the same stimuli—pain and fear. You strike out when you're hurt. I curl into a defensive ball. You pushed me away because seeing me reminded you of Andrew. I buried myself in Quincey, hoping no one would discover I was responsible for my husband's and son's deaths. Guilt tore me up, robbed me of sleep and appetite, and it fixed nothing.

"You have to let it go, Helen. Andrew and Daniel are gone. Nothing you or I can do will bring them back. The only thing left to do is not be afraid to move forward and live your life. And don't be afraid to love again." She met Adam's gaze and found love, support and approval reflected back at her. "Adam taught me that lesson."

He crossed the room and took her hand in his. "Mom, Dad, Madison has agreed to marry me. She's going to find someone to operate her practice, and I'm going to look for a job up here. We'll end up wherever the first opportunity arises."

Danny laughed. "Funny you should mention that. Your mom has the answer."

Excitement replaced the grief in Helen's eyes. "I do. Madison, if you're willing, I want you and Danny to swap practices."

"What?" Madison and Adam said simultaneously.

"I've been so morose and negative since…the funeral that Danny has been hiding in his office to avoid me. Our marriage has suffered. He's been trying to make me happy by giving me things when all I really want is time with him. I want him to cut back on his hours so that we can get back to the 'us' we used to be. The best way to do that is for him to take over Madison's patients.

"And, Madison, you can quit wasting your talents here in the country and take over Danny's practice, where you'll be challenged. That way everyone gets what they want.

"I get my husband back and Madison gets someone she can trust to look after her patients *and* her family of strays. And Adam gets to keep the job he loves and have the woman by his side who couldn't be more perfect for him if I'd picked her myself."

Dumbfounded, Madison couldn't speak. It was as if everything she'd ever dreamed of and more was being offered on a silver platter.

"What does Dad get out of this deal?" Adam asked.

"I get the love of my life back and plenty of time to tinker. Madison's barn has room for me to set up a shop. What do you say, Maddie? Care to swap practices?"

Hope and happiness welled up in her throat. She looked across the room to her future husband, then to Helen and Danny and nodded. "This is what families are supposed to do. We help each other out, but more important, we never, ever, stop loving one another."

* * * * *

LARGER-PRINT BOOKS!
GET 2 FREE LARGER-PRINT NOVELS PLUS
2 FREE GIFTS!

HARLEQUIN®

super romance®

More Story...More Romance

LARGER-PRINT BOOKS!

HARLEQUIN *Presents*

PASSION GUARANTEED SEDUCTION

GET 2 FREE LARGER-PRINT NOVELS PLUS 2 FREE GIFTS!

YES! Please send me 2 FREE LARGER-PRINT Harlequin Presents® novels and my 2 FREE gifts (gifts are worth about $10). After receiving them, if I don't wish to receive any more books, I can return the shipping statement marked "cancel." If I don't cancel, I will receive 6 brand-new novels every month and be billed just $5.05 per book in the U.S. or $5.49 per book in Canada. That's a saving of at least 16% off the cover price! It's quite a bargain! Shipping and handling is just 50¢ per book in the U.S. and 75¢ per book in Canada.* I understand that accepting the 2 free books and gifts places me under no obligation to buy anything. I can always return a shipment and cancel at any time. Even if I never buy another book, the two free books and gifts are mine to keep forever.

176/376 HDN F43N

Name	(PLEASE PRINT)	
Address		Apt. #
City	State/Prov.	Zip/Postal Code

Signature (if under 18, a parent or guardian must sign)

Mail to the **Harlequin® Reader Service:**
IN U.S.A.: P.O. Box 1867, Buffalo, NY 14240-1867
IN CANADA: P.O. Box 609, Fort Erie, Ontario L2A 5X3

**Are you a subscriber to Harlequin Presents books
and want to receive the larger-print edition?
Call 1-800-873-8635 today or visit us at www.ReaderService.com.**

* Terms and prices subject to change without notice. Prices do not include applicable taxes. Sales tax applicable in N.Y. Canadian residents will be charged applicable taxes. Offer not valid in Quebec. This offer is limited to one order per household. Not valid for current subscribers to Harlequin Presents Larger-Print books. All orders subject to credit approval. Credit or debit balances in a customer's account(s) may be offset by any other outstanding balance owed by or to the customer. Please allow 4 to 6 weeks for delivery. Offer available while quantities last.

Your Privacy—The Harlequin® Reader Service is committed to protecting your privacy. Our Privacy Policy is available online at www.ReaderService.com or upon request from the Harlequin Reader Service.

We make a portion of our mailing list available to reputable third parties that offer products we believe may interest you. If you prefer that we not exchange your name with third parties, or if you wish to clarify or modify your communication preferences, please visit us at www.ReaderService.com/consumerchoice or write to us at Harlequin Reader Service Preference Service, P.O. Box 9062, Buffalo, NY 14269. Include your complete name and address.

HPLP13R

ReaderService.com

Manage your account online!

- Review your order history
- Manage your payments
- Update your address

*We've designed
the Harlequin® Reader Service
website just for you.*

Enjoy all the features!

- Reader excerpts from any series
- Respond to mailings and
  special monthly offers
- Discover new series available to you
- Browse the Bonus Bucks catalog
- Share your feedback

Visit us at:
ReaderService.com